Also by Micheal Maxwell

Cole Sage Mysteries

Diamonds and Cole

Cellar of Cole

Helix of Cole

Cole Dust

Cole Shoot

Cole Fire

Heart of Cole

Cole Mine

Soul of Cole

Cole Cuts

Logan Connor Thrillers

Clean Cut Kid

East of the Jordan

Adam Dupree Mysteries

Dupree's Rebirth

Dupree's Reward

Dupree's Resolve

Flynt and Steele Mysteries (Written with Warren Keith)

Dead Beat

Dead Duck

Dead on Arrival

Dead Hand

Dead Ringer

Copyright © 2020 by Micheal Maxwell

All rights reserved. No part of this book may be reproduced in any form or by any means, electronic or mechanical, including photocopying, recording, or by any information storage and retrieval system, without permission in writing from the publisher.

ISBN: 9798564234580

COLE MINE

MICHEAL MAXWELL

Chapter 1

Kelly Mitchell found herself in a strange and wonderful new world, a world she only read about in books and magazines. She was on a mission, and for that, she was willing, even eager, to step outside the safe world of her Lombard Street apartment and venture into a place she could only find with the guidance of Google and the GPS on her phone, *Rosenberg's Kosher Deli.*

Her fiancé, Cole Sage, loves kosher food. The robust flavors of Eastern European Jewish cooking were a go-to source of gastronomic pleasure, second only to ravioli and ice cream. He often told Kelly of his love of kashe varnishkes, square potato knishes, kishke covered in paprika sauce, thick pastrami sandwiches with a dill pickle, and how he missed his favorite Chicago delis.

It was a special occasion, his birthday, and for that, she was pulling out all the stops and spread a table with all his favorites. As she pushed the door open and slipped into Rosenberg's, the smell of fresh bagels, rye bread, and steamed cabbage brought a wide smile to her face.

Cole, you're right again, Kelly thought.

"Hello, pretty lady, what can I do for you today?"

"Hi. A special birthday dinner!" Kelly said brightly.

The little man behind the counter flashed an elfish grin. The naughty twinkle in his eye didn't go unnoticed by the feisty Ms. Mitchell. He was well into his seventies and looked as if he enjoyed every year of it. His wiry salt and pepper hair was cropped much shorter than his massive white mustache.

"Any dinner with a lady as pretty as you would be special. What's on the menu?"

"I was hoping you could help me with some ideas. My fiancé likes kashe varnishkes. Do you have them?"

"Does a one-legged duck swim in circles? Of course. Next?"

"How about kishke?"

"Who is this lucky guy? What kind of sauce?"

"My fiancé, Cole Sage. I think you know him. Paprika?" Kelly asked.

"Perfect! I should have known! Cole and I have been friends since he came to San Francisco. For a Gentile, he's got an awfully Jewish palate."

The tinkle of the bell above the door sounded, and the color from the little man's face behind the counter drained. Kelly turned to see four skinheads enter the deli. Their hair was buzzed short, nearly shaved, and they all wore similar clothes: heavy black lace-up boots; jeans rolled above the boot tops; white T-shirts with various punk bands; and black, quilted cloth, waist length jackets. Various anarchy and swastika patches covered the fronts of the jackets. They were trouble, and Kelly knew it.

"Irwin! Old buddy, how ya doin'?" The greeting was less than friendly.

Kelly turned to see the man behind the counter reach for a long knife. She hoped he wouldn't be foolish enough to try and take on these thugs.

"We told you nicely we didn't want your rat-infested Jew food in our neighborhood. You don't seem to get the message. And what's with trying to call the cops? Tsk, tsk not friendly. We gave you the chance to move peacefully, but now you have hurt my feelings. If you had American food, I might order something." The young man's voice was kind and friendly, but his words and demeanor were ominous and threatening as he smiled wickedly at the old man.

"I haven't got time for your foolishness!" Irwin said boldly.

"Oooh, tough little Jew."

"Get out!" Irwin shouted.

The leader of the group pulled a foot long black object from behind his back. In the blink of an eye, the black tube turned into a nearly three-foot-long chrome baton with a marble-sized knob on the end.

"Now, that is not friendly. You act like you don't want to serve red-blooded, white Christian Americans. Is that what this is, Irwin?" the tallest of the four said, stepping forward.

A boney, pimple-faced kid of about eighteen stepped back and stood with his back to the door. Heavy boot planted firmly against the bottom corner, he crossed his arms and grinned at Kelly.

"What do you think this is?" Kelly demanded.

"We don't need any lip from a rich Jew bitch. Just shut up!" the thug with the telescopic baton shouted.

"I'm not Jewish, not that it matters; I was raised Baptist. I see no fruits of being a Christian in your behavior or insulting mouth. I think you and your buddies need to go and pick on somebody your own size."

"Look, old lady…"

"Old lady? That's it, you little punk. Go home!" Kelly's face burned with anger.

The leader bounced the baton on his shoulder as he glared at Kelly. In a swift, powerful swing he brought the baton forcefully down on the curved glass in front of the deli case. He pulled back for a second attack before the sound of exploding glass stopped echoing through the small shop.

"Stop it!" Kelly screamed, stepping in front of the raging young man.

Without hesitation, he shot his fist through the air, hitting Kelly hard just below her right eye. The blow knocked her off her feet, and she landed hard against a rack of bread and bagels, hitting the back of her head. She rolled as it toppled and lay motionless on the floor.

Blow after savage blow, the row of deli cases exploded into shards of thick glass.

"Hatichat Hara!" Irwin yelled, swinging the large butcher knife.

"You want some?" the baton-wielding thug screamed, jabbing at the old man.

"I'm not afraid of trash like you! You are not American, you Mamzer!"

"Speak English, Kike!" The thug laughed fiendishly.

As Irwin swung the butcher knife ineffectively at his attacker, the two other thugs methodically used their cupped hands and forearms to scrape the shelves in the shop bare. As they plowed through the store, they stomped and kicked cans and shattered jars in every direction.

Kelly tried to get to her feet, and the baton thug gave her rump a hard kick with the sole of his boot. "Don't even think of getting up, bitch!" he said, kicking Kelly with a crushing blow to the ribs. "Done?" Baton shouted toward the back of the store.

"Just about!" came a reply.

Reaching the back wall, the pair finished emptying the shelves, took old fashioned bottles of Cel-Ray and began throwing them across the store, watching them explode against the wall. Not satisfied with their destruction, they began smashing the fronts of the coolers.

Irwin came from behind the counter to meet his Goliath head on. In a flash of chrome, the baton came around and struck the valiant old man in the side of the head just above the ear and sent him to the ground like a hundred-pound bag of Passover cake meal.

"That should do it!" Baton shouted. "Let's go!"

The doorbell tinkled, and the first of the four exited the shop. As Baton reached the door, he took one last mighty swing and knocked the little bell off the wall.

Kelly rolled and tried to clear the fog in her head, but the pain in her side made her nearly pass out. Rising, she saw the crumpled form of the sprightly old merchant, now small, frail, and motionless. She half-crawled and half-rolled over the broken glass to where he lay. She turned him slightly and felt for a pulse. He was still alive.

"Thank God," she whispered.

Fumbling in her purse, Kelly felt for her phone. Unable to find it, she angrily dumped the bag's contents on the floor. Grabbing the phone, she pushed 911 and waited.

"There's been an attack at Rosenberg's Deli. The owner is hurt, send an ambulance."

Kelly dropped the phone. She gently raised Irwin's head enough to cradle it in her lap as she leaned against the shattered display case. Her anger brought tears of rage as they rolled down her throbbing cheek. She closed her eyes and gently stroked the old man's head as they waited for the ambulance.

Chapter 2

"If there is one thing you can count on in life, it's that plans for the most part never work out."

This could almost be Cole Sage's motto. Since getting the job teaching journalism at Stanford University, nothing has gone according to his plan.

Housing in Palo Alto is not only expensive, but it is also difficult to find. If it was just a matter of finding an apartment near campus, Cole could have found a dozen places he could have lived in. Granted, he wouldn't have like them, but it was a roof over his head and he wouldn't have to make the hour plus drive back and forth to his place in the Marina in San Francisco.

His engagement to Kelly Mitchell changed the equation completely. They agreed they wouldn't live together until they were married. Old fashioned? Maybe, but Kelly's strong Biblical faith made a strong case for separate housing. Cole was learning more and more about what made her tick as time went on. His faith, too, was now a consideration in the way he looked at living his life. Something he would never dream possible five years ago.

Murphy's Law says if anything can go wrong, it will, or something like that. Cole rejected the notion, but it seemed Mr. Murphy was trying to make a believer out of Cole. Most of the arrangements with the University seemed to get reinterpreted somewhere between his leaving the Chronicle and the first day of classes.

The salary stayed the same, but the office he was originally shown was assigned to a squeaky wheel member of the English department. The administrative assistant position, originally promised for Hanna Day, seemed to disappear with her death. Instead, he found he shared a secretary with three other part-time staff members.

"Budget restraints, you understand. The position will be reinstated more than likely with the new fiscal year. The budget always loosens up."

Same old political nonsense Cole fell victim to his entire newspaper career. It didn't matter; without Hanna, he really didn't want or need an assistant.

Randy Callen, too, got shafted in the move. He was politely resigned to it, but Cole found it embarrassing and regretted asking him to come along. The position promise morphed into a research assistant in the library. The tech equivalent of Stephen Hawking being asked to teach Junior High Science.

All in all, the move was a disappointment, as were his classes. The promise of grad students being fine-tuned for their degree was put on hold due to accreditation issues. So, as the second semester began, the great Cole Sage found himself with two sections of Journalism 101 and one section of Journalism 201 and a section of Copy Editing. The bright spot was being the faculty advisor to the student-run newspaper. He was finally an editor. To Cole's great disappointment, though, there wasn't a grad student in sight.

The first semester, he was assigned a teaching assistant, an arbitrary decision made by the Dean. Cole neither interviewed nor participated in the selection. He was a nice enough young man, did as requested, not the most detail-oriented, not the most punctual, but in the end, it didn't really matter because Cole didn't have a whole lot for him to do.

Cole took a deep breath and looked out over the forty or so students in the small lecture hall. The sun was shining out the narrow windows at the top of the high walls. The billowy spring clouds cried out to be enjoyed on the lawn under a shady tree or with friends on a bench in the sunshine. Cole glanced at his watch. Ten minutes to go is an eternity when you are dragging a bored class of freshmen up the hill of journalistic history.

"A journalist bears a great responsibility. A grandiose, overused, hollow, abused, becoming-meaningless cliché. So what does it really mean? Mr. Cellphone there in the third row."

Cole Sage glared from the table where he leaned. A pretty girl in a red Stanford T-shirt nudged the young man on the cell phone. She indicated Cole with a jerk of her head in his direction. Mr. Cellphone glanced up and shrugged.

The class erupted in laughter.

"What?" Mr. Cellphone asked when the girl whispered something to him. The room laughed again.

"He asked you a question, numbnuts," a guy with a curly blonde white boy 'fro called from the side of the room.

"Oh, yeah. Sorry, can you repeat the question?"

"What kind of scholarship are you here on?" Cole asked.

"Water Polo."

Again, the class laughed at their clueless classmate.

"I knew it had to be…" Cole's voice trailed off as he looked around the room. "Same question, young lady who tried to save your friend."

"To tell the truth." The bright-eyed girl didn't hesitate in responding.

"Whose?"

"Sir?"

"Whose truth?"

"Well, mine of course," she said confidently.

"Therein lies the problem of the media today. Left, right, reactionary, anarchist, socialist, capitalist, and everything in-between all have their version of the truth. The problem is, it's all filtered through the truth of their ideology. The truth as facts has been lost to agenda. Sometimes this version of the truth is so far from the facts that it is unrecognizable. So what do you do as a journalist? Do you embrace the chance to spread the gospel of your personal set of truths, or do you report the facts? Mr. Cellphone, a chance to redeem yourself."

"Tell the truth."

"Right," Cole said in disbelief. "Someone else."

"People have a right to know what is going on."

"Daniel Ellsberg," Cole replied. "Google him. Anyone else?"

"Facts are not always the whole story. Point of view helps guide the reader through a maze of information they may not be qualified to interpret for themselves," a handsome, well-dressed young man in the fourth row offered.

"Let's see, class, racist, sexist, ageist, misogynist, bourgeois, elitist?" Cole smiled at the young man. At that moment, his cellphone vibrated in his pocket. He glanced at his watch. "Ponder that question. I want you to give me five hundred words explaining the responsibility of a journalist to the truth. Thursday, that's where we'll start. Have a good day."

Cole turned his back on the class as they made their way out of the room and looked at the phone number. Leonard Chin. Cole tapped Chin's number.

"Leonard."

"Everything is fine, but Kelly's at St. Martin's Emergency. She's asking for you," Lieutenant Leonard Chin said.

"Kelly? What are you doing with her? What's happened?" Cole pressed, making his way for the door, pushing his way past the stragglers in the class. "Leonard, are you there? What's going on?" he asked once in the hallway.

"Marty Sanchez called me. He was the first black and white on scene. She ran into a bunch of punks in a store. I'll explain when you get here. She's fine. Gotta go. I got a call from headquarters."

Chin was gone.

Chapter 3

"Excuse me," Cole said sharply after waiting longer than he thought necessary.

"Yes?" The woman looked up and sneered at Cole.

"I need to see Kelly Mitchell. She was brought in within the hour."

"And you are?"

It was clear this woman was not going to be accommodating. If he said fiancé, boyfriend, or anything other than family member, he was in trouble.

Without missing a beat, Cole stood a little straighter and said, "Her attorney. And you are?"

The woman glared at Cole. "Does she know you're her attorney, or did you just happen to follow the ambulance here?"

"Ms. Mitchell and I have a longstanding relationship, along with that of her son, Dr. Benjamin Mitchell. I suggest we cease with your charming attempt to get acquainted and you direct me to my client."

"Through the doors, bed five."

Without a word, Cole turned and made his way across the room and to the large stainless-steel doors. As he approached, there was a whoosh of air and they opened.

A big red 5 was painted on the highly waxed tile floor. A pale blue curtain was pulled around the end of the bed. Cole stood for a long moment before clearing his throat and stepping to the side of the bed.

"Hey there," Cole said softly.

"Hey yourself. I'm so glad you're here." Kelly started to smile, then burst into tears.

Cole sat on the edge of the bed and took her hand. "It's okay, I'm here. Are you all right?"

"They won't let me go home." Kelly sniffled, trying to regain her composure.

"That's probably for the best."

"Says who?" Kelly said, showing her frustration.

"What did the doctor say?" Cole patted her leg through the blue thermal blanket.

"I haven't seen one yet. They put me in here and just left me."

Cole took a deep breath and let his anger wrestle with his relief for a moment. He found it difficult to look at Kelly's bruised cheek and purple swollen eye. He gently stroked her hand while holding it in the other.

"It must be bad," Kelly began. "You haven't looked at me once."

"You're pretty bruised. Are you hurt anywhere else? I mean, that's not visible?"

"I'm certain I have broken ribs. Other than that, it's just my pride. I am so angry. This is 21st Century San Francisco, not Munich 1939, for heaven's sake."

"What were you doing? Where were you?"

"I was surprising you for your birthday."

"It worked," Cole said, trying to ease the tension a bit.

"How is Irwin?"

"Who's Irwin?" Cole asked.

"The man who owns the deli."

"Rosenberg's? What happened to him?"

"He got really hurt." Kelly's eyes filled with tears again.

"I don't know. I came straight to you. Leonard called and gave me almost nothing except you were here and you were okay." Cole hesitated, not wanting to upset Kelly further. "What in the world…?"

"Nazis, or Neo-whatevers, skinheads, you know, punks in stormtrooper boots."

"Got it."

"They came in the deli, four of them, threatening Irwin and then started breaking everything."

"And how did you get involved?"

"I told them to leave."

"Geez, Kelly."

"I couldn't just stand there and let them say the vicious, hateful things they were saying to Irwin. I just saw red."

"So they smacked you," Cole said, more as a statement than a question.

"What would you have done in my position?"

"Probably gotten killed. That's not the point. I wish you would have…"

"What, done nothing?" Kelly cut him off.

"Not pick fights with a gang of thugs."

"Am I interrupting anything?" Leonard Chin stepped from behind the curtain.

"Hello," Kelly said, trying to appear cheery.

"So what do we know, Leonard?" Cole asked.

"Not much. No witnesses, present company excluded. Sanchez says they really tore the place apart." He directed his comments to Kelly. "When you feel like it, I would like you to flip through some of our mug shot binders, but not 'til you're feeling better," Lieutenant Chin said, smiling at Kelly. He was showing an uncharacteristic soft side.

"How is Irwin?" Kelly asked.

"Pretty rough shape. He took a bad blow to the head," Chin replied.

"What have they said about you?"

"I haven't seen a doctor yet. I really need to see Irwin. Is anyone with him?"

"His family has gathered. You need to wait until you've been examined. Looks like you took a pretty good blow yourself," Chin said, looking at Kelly's swollen face.

"I'm going to see about a doctor," Cole announced, showing his discontent.

As Cole left, he pulled the curtain back a bit. Chin moved to the chair beside the bed.

"This is a hate crime, plain and simple. You have to charge these punks with that when you catch them. Promise?" Kelly's anger started to bubble up.

"Let's catch them first. Do you think you can ID them?"

"I don't think I'll ever forget them," Kelly stated emphatically.

"We have a pretty good idea who we're looking for. They're most likely members of a group calling themselves W.A.R., a bunch of thugs that have been terrorizing non-white and Jewish businesses in Rosenberg's area. We can't get anyone to testify. They are all afraid of retaliation."

"W.A.R.?"

"Warriors of the Aryan Revolution. White supremacist."

"You know them?" Kelly asked.

Unfortunately, yes. But this time they have crossed the line. This is the first time they have seriously hurt anyone; usually, it is just destruction of property, graffiti, and threats. This time, we've got felonies."

"Well, I'll testify. You can count on it!" Kelly promised angrily.

"Let's get you checked out and feeling better. That's priority number one." Chin smiled and nodded.

"Thank you, Lieutenant. You are a good friend."

"Just part of my job, ma'am." Chin did a pretty good Joe Friday impersonation, to Kelly's delight.

The curtain pulled back, and Cole was standing with a white-headed doctor, and behind them stood Ben Mitchell, Kelly's son, the doctor.

"Look who I found," Cole announced.

"Hi, Mom. This is Doctor Milford. He's a good friend and a wonderful doctor. I wouldn't trust just anyone with my mother, you know."

"Hi, sweetie. I'm fine, no need for all the fuss."

"Dr. Milford will decide that."

"Hello, Mrs. Mitchell."

"Please call me Kelly."

"All right, thank you. If you gentlemen will give me a moment, we'll have a look at our patient," Milford requested pleasantly.

Cole, Ben, and Leonard Chin stepped out of the examination area and found a quiet place to talk.

"Someone want to fill me in?" Ben began.

"Wrong place at the wrong time. Your mom was in Rosenberg's Deli when it was visited by a group of Aryan thugs. They started out threatening and trying to intimidate the owner. Your mom stepped in, and one of them clocked her and then proceeded to kick her several times in the ribs." Chin paused. "The owner didn't fare as well. It looks like he won't make it. So, we have a whole list of felonies, possibly murder, we can get the punks on. Add to that hate crimes, and they are going to be off the streets for a long time."

"So they can do more recruiting inside," Cole added sarcastically.

"This time, Mom's righteous intervention got her hurt. I knew she would put her nose in it someday and come out the loser." Ben shook his head.

"I don't want to put undue worry on you guys, but they are a dangerous organization. We will be placing an around the clock detail on Kelly. I'm not saying they will try anything, but I wouldn't put it past them. You be on the alert."

"She can stay with us when they release her. We are out of the city."

"I would prefer she stay at home. I can't protect her otherwise."

"This is insane." Cole tried to contain his anger. "If we know who these clowns are, why can't you grab them?"

"Come on, Cole, you of all people should know there are procedures, due process and steps to ensure a conviction. I get you're mad. I'm mad, we're all mad. This just needs to be done the right way. It won't take long; I guarantee it. Kelly can ID them, I have no doubt. Then we arrest them."

"Yeah, yeah, I get it," Cole grumbled.

"And promise me you won't go off half-cocked and do some Cole Sagism and get yourself hurt or mess up our case. I need you to keep out of this. You got me?"

"I'm sorry. Yes, you have my word. You really think you'll put them away?"

"Long as I can. San Francisco is no place for far-right anything." Chin grinned. "We got that on our side, for sure."

Ben pointed back towards his mother's bed. Doctor Milford was looking in their direction.

Cole moved quickly to where the doctor stood. "Well?"

"Her face took a hell of a punch. She has a pretty good concussion. No permanent tissue or bone damage. The bruising will get worse before it gets better. Her ribs, now that's another story. I've ordered X-rays and a sonogram. Steel-toed boots can do some real damage. I'm sure at least two are broken. We need to make sure there is no internal damage. She is in good shape for a woman her age, so her recovery will be faster than most. Still, I am concerned what may have happened below the ribs. We'll know in a couple of hours."

Ben's phone buzzed. "I need to get back to the hospital. Robert, thank you." He extended his hand to Milford. "Let me say goodbye to Mom, and I'll be on my way. Cole, call if you need anything. Can you let Erin know what's happened?"

"No problem."

"Thank you, Lieutenant." Ben shook hands with Chin and moved behind the curtain around Kelly's bed.

"I'm going to grab some mug shot binders for Kelly to look at. Any problem with that, Doctor?"

"We'll have her ribs bound up, and she'll be pretty uncomfortable. She already told me she didn't want anything stronger than Tylenol." Milford smiled. "Tough gal, that one."

Cole chuckled. "Too tough for her own good, it seems."

"Well." Milford shrugged. "I need to see to her being admitted and getting a room. I'm sure I'll see you later."

"Thank you, Doctor," Cole replied.

Chapter 4

Outside of Starbucks, a ragged, filthy man sat on the sidewalk in front of an empty auto supply store. His few possessions seemed to be bundled within a sleeping bag. A bone-thin dog, with its leash tethered to the bundle, lay sleeping at his side.

The sight of degraded, homeless, street people, junkies, and the mentally ill on the streets was nothing new. The fact that Mason Muller grew more and more repulsed by them with each passing day didn't keep him from sipping his one hundred and ninety degree Kenyan roast coffee with soy and two packs of raw sugar. He stared out the window at the man.

As Muller watched, he noticed the man was fumbling with something made of glass. Small and round at one end, he realized it was a pipe. The man held the glass bowl over a small orange plastic lighter. After a few seconds, smoke began to waft from the end of the pipe. The ragged man put the pipe to his lips and inhaled deeply, all the while rocking back and forth in a primal rhythm. After a minute, he repeated the lighting process and again took another hit from the pipe. His rocking stopped and leaned back against the window of the abandoned shop.

Cars passed on their way to the Save-a-Lot Supermarket and Walgreen's just beyond. If the drivers noticed, they didn't react. Muller was appalled. It was broad daylight, the middle of the afternoon, on the sidewalk in his city! This piece of human refuse was taking drugs. He looked around the macchiato drinking, Chai sipping patrons around him, and no one was paying any attention to the man just across the driveway.

"Kristen, Caramel Frappuccino!" the barista called out.

A cute, perky blonde with a ponytail, running shorts, and a Stanford T-shirt bounced to the little round table and the end of the counter and smiled with appreciation. Life was going on as if the man didn't exist. Muller's anger began to rise.

That's why these people are able to get away with this behavior, he thought, *nobody even notices. Silence is approval.*

He took his cell and dialed 911. "I want to report a man on the sidewalk in front of the empty O'Connor Auto store on Fulton. He is smoking crack or something from a glass pipe." Muller paused. "Yes, that's my emergency. He's a menace." Another pause. "I want him arrested, that's what. What do you mean there aren't enough officers to deal with this kind of call? Are you kidding me?" Muller was outraged. "Hello, hello?" The emergency dispatcher hung up on him.

Muller stood. *Something must be done,* he thought. He left his briefcase and coffee on the table and went to the door. As he stepped into the bright sunshine, he realized he had no plan, no idea of what he was about to do as he walked toward the man.

He stepped onto the sidewalk and took a moment to survey the situation. Between the dog and the man lay the glass pipe. Muller took two short strides and stomped the pipe with rage. In that instant, he spotted the tin foil in the man's lap. As the dog leaped to its feet, the man began to rouse from his stupor. Muller bent and snatched the drugs from the man's lap and wadded the foil into a ball.

"Hey, what the hell?!" the man bellowed angrily. He tried to stand but was met with the hard sole of Muller's heavy wing-tip oxford on his chest.

"I want you out of my town!" Muller growled.

"You a cop?" the man shouted. "You don't look like no cop. Give me my crystal!"

"I am a concerned citizen of this community, and I'm telling you to leave my city."

"Or what?" the man said defiantly.

"Or the next time I see you, I will kill you." Muller's words were terrifying. There was no doubt in the man's muddled mind Muller meant exactly what he said.

Shocked by his utterance, Muller stood motionless. The derelict scrambled to get to all fours and crab-walked several steps before he was able to get to his feet. Without looking back or giving a thought to his bundle or dog, the man rounded the corner.

Muller's hands trembled. His breathing was shallow and rapid. He looked back at Starbucks; no one was looking in his direction. No cars passed. He looked down at where the man leaned against the wall.

There was a large, spreading wet spot. The dog looked up at him and barked. Muller bent and untied the dog from the bundle. The dog dashed off to find its master.

The bundle sat green, dirty and abandoned. Muller picked it up by the strap and started back to the coffee shop. To the right of the driveway was a block enclosure with a chain link gate. With the fiery anger of a prophet of old, he threw the bundle over the gate and into the dumpster.

"Carl, double shot French Roast." The sound of the barista was calm and cheerful as Muller re-entered the coffee shop.

As he made his way back to his seat, no one looked up or even noticed his presence. The middle-aged woman in the tailored charcoal suit, working on her laptop at the table next to him, glanced up and smiled, then returned to her work.

Nothing on his table was different. He took a sip of his coffee. Still hot. Mason Muller left an angry citizen and returned a victor over the forces of poverty, ignorance and drug addiction. He was able, by his action, to hopefully rid the city of one derelict drag on society. Yes, he would wander off to another neighboring town or city, but Palo Alto was cleaner by one cockroach. Although still trembling with adrenaline, Muller felt good.

"The only thing necessary for the triumph of evil is for good men to do nothing," Muller said softly. He did something, and it felt good.

The nameplate next to the door says Col. Mason G. Muller, Retired. War is a funny thing. It makes heroes out of warriors, and officers out of nobodies. Such was the case with Muller. An Idaho boy who loved the ROTC in high school rose to the top of the state ranking. It wasn't hard to get an appointment to West Point; after all, the whole point of ROTC is to grow the next crop of warriors for the volunteer army.

Never the best student, he worked harder than his peers and was good enough to rank in the top twenty percent of his class at West Point. Muller showed a real aptitude for geography, cartography, and urban studies. It seems that the boy from the woods developed a deep and almost organic understanding of modern cities, their layout and the movement of population centers around the world.

His path to the Pentagon was only detoured by a posting in Kuwait during Desert Storm. The nearness of battle drove Muller to distraction. He would beg his fellow officers to take him to the front lines. He put in for a transfer that would allow him a combat command. It was, of course, rejected, on the grounds that his training and insights into the towns and cities of Iraq made him a vital asset to the war effort. Muller grudgingly agreed with the decision. This did not, however, keep him from going out with junior officers for countryside pistol competitions. He would joke that he was born with a pistol in his hand.

After the dust settled in Iraq, the Pentagon appointment was put on hold. An opportunity presented itself for Muller to return to West Point as a visiting professor. It was a chance for him to do something he loved. He found it a perfect situation, teaching and working on his Ph.D. at the same time. It was during this stint at West Point he met Belinda.

It wasn't a fairy tale meeting or a particularly romantic courtship. It was, in fact, just what they each needed. Their individual needs, a way of expressing and receiving love, fit just like the white gloves Muller wore to the Officers Ball the night he met her. They were introduced by a fellow Muller barely knew. In retrospect, he was sure the guy thought he would pawn Belinda off on him so he could be alone with his own date. Whatever the case, the two became inseparable. They married a year later.

Once married, the appeal of all things military faded for Muller. The uniforms and rigor of West Point seemed unnatural compared to the loving looseness of home. Belinda's passion for life, art, and baking seemed so much more real to Muller than the marching, pomp, and ceremony of The Point. For Belinda's thirty-fifth birthday, he presented her with a slightly mangled envelope. Inside was the welcome letter from the University of Colorado and the contract for his new position there.

The next five years were spent in blissful peace. He loved his teaching assignment. They hiked, and he again found the love for fishing he forgot he possessed. Belinda gardened, painted and baked bread for a Farmers Market booth. They traveled summers and enjoyed nights by the fire, and reading in the winter. Theirs was the kind of life Muller always dreamed of.

One morning, the passion of their lovemaking was followed by cuddling and hugs. As Muller gently stroked and caressed Belinda's breast, he felt a hard lump. The cancer spread quickly to other parts of her body. In the year following the lump's discovery, she lost so much weight, she was almost unrecognizable. They would rock as she sat in his arms in his big reclining chair. He wept silently as the frail little sparrow of a woman napped in his arms.

At times the pain seemed, to Muller, more than she could bear. The home they made became a place of anger, resentment, and sorrow. The classes he once loved, and the campus he walked, only helped confine his heartache and despair.

One morning, he slipped out of the house to teach his morning class as she slept peacefully. The drugs the doctors gave her helped her sleep but only dulled the ever-present pain. As he opened the front door only a little over two hours later, the feeling in the house just wasn't right.

He called Belinda's name, but there was no answer. *She should be awake by now,* he thought. He called again as he made his way to the bedroom. There seemed to be no air in the room as he entered. Belinda lay propped up on her pillows. Her hair long gone, she wore a floral print scarf around her head. The bright pink lipstick was an odd contrast to her ashen gray skin. The blankets were pulled up under her arms and neatly folded over.

The bottle of oxycodone he so carefully monitored lay empty on the nightstand next to her. Mason Muller's beloved wife and soulmate chose to leave this world on her own terms and to leave him alone without a word of goodbye.

Nine months later, in a chance meeting at a small diner off campus, Muller became reacquainted with a fellow officer he served with during Desert Storm. Arlen Coffiere and his wife Sandra were vacationing in Colorado during the spring break. He, too, turned to teaching upon retiring from military service. After bouncing around for several years on short-term contracts, Coffiere landed at Stanford University. He taught Military History and 20th Century World Conflicts.

Muller invited them to dinner at his home, something, until now, he couldn't bring himself to do since Belinda's death. Somehow, this chance meeting seemed directed by fate. That night, as he told his story, it became apparent it was time to leave Boulder. Sandra insisted Arlen pick up the phone and call a couple of colleagues to see what could be done to get Muller an interview. It took a year, but Mason Muller was added to the faculty of Stanford University. He found a small house about three miles from campus and settled into a solitary life in Palo Alto.

Now the town he has come to love is being poisoned by drugs.

Chapter 5

Kelly was finally admitted, and after an hour in her new room, she was getting restless. The poor nurse was no match for Kelly's combination of charm and perfect argument for why she should be allowed to be wheeled down to Irwin Rosenberg's room.

"Only if you let me push." the nurse insisted.

"Just so long as I get down there," Kelly pleaded.

Outside the room where the nurse stopped, three people were gathered talking. A small dark-haired woman obviously had been crying.

"How's Irwin doing?" Kelly asked softly.

"Not good." A handsome man of around forty turned to face Kelly. "Jake Rosenberg, his son. This is my sister Ann and her husband."

"I'm Kelly Mitchell. I was in the deli when he was attacked. I'm so sorry. No, that's not true. I am so angry." Kelly's voice trembled as she fought back tears.

"So you saw what happened?" the crying woman asked.

"Yes. Your father is a very brave man. He stood up to those thugs and didn't back down until…" Kelly's voice faded away, deciding to not continue.

"For all the good it did him," Ann said angrily.

"Are you okay?" Jake asked.

"A knot on the head and a couple of broken ribs. I'll be fine. I am so worried about Irwin. That guy hit him really hard."

"Dad's in a coma. His brain is swelling, and the doctors put him in a coma, hoping to reduce brain activity. The idea is the medications will work better if he is under."

"Can I see him? I would like to pray for him," Kelly asked.

"He would like that. The Cantors' son has always been big on prayer." Ann gave a crooked smile.

"And you?"

"Not so much," Ann said.

"Would you mind if I prayed with you?"

"Jake?" Ann deferred to her brother.

"Certainly couldn't hurt."

Without hesitation, Kelly reached out and took Ann's hand. Ann took Jake's. "Our great and mighty God, God of Abraham, Isaac, and Jacob, we come to you on behalf of your servant Irwin. You, who David told us knitted us in our mother's womb, who placed the sun and stars in the sky, please touch our dear father, and friend, if it be your will. But if you should need him more than we here on Earth, take him to your bosom and ease our pain with the knowledge of your love. Amen."

"Amen," Ann's husband repeated.

"Are you sure you're not Jewish?" Jake patted Kelly's hand before releasing it.

"He's the same Almighty for all of us." Kelly smiled softly.

Kelly rolled forward, catching the nurse off guard. The room was very dim, and Irwin lay under a soft light. Kelly rolled forward as close as the machine surrounding the bed would allow. She stood, squeezed up to the head of the bed, and bent, giving Irwin a kiss on the forehead.

"They say people in a coma can hear when people speak to them. If that's true, you keep fighting. There are two kids here who love you very much. Don't let those awful men win." She reached out and gently placed her hand on his shoulder, closed her eyes and prayed silently. A minute later, she returned to her wheelchair.

"I'm down the hall in 462. Please let me know how your father's doing, won't you?" Kelly said, returning to the hallway.

"Certainly. Thank you for thinking of Dad."

"We've got to get you back. I'm gonna get skinned," the nurse whispered hoarsely.

"Then we better hurry."

Back in her room sat Leonard Chin. On his lap was a thick black binder.

"You'd think we'd have these on a laptop or tablet or something." He stood and moved out of the way as the nurse helped Kelly back into bed.

"This is a stupid amount of fuss for a couple of bruised ribs and a punch in the face."

"Concussion and two broken ribs. Now you need to stay put." The nurse was not shy in letting Kelly know there would be no more trips in the wheelchair.

"You and Cole make a fine pair. You're both stubborn as pit bulls." Leonard Chin was smiling, but he was serious. "I brought you a mug book to flip through in your spare time."

"Funny, I have nothing but spare time. They have got to release me soon. I'll go crazy in here." Kelly lifted the thick black binder and groaned. The expression on her face was a giveaway to the pain it caused her.

"That's why you're not going home," the nurse chided.

Kelly adjusted the bed with the remote. As she flipped open the binder, she glanced up at Chin. "Leonard, is there a lot of this? I mean, here in San Francisco."

"More than hits the paper."

As Kelly's eyes scanned the page of mug shots, she said, "So many wasted lives."

Page after page she flipped until she suddenly slapped the page. "There you are! Here's one, Leonard. For sure, this is the guy by the candy rack. I'm sure of it."

"Let's see." Chin stood and approached the bed. "Justin Manning, aka Stone Manning, aka Thumper. Got it." Chin wrote the name in his notebook.

"One down, three to go."

The more pages Kelly turned, the more frustrated she became. She reached the end of the massive book without finding another face she recognized.

"It's okay," Chin assured her. "We can try later."

"No, I'll do it now. I obviously overlooked them. They all start to look alike after a while. Let me go through them again." She immediately turned the binder over and began again.

Cole quietly entered the room and sat at the opposite side of the bed from Chin. He watched as Kelly now let her fingers run across every face in the book, stopping on occasion to give a face a closer look. Ten minutes in, she looked up.

"I think this is the guy who hit us, the guy with the baton. No, I'm sure of it. The long hair fooled me the first time. His eyes, those are the eyes. This is the guy, Leonard. This is the guy."

"Peter Travis, aka Travis Peterson, aka Spear." Chin stood. "I know this guy. You're sure?"

"Positive." Kelly gave Chin a nod of her head.

"This has been a long time coming. We got him this time." Chin turned to Cole. "I have sat across the interview table from this guy a dozen times. He's as vicious as they come, terrifies any potential witness into refusing to talk. This is going to make a lot of folks very happy."

"Missus Mitchell? Can I have a word?" Kelly's nurse and wheelchair driver stood in the doorway.

"Of course."

"The old man, Mister Rosenberg? He passed, darlin'. I'm awful sorry." The nurse bowed ever so slightly and slipped out of the room.

"It looks like we have a murder," Chin said to Cole as Kelly put her hands over her face and wept.

Chapter 6

"Morning, Cole." Randy Callen stood at Cole's office door, sipping at a steaming cup of coffee. "I thought I would come to say hello before I went to the library."

"Hey, buddy. Come in, please. Close the door." Cole Sage was an "open door policy" kind of guy. If he was at his desk, the door was open if he were alone.

Randy pulled the door closed, then took a seat across from Cole.

"I've been meaning to come to see you. There is no excuse for why I haven't except cowardice, embarrassment, and shame." Cole pulled his chair up close to the desk. "I owe you an apology."

"How's that?" Randy sensed a level of sincerity rarely expressed, much less spoken, by Cole.

"This didn't turn out quite as planned."

"Look, Cole, don't…"

"Let me say my piece, please," Cole interrupted. "The newspaper business is all that I have ever really known. Sure, I write about crooks and cons and the world's highs and lows. Problem with being an observer is, you don't live it. You don't feel the pain, you don't feel the gut punch of disappointment. That's why, I guess, this whole thing has been swept under the rug for six months. I keep thinking it is going to turn around or somebody will say, 'My bad, let's straighten this out.'

"Here's the thing, I feel responsible for your falling down the shaft with me. So, I guess what I'm saying is if you want to bail, don't stick around for any loyalty to me that is keeping you back. I love you like a son, I'm proud of who you are and what you do, but this crap bucket we've stepped in is getting really old for me. I can't imagine the come-down it is for you."

"Hey, I've learned more about Renaissance art and painters, the causes of World War I, and the Ben Johnson–William Shakespeare authorship argument than I ever dreamed of." Randy gave Cole a melancholy grin. "Hey, you were the only one at the Chron' I got along with anyway. I basically did the same thing there, only now I have a whole lot more pretty girls to look at. Don't worry about me; I make more money, I see daylight all day long. The computer sucks, and I only have one monitor at a time, but the campus is way nicer to hang out on breaks."

"You know I see right through you."

"Better than anybody. It's kind of scary. Please don't feel bad. We're a team, right? We're just having a slump season. Who knows, next year we could win the pennant."

"I want you to promise me that if you get the chance to do something more in keeping with your talents, you'll grab it. Swear?"

"Nope. If you can stick it out, so can I. I've got a lot of years to fill. You, old timer, can count yours." Randy laughed.

"Thanks, partner!"

A knock at the door stopped any chance of Randy having a pithy comeback. The secretary Cole shared with three other faculty members housed in the second floor Humanities building was leaning into the office.

"Excuse me, Mr. Sage, a mandatory, all faculty meeting has been called for this afternoon. You're in group 'C', so your time is at 3:00 in Turing Auditorium."

"Thank you, Suzanne. What's it about?" Cole asked.

"I'm not quite sure, but it was called by the president, so it is something big." The secretary raised her eyebrows, shrugged and closed the door.

"Hey, I gotta get rolling. We can do this, little buddy!" Randy stood and gave Cole a mock salute."

"Yeah, maybe I'm just still adjusting."

"You know what you need? An old fashioned Cole Sage investigation. On…no, I got it, write a book! Anything to get your mind off all these knucklehead kids around here."

"I kind of miss the chase," Cole agreed.

"I'm off. Want the door open?"

"Yes, please. Let's have lunch on Friday."

"You buyin'?"

"Do I ever not?"

Randy laughed heartily. "Then I'm in."

Cole looked down at the stack of papers on his desk to grade. "Hey, Suzanne, that new guy this semester, Ethan, my new TA, did he come in? It's been three weeks, and I've seen him twice."

"He came in yesterday while you were in class. He's scheduled again tomorrow." Suzanne appeared at the door.

"How convenient. Is this typical of teaching assistants?"

"Kind of, not really, but this one is *really* worthless. Anything I can help with?"

"No, thanks. He seems like a nice kid, but he has to earn his keep somehow. If you see him, would you tell him I need to have a chat with him? I have some stuff he could be doing."

Two classes and lunch later, Cole made his way to Turing Auditorium. He was a few minutes early and took a seat on the aisle about three-quarters of the way back.

"Afternoon," a woman in a dark skirt and red jacket said as she passed Cole.

"Hi."

The woman turned. "I don't think we've met. I'm Susan Stout, British Lit."

"Cole Sage, Journalism."

"Mind if I join you?"

"Not at all. Any idea what this is about?" Cole asked.

"The chatter is another student died of a drug overdose."

"So we have a mandatory meeting?"

"Odd, isn't it? There must be more to it than that."

The pair chatted as more and more people began arriving. The faculty sat spaced far apart. A few of the younger members came in together chatting and laughing and drew severe looks from the old school faculty.

At exactly three o'clock, the side door opened and three men and a woman walked out.

"Good afternoon, everyone. Thank you for being prompt. We shall not keep you long." The door slamming shut in the back of the auditorium punctuated the man's remarks. "Mr. President."

A powerful man in a perfectly tailored suit and thinning gray hair approached the podium. "I have taken this unusual step of bringing us together to address a most disheartening situation. This morning, I received news that a student on our campus has died of an opioid overdose. Ethan Fraioli, a doctoral candidate, was found this morning by his roommate. Our thoughts and prayers are with his family."

"My God," Cole whispered, "he was my TA."

"Ethan is the third student this year to die from this plague on our nation. This is not Appalachia or a trailer park in the Central Valley; this is our town, our campus, our student. We, as the adults, as *parentis locos*, need to be vigilant. We need to speak out and address this scourge. I would ask that this week as your classes gather, you take a moment to remember this young man so full of potential, so full of promise. These drugs so easy to obtain are flooding our streets, and now our campus.

"This isn't a simple joint smoked at a party, a line of coke on a dare; this is a deadly, powerful, addictive narcotic. 'If one is good, two is better', can kill. The opioid family's grasp is subtle and beguiling. The dose that calms and stones today isn't enough next week. More pills, another shot to boost the effect's quality or strength cannot be assured, and all too often death follows.

"We have contacted several volunteer drug counseling organizations. They will be on campus to advise, correct misconceptions, and offer treatment to anyone who has let this plague into their life. We have materials available, cards for counselors and schedules available as you leave.

"I have Dr. Kelmann, Dean of Medical Studies, Ms. Weltmire of Student Services, and Peter Franklin, our Director of Campus Police, with me today. We will try to answer any questions or entertain any suggestions you may have. Please stand and give your name so we all can see, hear, and know who is speaking."

"Phyllis Chamber, Romance Languages. I really don't feel comfortable talking about drugs in my class."

"Well," Ms. Weltmire began, "a simple announcement, a word of condolence, and a warning to the dangers of these drugs can make the difference between life and death. I think we can all step outside our comfort zone to save a life, don't you?" The president pointed. "Yes, on the left."

"What are the police doing about this problem? Sorry, Clinton Avila, Geography."

"Does anyone in this room think a Stanford grad student is the first person who comes to mind when you think of drug trafficking? Some of these drugs are coming from Mom and Dad's medicine cabinet. The opioid epidemic isn't just backstreet junkies anymore. Doctors are prescribing these dangerous substances as if they were Vitamin C! Oxycodone, OxyContin, Percocet, Hydrocodone, Vicodin, Lortab, Codeine, Fentanyl. All can be, and are, abused. It's estimated 310 million prescriptions for opiates were written last year! Some of you in a room this size probably have one or more in your medicine cabinet.

"This stuff is the ultimate gateway drug. Heroin is a lot cheaper than pharmaceuticals on the street, and that is what this stuff leads to. So, what are we doing? Everything possible, but you want to know who the biggest pushers are? Your Doctor." Peter Franklin was angry, and it showed.

"If I may, Peter is right," Dr. Kelmann said, stepping to the microphone. "We have begun instituting steps at every level to instill in our doctors-in-training that the prescriptions of opioids are the last acceptable line for the comfort of a patient. I would suggest that they are far, far too easy to get and in most cases can and should be replaced with another non-narcotic medicine."

The man a row in front of Cole stood and spoke in a loud, confident tone. "Mason Muller, Social Sciences. This all sounds nice, but a third kid is dead. Our city has become a dangerous, uncivilized snake pit of gangs, drug dealers, and welfare criminals. It is far past time to educate and counsel. We need to clean up our city, give mandatory prison sentences, and let this scum know they and their poison will not be tolerated.

"Now, somebody gave that kid the pills. Find them. Send them to jail. Will we? Hell no! Because they are white upper middle class, sons, and daughters of the movers and shakers in their community and ours. They will get a slap on the wrist and a half-hearted lecture, and then it is business as usual. If they were black, they'd be behind bars. When was the last time a Stanford student served time, Mr. Franklin? When was it? When was your last actual arrest and conviction for drugs? The people of this country are getting fed up with two systems of justice.

"Dope is sold openly on the streets of this city. If I know it, so do the cops! I, for one, am sick of this namby-pamby bullshit approach to dealing with crime. If the doctors are the problem, yank their license. Will it happen? Hell no! They make too much money. I, for one, am not going to listen to any more of this." Mason Muller stepped to the aisle and made his way to the door.

Cole glanced over at Phyllis Chambers. "That's going to be a tough act to follow. Who was that guy?"

Phyllis shrugged and put her finger to her lips to hush Cole.

The president returned to the microphone and tried to bring some order to the chaos created by Mason Muller.

"Please, everyone, if I can just have your attention." Slowly, the room grew quieter; a few last comments were exchanged, then he continued. "I realize this is a really sensitive issue. Please just try and reflect and do your part as you see fit."

"He should have stayed. That, my dear, is namby-pamby."

Cole chuckled and stood. He'd had enough, too. Outside the building, he called Kelly and arranged to have dinner. The walk back to the office was solemn. The campus felt like a dark cloud hung overhead even though the sun was shining.

Chapter 7

The walk across campus was a time of reflection for Cole. *What kind of a madhouse have I been committed to?* he thought. A kid is dead, several in fact, and the faculty attacks the cops. That was neither the time nor place for questioning and condemning policing or drug policies. Cole's thoughts swirled at the realization that a young man who reported to him was dead. Once again, drugs took the best and brightest.

Stephen Walker came into Cole's thoughts. Long buried in memory, the painful connection was now a glaring reality. Stephen and Cole were friends, good friends. The late sixties were a time of experimentation and a newfound sense of freedom for thousands of kids who found themselves away from home for the first time and exposed to new ideas, teaching and temptations their parents could never have imagined.

Cole knew Stephen was a partier. He always knew where the next party was and was usually in attendance. From freshman year to the beginning of their junior year there was a marked change in Stephen's appearance, attitude, and friends. As Cole became more involved with Ellie and he became more committed to his studies, their friendship seemed to be one of the casualties.

One winter evening, late, there was a knock on Cole's door. It was Stephen. He was wet, shivering and looked like death was holding his hand.

"Do you know what time it is?" Cole scolded.

"I need a favor," Stephen panted.

"Well, you better come in. You're soaked. Where have you been?"

"My roomie kicked me out. Look, I need ten bucks. Loan me ten bucks," Stephen said, bordering on a demand.

"At three in the morning? What are you going to do with ten bucks?"

"What the hell do you care? Just loan me ten bucks!" Stephen shouted.

"First you tell me what it's for." Cole was beginning to sense desperation beyond necessity.

With a rapid, desperate motion, Stephen yanked up his sleeve, exposing needle marks. Lots of needle marks, bruised and infected. "Happy? I need a fix, I need medicine. I need to get right."

"What you need is to get some help. I'll go with you. We'll get you to the hospital," Cole said with a kind demeanor.

"Oh sure, goodie, goodie Cole always with the right answer. I don't want or need your help!" Stephen screamed. Cursing and waving his arms like a madman, he continued to demand money.

There was pounding on the walls on both sides of the dorm room and demands for silence, adding to the escalating confrontation.

"I'll get you help, but I'm not giving you money for dope," Cole pronounced emphatically.

Stephen screamed a profanity in Cole's face and left the dorm, leaving the door open.

It wasn't much later that Cole learned his friend died. An overdose in a squat house on the backside of an alley left him dead and undiscovered for several days.

For many years, Cole wondered if he could have done more to save his friend. While writing a story on the scourge of heroin in Chicago, he came to the realization that the drug had a stronger hold on its users than friends, family or good intentions of onlookers.

Cole thought of the foolishness and brilliance of Nancy Reagan's "Just Say No" campaign in the eighties. Foolish for those caught in the web of poverty, peer pressure, and addiction, brilliant for people who, if challenged early, would save them from heartache, pain, and potential death. Cole was eternally grateful his fear of alcoholism or drug addiction kept him from experimentation.

When he arrived back at his office, Suzanne was waiting by his door.

She gave a hard jerk of her head in the direction of the small office used by TAs in the department.

"What?" Cole whispered.

"Visitor," Suzanne mouthed.

Cole moved toward the tiny office, but it was too late.

Mason Muller came straight from the meeting. He entered the TA's office and flipped papers and opened drawers until he figured out which of the three small desks belong to Ethan.

He searched the drawers one by one until he found, hidden in the back behind a wadded up T-shirt, an amber pill bottle with a handwritten label COTTON BALLS. Muller knew from his research it was slang for OxyContin tablets. The cap was off the bottle, and it was empty except for a torn piece of notebook paper. He put the paper back in the bottle and shoved it in his jacket pocket.

"Idiot," Muller grumbled.

He explored the last drawer, but it held only a couple of newspapers, notebooks and a fist full of candy bar wrappers.

"Excuse me. What are you doing in here?" Cole was less than pleased at the sight of Muller.

Muller turned. He was considerably taller than Cole. His hard features bore a look that warned the world he would not be trifled with. Though nearing sixty, the muscles beneath his suit jacket showed he still retained a military commitment to fitness.

Cole's experience with military personnel, active or retired, never left him with any endearing memories. Not that he was anti-military, he just never found dealing with them in his best interest. Perhaps it was his unorthodox sense of discipline or his less than enthusiastic embrace of being told what to do. He already formed an opinion of Muller, and it was not favorable.

"Looking around." Muller glared at Cole.

"And what gives you the right to come snooping around in other people's desks?" Cole was trying not to let him have it.

"I'm a faculty member. I have -"

Cole cut him off. "You have nothing here. Muller, right? You're Social Science? That's two buildings over." Cole looked at the desk. The clutter made it difficult to tell what was its natural state, and what, if anything, Muller was responsible for. "I think that is where your rights are."

"I'm done here," Muller said, moving toward the door and Cole.

"I hope you weren't foolish enough to take anything from this room."

"You want to try searching me?" Muller stood ramrod straight, defiantly challenging Cole.

"No, that bluff tells me everything I need to know." Cole smiled knowingly.

Muller pushed past Cole and made his way out of the building. Cole watched his exit, making mental note of the time.

Suzanne was standing at her desk, phone in hand, ready to call security if the need arose. "What was that about?" She asked as she set the phone down and approached Cole.

"It was about him snooping around in Ethan's desk. What's with that guy anyway?"

"Isn't it awful?"

"You heard?" Cole said flatly.

"There are no secrets around here," Suzanne offered. "I feel terrible saying those mean things about

Ethan when he was already dead." Suzanne followed Cole to his office door.

"Death doesn't change the truth," Cole stated somberly. "Just because someone dies, it doesn't change who or what they were, or wash away their sins."

"But he wasn't a bad kid." Suzanne wasn't sure where Cole was going with his comment.

"People always give sainthood to the dead. I went to the funeral of a convicted child molester and murderer in Chicago once. He'd hanged himself in his jail cell. The priest went on and on about how God welcomed this poor lost sinner into his bosom. I almost puked. If anything was happening to that animal, it was the devil stoking up the welcome fires in his corner of hell."

Suzanne could see she touched a nerve. She decided it would be best if she kept her response to herself.

"Do I have any calls or anything?" Cole asked.

"No, not at the moment."

"Good, I'm going to take off. How do we go about getting another TA?"

Suzanne looked at Cole like he slapped her across the face.

"Too soon?" Cole said with a grimace.

"A bit. I will call Graduate Services in a day or two," she replied.

"Say, what do you know about Muller anyway?"

"Not much. My friend Melanie did a short-term sub in his department. I'll ask her when she comes back."

"Thanks. Listen, sorry about the -"

"It's fine, we all react differently to bad news. I laughed when my mother called to tell me my aunt died. I was in college. It was finals, and I had just been dumped by the guy I was dating. Too much stress, you know? We're good."

Cole grabbed his keys from his desk drawer and his briefcase. "See you tomorrow."

He almost made it to the door when two men stopped him. "Cole Sage?"

"Yes."

"Detectives Wilcox and Preete, Palo Alto PD. Got a minute?"

"I was trying to sneak out early, but yeah, I got all the time you need. Let's go to my office."

"Great, thanks."

Greg Wilcox was in his early forties, tall, athletic looking and seemed the friendlier of the two. Good cop, bad cop? *A little early for that,* Cole thought. Beau Preete, on the other hand, was tired, wrinkled, smelled of stale tobacco and wore the look of a career already gone too long. The two men stood at Cole's desk.

"Have a seat, gentlemen," Cole offered.

"I understand Ethan Fraioli was your teaching assistant, that right?" Wilcox asked. It was clear he was taking the lead. Preete slouched in his chair and looked around Cole's office, showing little or no interest in the proceedings.

"Yes, he was assigned to me about a month ago, just after the new semester."

"What do you know about him?"

"Not enough, evidently. He was, let's see, not a great TA. Pretty hit and miss on his office hours. Nice enough, I guess."

"Did you suspect he was a drug user?"

"Tell you the truth, he wasn't around me enough to make a judgment on much of anything. What killed him exactly?"

"It appears he was snorting oxy," Preete grunted.

"Whoa. Sure didn't see that coming. That's pretty hardcore, isn't it?" Cole leaned forward.

"What is it you teach, Mr. Sage?" Wilcox asked, ignoring Cole's comment.

"Journalism, and I advise the student newspaper staff."

"Been here long?"

"Nope, first year."

"Where did you teach before Stanford, if I could ask?"

"I didn't. I was at the San Francisco Chronicle, and the Chicago Sentinel before that."

"A real newspaperman." Wilcox smiled. "Sorry, it was just my curiosity. I knew you weren't a lifer here."

"How's that?"

"You're not a big enough asshole," Wilcox stated without expression. "Did Fraioli have a desk or anything, somewhere he did his work? A locker, file cabinet or anything?"

"Not that he did a lot of work, but he did have a desk. I'll show you." Cole stood and moved toward the door.

"I'll wait here," Preete grumbled.

Wilcox didn't even look in his direction. Outside the door, he smiled at Suzanne.

"Did she work with Fraioli?"

"Not really. Several of us share her secretarial skills, so she's a busy lady. She prepared his calendar and time card each week, for all the good that did. Beyond that, you'll have to ask her."

"Sounds like you didn't like him much."

"No, it's not that, I guess I'm not an academic yet. I come from the old school where you worked or got fired. You certainly didn't get a Ph.D. by not showing up. On the right," Cole said, pointing into the TA office. "I'm afraid somebody beat you to the search, though."

"How's that?"

"A faculty member named Muller. I found him snooping around when I got back from the faculty meeting."

"He's got an office in this building?"

"That's the thing, he has no business in this building. He's Social Science. Their offices are a couple of buildings over, so are their classrooms."

"You're quite the investigator," Wilcox chuckled, beginning to open the drawers of the small desk.

"Old habits die hard." Cole liked the detective. He was no nonsense and gave off a confident directness Cole appreciated.

"Not much here. His apartment was the same way. I'm guessing you didn't know anything about his personal life, friends, stuff like that?"

"Not a thing. As I said, he was nearly a stranger around here."

Wilcox closed the bottom desk drawer. "Either that other guy found something and took it or found as much as I did. I'll have Forensics test for residue. I don't expect much, but if we can get a small sample, we can often tell the manufacturer, which helps narrow down which dealers are working different markets. This place would be fat city if somebody got in."

"What's the attraction to oxy and heroin? I had morphine in the hospital and hated it."

"It makes the world go away. A lot of these kids have lived under pressure for so long, they can't turn it off. Straight As come with a high price. Getting into Stanford doubles their value. So a little white pill that totally relaxes and releases all those years of being a tea kettle is very attractive to a lot of these kids. No Mom and Dad to monitor them, they can spend the weekend in their dorm room in the dark on the bottom of the ocean."

"How many kids around here do you suppose have an opioid problem?"

"At the rate, they're dying? Quite a few." Wilcox shook his head. The two men moved back to Cole's office. "All done." Wilcox roused the dozing Preete. He rolled his eyes at Cole.

Cole smiled knowingly and said, "I *am* sorry about the kid's death. I had no idea it was the third this year."

"Not the kind of thing these smarter-than-the-rest kids and their parents want to hear about. The administration tried to keep a lid on it." Wilcox extended his hand to Cole. "Thanks for your help."

"Whatever I can do."

Preete gave Cole a jerk of his head and made his way to the door.

"Ball of fire," Cole said with a smile.

"I heard that," Preete said without looking back.

Wilcox shrugged. "Never-ending supply of surprises."

Cole went to his desk, completely forgetting about leaving early. He turned his computer back on. As he waited for it to boot up, he stood looking out the window. Below, he saw Wilcox making his way up the walk to the Social Science building. Preete was a few steps behind, dutifully tagging along.

Chapter 8

"Who died?" Kelly said, opening the door.

"My teaching assistant."

"Oh, Cole, I am so sorry!" Kelly threw her arms around Cole's neck. "I should never joke. Please forgive me." She went up on her toes and kissed him on the cheek.

"You're taking it a lot harder than I did. That's not what's bothering me, but nice to know how well I wear my thoughts and concerns on my face."

As Kelly stepped back, she grimaced. "Ouch. I guess that stretch was too early for my ribs." She held her side and winced.

"It's only been a week," Cole scolded.

"I have been in kind of a funk all day, too. I feel really bad I missed Irwin's funeral."

"You were in the hospital."

"I know, but I still feel bad."

"So, you want to go out?"

"Let's stay in. I can make a Shrimp Louie. I baked some bread today."

"Sounds great. Now, why are we really staying in?"

"We need to do some planning. If you are serious about getting married in a hurry, we need to get our plans set."

Nothing was settled that evening, but over the course of the next week, Kelly and Cole spent hours over plates of Ravioli, mugs of coffee and chocolate chip cookies. They walked miles around Golden Gate Park and snuggled on the couch for several evenings before coming to a decision. If they were ever going to get into an argument, this was the best place to start.

As they planned for their wedding, preferences, dislikes, a lot of never discussed feelings about weddings came to the surface. At times it seemed Cole stomped on Kelly's feelings without knowing, only later to find his ideas snuffed like a stinky candle. Through it all, they laughed, teased and good-naturedly pouted. Never was an angry word exchanged.

With all compromises negotiated satisfactorily, the ceremony would take place on Muir Beach. Kelly's pastor will officiate, with only Erin, Ben and Jenny in attendance. A reception would be in a month or so, allowing out-of-towners and friends to have time to plan ahead if they wished to attend. They would plan on a honeymoon when school was out.

"Then we agree?" Kelly smiled.

"Of course, do we ever not?"

"Well…" Kelly giggled.

"I love the whole idea. You can do your invitation thing. I can dig out mailing addresses. You can even pick the where and when. Happy?"

"In other words," Kelly frowned, "you want nothing to do with it."

"That's not fair. I'll help pick out the paper plates at Costco. You can oversee my choices for what we should have to eat!" Cole announced enthusiastically.

"You want me to oversee something? Is that possible?"

"Look, you're the event Queen. You really don't want me planning something so important by myself; otherwise, it would be catered by Uncle Louie's BBQ, augmented by open bags of Kettle Chips and bowls of peanut M&Ms everywhere. I want some say in it, but you want something classy and nice. I just want to see all our friends in one place and having a good time."

"So do I. But these things do require some planning. I appreciate your concern for my wishes. I really do."

"So long as there is no pink, frilly lace or artificial flowers, I'm good. Oh, and the dress is as informal as possible."

"Don't worry, you won't be wearing a tux!"

"See how easy that was? I bet your hyper stepdaughter, uh, daughter-in-law, what are you going to refer to Erin as? Anyway, she will be hard to keep out of the mix."

"She is my daughter-in-law, too hard to change now, number one. Number two, she is eight month's pregnant, greatly limiting her mobility. So I won't count on her for much."

"OK, you tell her that!" Cole laughed at the thought of Erin being told to take it easy.

* * *

The gusts of wind came off the Pacific, overturning umbrellas and snapping kite tails. The sky was bluer than an Etta James ballad, and what few clouds there were seemed to rest gently overhead, watching the group assembling on the beach. It was what some would say a perfect day for a wedding.

Pastor Rick Callaway walked along the beach edge, his jeans rolled up, his bare feet moving through the water's edge, his head bowed, his eyes mindfully watching the sea foam just ahead of each step. He clutched his raven black Bible under the arm of his crisp tuxedo shirt. He wore no tie, and the tail of the brilliant white shirt was not tucked in. He didn't notice when the rest of the wedding party started arriving.

Erin and Ben were the first to arrive. Jenny ran as fast as her sandaled feet and long white dress would allow to the water's edge. For Erin, the soft sand and eight months of very large baby approaching delivery made the going rough. Ben tried to lend a hand but was more of an irritation than help. Even pregnant Erin looked angelic in her long white dress and crown of yellow daisies.

The flowers were a gentle sign to Cole that her mother Ellie would approve of Cole's marriage. Daisies were always Ellie's favorite. At her funeral, Cole presented her with oceans of the beautiful yellow flowers. Now, as he begins a new life with Kelly, the sight of daisies on his only child was her way of giving her mother's blessing. Adding Jenny's slightly askew daisy headband to the mix gave Erin a completion of the circle. The child would have one set of grandparents that contributed the love, history, and blood from both sides of her family, a unique and precious heritage for sure.

The pair of green camo Crocs Ben wore was quickly discarded when the sand got deep. He wore the requested jeans and tuxedo shirt and carried the overstuffed denim bag Erin packed for the day on the beach. He promised Erin he would return to the car for the folding chairs after the ceremony.

The squealing and screaming of Jenny's excitement of being at the beach alerted Pastor Callaway that he was no longer alone. He waved and started toward Ben and Erin. A couple from the Sausalito Christian Fellowship made the trip to Muir Beach with their pastor and prepared a lovely canopy of flowers and a small carpet for the ceremony. The photographer appeared unannounced and started sizing up the impromptu outdoor sanctuary. It seems everyone was in place except the bride and groom.

"Hi, I'm Rick Callaway. I think we met at church a couple of times."

"Yes, indeed. I remember. I'm Erin, and this is my husband Ben."

"Anyone seen the bride and groom?" Callaway asked.

"We all caravanned up, but Mom has this idea Cole shouldn't see her until the service. How she'll manage that, I don't know. They came in the same car!" Ben chuckled.

"I have no doubt she'll manage," Callaway replied as he nodded knowingly.

"We passed a beautiful girl on a bench playing guitar. She was really good. Ben, why don't you go see if you can hire her to play a couple of songs?" Erin suggested.

"No need, she's with me. We got this all covered. Kelly saw to that. Cole picked the song."

From off to their right, Cole appeared at the top of the trail leading down to the beach. He waved and smiled like he'd discovered buried treasure.

"Thanks for coming!" Cole offered as he approached.

"It's part of the package," Callaway quipped.

"You clean up pretty good!" Erin said, seeing Cole in the jeans and tuxedo shirt uniform of the day.

"None of my doing. It's all Kelly." Cole reached out and hugged his daughter. "You look like an angel," Cole said softly. "I love the daisies. Thank you."

Erin's eyes flooded with tears. "Oh, Daddy, thank you. I hoped you would understand."

"Sweetheart, you are your mother's daughter. Of course I understand, and she would have loved it." Cole gently kissed Erin on the cheek.

Cole shook hands with the pastor and glanced around the beach. A few feet away, Ben watched Jenny dodging the waves as they lapped upon the sand.

"Hi, Ben. Where is that mother of yours?" Cole called.

"Probably up at the house watching us through binoculars, waiting to make her grand entrance." Ben laughed and moved over to Cole and gave him a bear hug.

"And I change in the parking lot between two open car doors!"

"How did you manage to rent a house right on the beach?" Ben asked.

"I can take a bit of the credit for that one." The pastor grinned. "The Martinellis at the church volunteered their beach house for the honeymoon when I told them I was doing the service here."

"Can it get any better?" Ben chuckled.

"Not much." Cole smiled.

The four adults moved to the canopy. Erin called Jenny to join them. To Erin's delight, not only did she obey, there wasn't the slightest bit of dampness on her dress. Erin straightened the crown of flowers attached to Jenny's curly blonde hair, all the while trying to keep her from going to her grandfather.

"Grandpa!" Jenny cried as she wiggled free of her mother's last-minute adjustments.

The little girl flew into Cole's open arms, and he picked her up and twirled her around and around.

"Where's Grandma?" Jenny asked as Cole set her down.

"Good question."

"You can't get married without her. What if she doesn't come?"

"Then I guess we will go get an ice cream cone and take a walk down the beach."

"Don't worry, Grandpa, she'll be here. I think she loves you a lot."

"That, my angel, is a comfort." Cole gave the little girl a smile only a proud grandfather can give.

The young woman with the guitar approached and said by way of a greeting, "She's right behind me."

A moment later, Kelly Mitchell, mother of Ben, mother-in-law of Erin, and grandmother of Jenny appeared over the rise. As she made her way down the sandy path, Cole felt a lump come up in his throat. This woman healed his broken heart after the death of the woman who held it captive for thirty years. Though they were never married and spent far more years apart than together, Ellie was Cole's only other real love.

He jumped from fleeting images to the memory of the truth that it was Ellie who made the contact he yearned for so long; without it, he would have lived without Erin, the daughter he never knew was born. He would have never been freed of his pain of the lost years without Ellie. Now he watched as the mother of his daughter's husband, the grandmother of his beloved granddaughter Jenny, made her way to take his hand. Kelly was the one who brought happiness back to Cole's life, she showed him faith that now was a part of his life as he never imagined possible. Most of all, she loved him as he was, good, bad, faults and all. She knew his heart and saw who he truly was.

Her beauty was a natural outpouring of her inner spirit. This gracefully stunning woman, whose smile never ceased to charm Cole and lift his spirit, was to be his. Her height and elegant frame fit perfectly in Cole's arms. The touch of her hand and softness of her kisses left the old newspaper man's cynical nature in ashes at her feet.

As Kelly came the last few feet to Cole, he could hardly breathe for the beauty of this woman. She wore a soft white lace dress. The rounded neckline framed her long neck like an art deco statue. The sleeves clung tight to her toned arms, and the dress hung close to her near perfect figure. A tear rolled down Cole's cheek as he wondered, *How could she love me?*

Kelly approached Ben and took both of his hands and whispered something no one could hear.

Jenny grabbed her around the waist and exclaimed, "I told him you'd be here!"

The group laughed at the expression on Kelly's baffled look. She turned and faced Erin. She took her very pregnant daughter-in-law in her arms and kissed her gently on the cheek.

"I love you, too," Erin said softly.

"Well, shall we begin?" Pastor Callaway suggested brightly.

Kelly moved toward Cole, and without a word, he reached out and took her hand.

"Today is a little different than the usual wedding ceremony I perform. I am pleased to see two people I have come to know and love now join together before God and their family in marriage. In my twenty-something years as a pastor, I have never seen the parents of a married couple marry. The extraordinary thing is that Jenny has double grandparents, or is it triple?" The group laughed.

"I don't get it," Jenny whispered to Erin.

"I'll tell you later."

"Let's take a moment before we begin and call upon God's blessing on this marriage," Callaway began. "Heavenly Father, we come to you today with joyous hearts. We thank you for this family that believes in the power of your Word and the guidance of your wisdom. Please be with us now as we join this couple in the holiest of bonds, that of marriage. Amen." Callaway nodded at the lovely young lady, dressed in a long white dress that matched that of Erin and Jenny, holding a guitar.

"When Pastor gave me the song Cole requested, I must admit I had never heard of it or the person who wrote and sang it. But as I began reading the words, I realized there was an incredible amount of truth in them. I hope my voice will convey the love I have for the two of you and the example you are to so many of us in the church. Thank you for letting me be part of this wonderful day." She slid the capo down the neck of her guitar and strummed softly.

"Some kind of love starts as friends, that kind of love never ends, it comes on as slow as roses in snow, some kind of love starts as friends." The young woman's voice was as pure as the sea air. The words of the John Stewart song, so carefully chosen by Cole, touched the heart of everyone present, and they all recognized that the lyrics were the perfect picture of the love Cole and Kelly had found.

Standing hand in hand with Kelly, his mind drifted back to the night she called him the week after he returned home from Ellie's funeral. It was a simple invitation to a dinner party. The sound of her voice on the phone and her carefully chosen words impressed Cole. He remembered thinking some lucky fellow should snatch her up. He smiled at the memory and thought of the first time he kissed her. He thought of her covered in dirt and paint in the Oklahoma farmhouse they cleaned up. It was then he knew he loved her. He could see it now. She was the living embodiment of her faith, and that made his all the more important.

He glanced over at Erin, his beautiful, amazing daughter, and she was gazing at them as tears ran down her cheeks and gently kissed the corners of her smile. Cole returned her smile and squeezed Kelly's hand. She was standing with her eyes closed and a smile that came and went as she took in the lyrics of the song.

The singer tossed her long blonde hair from her face as the wind gusted. Her voice rose as she sang the last line of the song, "That kind of love is the hardest to find, through laughter and rage, it mellows with age, some kind of love never dies." She let the guitar softly fade into the wind. She touched her lips and blew Kelly and Cole a kiss.

"This may come as a surprise, but Kelly and Cole have written their own vows for each other. Jenny, can I have the rings?"

"Yes, sir." She handed the pastor the small lace bag Erin gave her moments before.

"Kelly, would you like to start?" She turned and faced Cole.

"I would. I, Kelly, am happy to take you, Cole, for my husband, lover, and friend for the rest of my life. You can count on me to be there for you when the days are bright and filled with joy, and when the clouds of grief, despair, and uncertainty come along. They will come along, and with God's grace and our faith in His undying love, we will draw closer together and weather the storms. I promise to bring to our home peace and serenity in a world gone mad. I will be faithful and yours alone until the day I die. I love you, Cole mine."

Cole tried to clear the lump in his throat. He took a deep breath and paused for a long moment. "I, Cole, am a work in progress. My heart is so full of love for you, I can hardly breathe. The mystery of how God has put love in your heart for me is truly a miracle I will never understand. It is my solemn vow to you that I will do everything in my power to be the man you *need* me to be, *believe* me to be, and *deserve* me to be. With your help, I can and will do it. I pledge to protect you, love you, and though I may disappoint you, I will never do it intentionally. It is my prayer that our home together will be a place of welcome, hospitality, and care for all those who call us friends and family. I love you now as I will love you when I take my last breath, and I shall thank God every day for making you mine. I love you, Kelly."

"Kelly, do you take this man as your lawful wedded husband?"

"I truly do." Kelly slipped the gold band on Cole's finger.

"Cole, do you -"

"Yes, I do!" Cole said, cutting the minister off. "Sorry, please finish," Cole said sheepishly.

"I think you got it." Callaway smiled.

Cole grinned and slipped the ring on Kelly's waiting finger.

"When two people come together after a lifetime of love, experience, and loss, for them marriage holds an entirely different meaning than for the wide-eyed, passionate glee of youth. I know these two, and I know their stories. I was with Kelly at the hospital when Peter died. I remember holding her hand and praying and thanking God for Peter's life and the wonderful husband and father he was. I remember Ben quietly comforting his mother in the hallway, and I prayed God would provide her with another partner to continue her life with. Even at that painful moment, I believed Cole was out there, not by name, but by character and love for this special lady." Callaway smiled widely.

"I remember, too, the first time Kelly brought Cole to our church. I could see a reverence below the newspaperman's curious eyes. I could see from the platform that this church was in a format he had not seen before. Through the sermon, I kept one eye on him and saw in his eyes my words, with God's guidance, were touching him deeply. Though the congregation couldn't hear it in the closing prayer, I was thanking God for sending her the partner I prayed for just a few short years before.

"Now it is my pleasure to join these two together in holy matrimony. With the love of Almighty God and the power vested in me by the State of California, I pronounce you man and wife. God bless and keep you, and this wonderful family, for all your days."

"So, without further ado, you may kiss your bride!"

The small group clapped happily.

* * *

It was nearly dark when Ben and Erin pulled away from the beach house. Jenny waved and blew kisses until she was out of sight.

"Well, Mr. Sage, we are all alone until Monday morning."

Cole stood with his arms around Kelly's waist. He looked into her eyes for a long moment and kissed her. "Have you got anything planned, Mrs. Sage?"

"Not past the next couple of hours." Kelly grinned.

Cole reached over and opened the door. Without a word, he swept Kelly up in his arms.

"What are you doing?!" she squealed with delight.

"Something I've always dreamed of doing," he replied, stepping over the threshold. He gave her a quick kiss before setting her down inside.

"Mr. Sage, you are just full of surprises."

"I try my best, Mrs. Sage."

"Oh, look at this mess."

"Leave it 'til morning."

"Can't, it will spoil." Kelly shrugged and sighed. "It won't take long."

"Any long is too long," Cole conceded. "I'll put the dishes in the dishwasher."

"I'll put the food away." Kelly raised her palm for a high-five.

They chatted, teased, and stopped occasionally for a kiss. Within a few minutes, the task was completed.

"I think I will go freshen up," Kelly said coyly. "Join me in about ten minutes?"

"I'd like to see somebody try and stop me. Oh, wait! There's nobody here but us."

"Make it five, handsome." With that, Kelly went down the hall to the bedroom.

Cole paused after making sure the doors were locked and the lights were turned off. He gazed out the massive picture window in the living room. A bonfire down on the beach sent sparks and flames into the inky darkness of the night. The silhouette of a couple danced in the light of the flames. The hypnotic strobe effect took Cole back in time.

With each flick, he saw a face. Old friends, women he'd known, Erin the first time he saw her, Jenny's golden curls bouncing as she ran across the park, his mother, and his beloved Ellie. All have a piece of his heart. All have left him a better person. He was once told that just because you find someone new to love, doesn't mean they crowd out what came before. The heart is the one place you can keep filling that doesn't get crowded.

He smiled as he thought of the mini-reception, new friends, the pastor, and his family. Kelly was the first lady of it all. Her charm and easy way with giving love showed how big a heart can be. Now she was going to welcome him to her bed.

The thought of their coming together as man and wife gave him a shiver. He was flooded with excitement and fear. He longed for intimacy, a closeness he lived without for so long. He realized as he thought of what was about to happen, his fear was born of his immeasurable desire to show his bride the depth of his love. His actions in the next few moments must be about her.

Pleasure was a fleeting thing. The connection they have shared up to this point was that of two people connecting in their singleness. Now they were to become one. Cole breathed a prayer and turned to the light coming from the hall.

"Anybody home?" Cole said nervously.

"Just the happiest girl in the world," came the response.

Her bare shoulders and arms were neatly tucked into covers. "It's been a long time," Kelly said softly.

Cole's smile as he looked down on his bride was all the words she needed. He reached over and turned off the light on the nightstand.

Chapter 9

The honeymooners woke at around six Monday morning. They found that lying back to front like spoons in a drawer with Cole holding Kelly in his arms was the next best thing to heaven. They spooned for nearly a half-hour, then they showered, dressed and were on the road by seven, giving them plenty of time to get back in time for Cole's nine o'clock class. Breakfast was coffee and a breakfast sandwich at Starbucks. They chatted, laughed, and planned all the way to Palo Alto.

With twenty minutes before his class, Kelly dropped Cole off and promised to be back promptly at 3:00 to pick him up. With a newly invigorated stride in his step, Cole made his way to his office. It didn't look so drab and confining today. Maybe marriage agreed with him, Cole thought.

"Good morning, Cole!" Suzanne said cheerfully. "You've got a little pep in your step today."

"It is indeed a good morning, Suzanne. And like the song says, 'ain't nuthin' gonna bring me down'."

"I don't know that one."

"Ain't nothin' gonna break-a my stride, Nobody gonna slow me down, oh no," Cole sang. "Come on, you're a lot younger than I am. '84 or '85, Matthew Wilder? 'Break My Stride'? No?"

"I've always been a jazz and classical girl."

"Now, that explains a lot!" Cole laughed.

"What's that mean?" Suzanne asked defensively.

It was too late; Cole was already in his office.

"OK, folks, this is what you've been asking for. Next year, you will be the senior staff on the paper. A change of direction and new look are in your hands. As we move forward with this renovation, I feel I really need to give you some hard-learned counsel." Cole stood and moved to the large whiteboard on the wall. "First off, this is a student newspaper, staffed, written, and run by students. In the charter with the university, in exchange for office space, funding, and freedom of distribution, you are saddled with a faculty editor-slash-publisher."

The group gathered around the conference table, laughed and exchanged comments.

"For the most part, as you will learn, I intend to stay out of your way. I'm available, willing and able to guide and direct, settle squabbles and end disputes. Here's the bottom line. In the real world of newspapers, there is level upon level of management over your head. Every move is monitored, and you are accountable for your time and productivity. Obviously, we don't have that.

"What we do have is the chance at a good working relationship. That said, if there is a major policy decision to be made, a serious issue that is not in the best interest of the university, it is I alone who is responsible for making the call. Understanding that now will save us a lot of frustration, anger, hurt and misspent energy.

"If there is anyone here who feels they are incapable of yielding to the authority of the management above them, you probably should consider a different vocation."

"Yeah, but you wrote a lot of stories that ruffled a lot of feathers down through the years," a bushy-haired young man in a moth-eaten sweater interrupted.

"Absolutely. Death threats, nasty phone calls, and I even got punched a couple of times. That's not the point. The fact is, for every story idea I had that would cause a row, I had three rejected. When I did publish something edgy or controversial, it was with the blessing and power of the editor behind me."

"And you were OK with that?"

"Not always, but that is the way the game's played. If you don't like the rules, find another game. More than anything, newspapers are a business. Lose readers, lose money. Make a splash with a story that brings more readers, the paper makes more money. You're a hero."

The group chuckled and smiled.

"You could be a hero, Mitch!"

The kid in the holey sweater grinned. "Fat chance."

"OK, we've wandered a bit off the path. But that's good. What is it the academics call it? A teaching moment?" Cole smiled, but it faded as his attention was drawn to a commotion outside in the common area of the offices.

"Young lady, I am a member of the faculty, and I insist you tell me where Sage is!"

"This can't be good," Cole said jokingly. "In here," he said, reaching the door.

A large man with a severe expression walked toward the door. It took a moment, but Cole realized it was the man who searched the TA's desk and gave the bombastic speech at the faculty meeting.

"I'm Mason Muller," he said, shooting out his hand. "I don't remember being introduced."

"So you are. I'm in the middle of a meeting with the newspaper staff. Can this wait, whatever it is?"

"Good, I want this printed in the paper." Muller waved a sheet of paper at Cole.

Before he could react, Muller pushed past Cole and into the conference room.

"This campus is being flooded with hard drugs; Heroin, oxycodone, and the like. You, as the voice of the student body, have a responsibility to take a stand and voice the warning of this plague to your peers."

Cole could see Muller was just getting started. "Look, Mr. Muller, we are in a meeting. There is a protocol for submitting letters to the editor, and I would appreciate you abiding by them. Now, if you will leave your letter with the secretary, she will see it gets to the editor."

"Which one of you is the editor?"

Jody Zhuan, the newly elected editor, looked up at Cole. She didn't speak.

"Ms. Zhuan is our editor this semester. She will review your piece and get back to you."

Jody, being the only Asian at the table, instantly drew Muller's eye. "Here you are. There is nothing wrong with it. I pride myself on my command of the English language, punctuation and all. It can be printed as is."

"I will take a look, thank you," Jody said, forcing a smile.

"What's that mean? Take a look?" Muller was not pleased by her response, and his demeanor was shifting from firm to hostile.

"It means we have limited space, and our letters section is even more limited, so often we need to edit and shorten things that are submitted to us. It is the right of any publication, and our policy is so stated in the disclaimer at the bottom of every Letters page. So, thank you, and I'll take a look." Jody met Muller's glare and didn't blink.

Cole beamed; he was so proud of this young woman. She would certainly go far in the newspaper business, or any other endeavor she put her mind to.

"OK, so if we could get back to our meeting. Thank you, Mr. Muller, for coming by."

"Are you dismissing me, Sage?" Muller turned and glared at Cole.

"I think I have been more than tolerant of your interruption. So, I am politely trying to let you know your time is up. Next time, please call or email, and we will arrange a time and place to meet that will not disrupt my class, something I'm sure you would find most offensive and intolerable while you were teaching."

"Fine," Muller said hoarsely, fairly choking on the word.

He left the room, shoulders back in a near military march.

"I apologize for the interruption."

"Who is that guy?" someone asked.

"Sage is a bad-ass. He sure put him in check," exclaimed another.

"OK, OK. Jody, I can see you are the perfect choice for an editor. Well done, very professional."

Applause broke out around the table.

Jody looked up at Cole. "Mr. Sage, this is totally unacceptable." She held up the paper Muller left. "It is not a letter to the editor, but an op-ed addressing the students and staff. The tone is very hostile and inflammatory. It has very harsh racial and ethnic overtones that, frankly, I find offensive. Not only is it hostile, but it makes him look pretty crazy."

"Well, here we go. I didn't pay him to come in, I swear!" Cole's injection of humor seemed to calm the nervous charge in the room. "Jody, why don't you read what it says? We'll get back to the re-vamp tomorrow."

Just as their time ran out, it was unanimously agreed that Mason Muller was welcome to write an op-ed. His angry tone would have to be pulled way back. Cole volunteered to talk to him, but Jody insisted that, as Editor, it was her responsibility.

"This was a most productive session. It certainly took a whole different direction than I had planned. Thank you, everyone, see you tomorrow."

Cole went to his office and plopped down in his chair.

"Suzanne, you got a minute?" he called.

"You all right?" the secretary asked as she came into the room.

"Me? Yeah, fine. Have a seat." Cole smiled and gestured for her to sit down. "What did you find out about that guy, if anything?"

"He's in the Social Sciences department, a retired Major from the army. Ramrod straight, a grouchy loner, and a royal pain to work with according to a friend of mine over there."

"He made a speech at the faculty meeting, then stomped out. Seems like a loose cannon," Cole added.

"I guess he's been on a clean up the city, anti-drug campaign for about a month. His behavior in here, though, that was over the top, if I may put in my two cents."

"Do we just let it go? Or is there somebody who needs to know? I'm still foggy on the food chain around here."

"It might be a good idea to give Arlen Coffiere a call. He's the dean of Social Sciences and History. You might give him a heads up," Suzanne suggested. "I've seen hotheads like Muller cause a lot of turmoil. His dean could put an end to it before it gets ugly, especially if he saw his little outburst in the meeting."

"That's how it's done?" Cole questioned.

"That's what I would do. Did you read his letter?"

"Oh, yeah." Cole opened his eyes wide for affect. "He really has built up a head of steam. It's gonna hit the fan when he gets the word he needs to do a re-write and pull it back a bit, a big bit before we can publish it. Thank you."

Five minutes later, Cole was on hold waiting for Arlen Coffiere to pick up. Cole felt like a kid going to the principal to report a bully. He spent forty years fighting his own battles outsmarting or shouting down idiots who couldn't or wouldn't mind their own business. Chalk this one up to another loss of freedom surrendered to academia.

"Sage, what can I do for you?" The voice took Cole by surprise.

"I had a bit of a situation this morning. It was suggested I give you a heads up."

"All right."

"My newspaper staff class was interrupted by a faculty member named Muller. You know him?"

"Oh, yes. Mason can be quite forceful at times."

"You're quite the diplomat." Cole chuckled. "He demanded we print a piece he wrote regarding, but not confined to, the recent opioid deaths on campus. The student editor found the hostile, racial, socio-economic attacks unfit for the paper. She is going to request he tone it down and resubmit it rather than simply refusing to print. I thought it pretty brave of her. I just figured in case he makes a stink, you should be aware so you're not broadsided."

"I can appreciate that, but perhaps the best thing would be to just print Mason's letter."

Cole could see this was a pointless call. The tone of the Dean angered Cole. "The paper is an independent entity chartered by the University, for and by the students," he began. "We are not required to comply with or take orders from faculty."

"I appreciate that. Mason Muller is not a man to mince words or suffer fools. My advice is to just choose your battles. All the same, I'll have a word with him."

"That would be great. I'm new around here, and I certainly don't want to get a reputation for being difficult. I will hold the line when it comes to policy. I am a true believer when it comes to freedom of the press."

"Listen, he is a man of strong convictions. Sometimes people get the wrong impression. You might want to reconsider. But thanks for giving me a heads up. Anything else?"

"No, that's it," Cole said, recognizing the conversation was finished.

"All right, then. Have a good day."

"You, too," Cole said to a dead phone.

Cole couldn't have known he just complained to Mason Muller's closest friend and Army buddy. He just threw gasoline on the fire of the situation. Arlen Coffiere was feared on campus. When he fought, he won; when he suggested, it was done. Cole just made a powerful enemy.

Chapter 10

The decision for Cole to stay at Kelly's place instead of his was an easy one. Until they found somewhere near the university, comfort trumped convenience. A California King bed and big leather couch were better than the Spartan furnishings of the place Cole was staying.

Cole drifted into a deep sleep their first night back. When the ringing of the phone jarred him awake after three a.m., he was disoriented for a moment in the pitch black surroundings.

"Hello," Kelly said, clicking on the light. "Now!" Kelly squealed. "We're on our way!"

"What's wrong?" Cole muttered, trying to shake off the foggy blur of sleep.

"Nothing! Erin has gone into labor. They're already at the hospital. Get dressed!"

Cole leapt from the bed so fast, he lost his balance and needed to steady himself on the wall. "What time is it?"

"Three-thirty. Stop dilly-dallying and get dressed," Kelly said as she scampered for the bathroom.

The arms in his T-shirt seemed to have been sewn up as Cole struggled to get it pulled over his head. He stumbled to the hall bathroom. He splashed his face repeatedly, then combed his hair.

"Are you ready?" Kelly called down the hall.

The woman who seemed to take forever to get ready to go to the market stood at the end of the hall, fully dressed make-up perfect and looking like she just returned from an afternoon at the mall.

"I just went to the bathroom, Kell'. Give me a minute," Cole said, racing back to the bedroom.

Five minutes later, they were in the car and on their way. When they arrived at the Family Birthing Center, the parking lot was deserted. Before Cole could put the car in park, Kelly was out of the car and racing to the door.

"See you inside!" she said, slamming her door.

Cole turned off the engine, got out of the car, and made his way to the double-wide glass sliding doors.

Just inside, he found the poor receptionist being bombarded with Kelly's incessant questioning.

"Need some help?" Cole asked the poor woman calmly.

"Your wife is really spunky for this time of the morning," the woman in white replied.

"Sure is." Cole put his arm around Kelly's shoulder. "Mitchell, what room?"

"5-C, to your right, just down the way."

"See how easy that was? She really didn't need the history of the pregnancy," Cole said jovially. "Let's go see our girl."

Inside the dimly lit room, Erin lay in a big bed with no side rails or anything else resembling a hospital room. Ben sat in a chair, holding a sleeping Jenny in his arms.

"Hi, sweetie," Kelly whispered.

"Hi, guys." Erin was far calmer than her mother-in-law.

"How long have you been here?"

"About an hour. You got here really fast. Dad, did you break any speed limits?"

"Only a dozen or so." Cole gave her a thumbs up.

Kelly moved to where Ben sat and gave him a kiss on the cheek.

"Hi, Grandma," came a sleepy voice from Jenny.

Kelly gave her a kiss on the top of the head.

Always awkward in hospital situations, Cole stood, not really knowing what to say or where to go.

"Daddy, are you all right?" Erin giggled.

"Fine, just a little out of my depth here. I missed the first one, so technically this is the first one. This is the first one I have been in attendance for, I mean. Of course, Jenny is the number one grandchild. But this baby is my first experience at being at the birth of my very own grandchild. See what I mean, it is a really important thing for it being the first one and all. I'm really excited about being here. I am so out of the loop at this kind of thing. I mean, this is my first. Not birth, I've seen that before, but somebody I love, you know what I mean? Are you all right? Are they taking care of you? Ben is monitoring everything, right? I trust him. Sometimes hospitals can be scary places." Cole's adrenalin, nerves, and excitement were driving his emotions, and he was chattering like a madman.

"Dad, Dad, it's OK. I'm going to be fine. You need to relax before you blow a fuse or something. Come here." Erin patted the side of the bed next to her.

As Cole sat down, Erin took his hand. "I'm going to be just fine. Don't worry."

"I know," Cole said softly. "I just am so excited and afraid, I'm kind of jumpy."

"You afraid? I've never heard those words before."

"You're my only child. I know this happens all the time, but not to me – I mean you, you know what I mean?"

"Give me a hug before this gets ugly." Erin laughed.

"What's that supposed to mean?"

"It means," Ben began, "last time once the contractions really kicked in, she was mean as a snake and shouting words I didn't know she knew."

"I'm still sorry and embarrassed by that. I asked God and everybody in the hospital to forgive me," Erin explained sheepishly.

"So, what do we do?" Cole asked.

"Wait," Kelly said.

"Whoa! That was a good one," Erin grunted.

"Counting," Ben pointed up at the large clock on the wall.

The four adults in the room stared at the clock. Two minutes later, Erin grabbed Cole's hand and squeezed so hard, he thought she would break his knuckles.

"Time to call the nurse," Ben said.

"I'll go get her," Cole quickly volunteered.

Kelly laughed as Cole moved toward the door. "Big, tough Cole."

Twenty minutes later, Jenny led her grandparents from the room, at her mother's request, as the staff swiftly transformed the oversized bedroom into a more sterile delivery room. The lights would remain dim for the birth, but the preparedness for any emergency was a comfort to Cole as he turned to blow Erin a kiss.

Cole tried to read the day-old newspapers while Kelly and Jenny played games on her iPad. The clock seemed to run backward. Cole walked the hall, ate three bags of toffee covered peanuts and a Snickers bar from a machine in the hall as he paced. At the one-hour mark, a candy striper came with a cart full of juice, milk, cookies, and fruit.

Full from sneaking the sugary calories in the hall, Cole declined the cookies but did grab a carton of milk. Jenny had to be restrained at the sight of free chocolate chip cookies. The cart was rescued by Kelly, who limited Jenny to a banana, a milk and one cookie.

At five-thirty-five, Ben came out of the birthing room.

"Anybody want to meet the newest member of the family?"

"Me, me, me!" Jenny jumped to her feet and ran to her daddy's arms.

Cole looked at Kelly and smiled. "Well, Grandpa, let's go see."

Kelly went into the room first. It was cleaned up and returned to a big, spacious bedroom. The lights were brought up, and the first rays of the morning were filtering through the sheer curtains at the windows.

As he stood in the door gazing at Erin and the small bundle she held, he felt a huge lump in his throat and realized tears were running down his cheeks.

"Everyone, let me introduce you to Cole Aaron Mitchell."

"Oh, Erin, a boy." Kelly moved to the bed.

Cole couldn't move. His mind was exploding with the thought of the child being named for him.

"Come on, Grandpa!" Jenny said excitedly from the bed.

Cole took two steps and turned to Ben. He extended his hand to the new father, then grabbed him in a hug.

"Thank you, Ben."

"It was Erin's idea, but I was all for it. The Aaron part was all me, though."

"It is such an unexpected -"

"Daddy, someone is dying to meet you." Erin's smile was apparent without even looking.

Cole moved to the bed. Erin sat propped up with pillows. The bed was raised to a comfortable sitting position. She turned the blue bundle up to face Cole.

"Hi, buddy," Cole said, looking down at his grandson for the first time.

"What do you think?"

"He's incredible." Cole's smile could have lit the room. "He looks like...well, he has Ben's dark hair, your chin, and I think I see Jenny's nose." Cole turned and winked at Jenny. "What do you think, Sport?"

"I think we'll keep him."

Kelly softly cleared her throat. Cole turned to face her. The love on her face was the most beautiful thing he ever saw. As tears of pride, love, and happiness streamed down her cheeks, Cole realized everything he ever dreamed of was right here in this room.

After a few minutes of cell phone pictures with the baby, Kelly volunteered to take Jenny home with them.

"Let's let Mommy and Baby Cole get some rest," Kelly said. "You can come to stay with me for a little while, how's that sound?"

Jenny looked from Kelly to Erin, then the baby and then back to Kelly, "Well, OK. I'm kinda tired, too." Kelly moved across the room to Ben. "She's good with me for as long as you need," she said softly.

"I'll come by later. Erin should go home tomorrow." Ben hugged his mother.

Cole moved to the side of the bed and kissed Erin on the top of the head. "We'll see you this evening. You look like you could do with a bit of a nap."

"So do you. I think it took more out of you than it did me!" Erin laughed. "I'm so glad you could be here this time. It makes it so special. I love you, dad."

"I love you, too, sweetheart." Cole smiled. His heart was filled to overflowing.

Kelly and Erin exchanged a few words, Kelly hugged her and kissed Baby Cole's forehead.

"Then we're off!" Cole grabbed Jenny and swung her up in his arms.

To Cole's amazement, it took nearly twice as long to get home as it did to get to the hospital. He blamed the traffic. Truth be told, he couldn't afford the fines he would have received if any number of cops would have clocked him on the way to the hospital!

Cole took a nap on the couch, and the hour power nap helped energize him. *What a week!* Cole thought as he drove to work. *Married and a grandson. Can life get any better?*

Chapter 11

"It's a boy!" Cole said in greeting to Suzanne.

"You just got married, Cole?!"

"My new grandson, silly. My daughter Erin delivered at five o'clock this morning."

"What did he weigh?"

"I don't know," Cole said, realizing he missed that detail.

"How long was he?"

"I don't know."

"Are you sure it was a boy?" Suzanne teased. "What did they name him?"

"That I know!" Cole said proudly. "Cole Aaron Mitchell."

"Oh, that's wonderful. Congratulations."

"It is a great day."

"Hi, Mr. Sage." One of his students called, entering into the conference room.

"How much time do I have?" Cole asked in a sudden panic.

"About five minutes," Suzanne replied. "You're fine."

Four more students rounded the corner, chatting and ready for the newspaper meeting. Behind them came Mason Muller, with a scowl like an angry bull.

"Sage!" Muller bellowed.

The students froze where they stood. They all looked to Cole with expectant expressions.

"Great. What's he want?" Cole glanced over at Suzanne.

"Who the hell do you think you are?" Muller shouted across the room.

"I'm the guy who is getting tired of you showing up and disrupting my peaceful environment. What is your problem?"

"You had no right to contact Dean Coffiere regarding my letter!"

"First off, my conversation with the Dean is my business. It was your obnoxious appearance in my class that prompted my call. Regarding your request for submission, I informed the Dean of the responsibility of the paper to the student community and our policy for accepting letters to the editor or op-ed articles."

"Policy be damned. You will print my letter as is. I am a highly regarded member of this faculty, and my opinions carry considerable weight on this campus. You don't want to mess with me. You *will* regret it." Muller was furious, and his anger showed in the bright red of his face.

"Boastful and threatening can now be added to the list of your undesirable qualities. Are you about finished? Because I have a class starting, and I will not have you disturbing it and my students again. Clear?" Cole was not about to give Muller an inch. He would not be bullied, and he intended to send a strong message to that effect.

"How dare you speak to me in that tone!"

"Look, I've had enough of you and your bluster. Now..." Cole had no more patience for Muller. Reaching into his briefcase, he came out with two sheets of paper. "Here is your odious, racist, diatribe." Cole wadded up the papers Muller presented the last time they met. With a quick snap of his wrist, he threw the wadded up papers at Muller's chest. Unfortunately, his aim was off and the wad hit Muller in the middle of the forehead.

"We will print that over my dead body. I suggest you get out and go where it is you sulk, and leave me to my class." Cole's voice still wasn't at shouting level, but it was getting close.

Muller, totally unprepared for Cole's paper attack, growled, "This isn't the end of this! You will print my letter as is. Wait and see."

"Not likely," Cole said as forcefully as he knew how.

"Get out of the way!" Muller shouted at a student unfortunate enough to enter the office late.

Cole looked at his assembled class. "Give me a minute." He turned and went into his office and closed the door.

Realizing he'd just hit Goliath in the forehead with his paper stone, Cole began to laugh. "You have done it now."

The laughter seemed to ease Cole's anger and frustration. The complete absurdity of Muller and the politics of academia were so foolish in Cole's eyes, he couldn't believe he was a party to it all. He plopped down in his chair and threw his feet up on the desk.

Take ten, he thought. Maybe it was fatigue, maybe it was the emotion of the arrival of his namesake, but as Cole looked around his office, he wondered how he thought all this was a good idea.

It only took about seven minutes for Cole to regroup and join the kids in the conference room.

"Nobody say a word." Cole's voice left no doubt he was not in the mood for clever remarks. "I most humbly apologize for my most inappropriate behavior."

Mitch, wearing his same holey sweater, started to say something but thought better.

"It is a major character flaw in my make up that I will not be bullied, often to my own detriment. However, we as journalists, to whatever level we may rise, are bound by an age-old unwritten rule that what we represent is the soul of our being. What we, if called to make decisions, are made to the highest purpose of our better nature. Truth, fairness, an unimpeachable dedication, to looking out for the little guy. In the Bible, Jesus says, 'Whatever you did for one of the least of these, you did for me." No matter your beliefs, these words carry a meaning that we all can understand.

"Doctor Muller's words and position are indefensible. His demand for us to print his piece unedited is unreasonable. Our position is a trust given to us by the university. To protect and honor the students and community we reach." Cole looked around the table.

"By a show of hands, how many say they are unwilling to print an unedited version of Muller's piece Jody read to us?"

As if in one motion, every person at the table raised their hand.

"Then as your advisor and legal publisher of record, respecting your decision, I promise you I will stand by it come what may. Class dismissed."

The class stood and made their way to the door as several said thank you. Jody looked at Cole and smiled. Mitch stopped and looked for a long moment at Cole, then threw his arms around him and gave him a hug.

"Give 'em hell, Sage. We got your back." Mitch slapped him on the shoulder and left the room.

"You OK?" Suzanne asked as Cole left the conference room.

"No. Actually, I'm not. I'm angry. I am just not built to take crap off people like him. I've fought it all my life. And for the first time, I am in an arena where I have no idea what the rules are."

Without waiting for a response, Cole went to his office. He stood looking out the window at the comings and goings of the students below. He wondered if they were being prepared for a world of Mullers. Or, will they go out in the world lambs to be devoured by wolves?

The humming of his cell phone interrupted his thoughts. He smiled in anticipation of a call from Kelly. *No,* he thought as he reached for the phone, *she knows I'm in class, or should be.* He looked down at the screen: Georgia Kappas.

"Hey, 'Cuz, long time, no speak!"

"Hello, Cole."

It had been several months since Cole spoke with his cousin. Her tone and inflection was one of seriousness, and it concerned Cole.

"How's Ernie?" Cole thought he would jump right in, in case something was wrong with her husband.

"It's Mama."

Cole's heart sank. His aunt, his father's half-sister, was very special to Cole. He didn't want to hear what Georgia was about to say. He feared the worst.

"She's had a stroke."

"Oh, Georgia, I'm sorry. How is she?"

"Not good. She is paralyzed and unresponsive. She is in a coma. The doctors aren't giving us much help."

"What can I do?" Cole asked earnestly.

"Pray. That's about all there is. Oh, Cole, what will I do without Mama? She's been my rock my whole life. I'll be lost. You and her are the only kin I have in the world." The sound of sobbing filled the void of unspoken grief.

"How's Ernie taking it?"

"He cried like a baby, Cole. It would have broken your heart." Georgia sniffed. "The doctors say there is not much they can do. Mama's been moved to a rest home. They said to make her as comfortable as possible."

"Do you want me to come?" Cole offered.

"No, hon'. I just needed to hear your voice, tell you what was goin' on and ask you to pray. She wouldn't even know you were in the room."

"I was actually thinking about you. I miss you."

"I miss you, too."

A knock on the door interrupted the call.

"Yeah?"

"A call from the president. He wants to see you at 11:30," Suzanne winced.

"You must be busy. I'll let you go," Georgia said.

"You are far more important. Do me a favor. Tell my buddy Ernie not to worry, and give him a hug for me. Then," Cole paused for the wave of emotion to pass over him, "please give My Aunt Lottie a kiss on the cheek and tell her I love her. You know they say people in a coma can sometimes hear the things around them."

"I surely will."

"Before we go, my daughter, Erin had a baby this morning, a little boy. They named him Cole, isn't that something?"

"A fine name. I'm sure with a grandpa like you, he will grow to be a fine man, too. You take care. I'll call you if there is any change. Give my love to that pretty lady of yours."

"Will do. We'll talk again soon." Cole pressed the red button on his phone, ending the call.

"Time to take inventory," Cole said, pulling a yellow notepad from his desk drawer.

The long blue line he drew from top to bottom of the legal size notepad glared up at him in defiance, as if to say you can't do it. At the top of the page on the right, he wrote LIKE; on the other, NOT.

Without hesitation, he began to write words and phrases on the paper. There were things he liked about his current situation. Randy Callen was still around, Suzanne was a good secretary even if he did have to share her, and he felt a genuine affection to a couple of kids on the newspaper staff. The Not column, however, filled much quicker and was several lines longer. He hated Palo Alto, his Journalism classes were filled with English Majors looking to fill out their credit needs with a class rumored to be easy. The politics were responsible for the need to make this list. He missed writing. The thrill of the chase, the scoop, the bearing witness to the truth, all were no longer part of his life.

He missed Hanna terribly. Though no one could have seen her death coming, he somehow felt responsible on some level. The guilt ate at him. She was his right hand, his sounding board, and the best assistant he ever had. Her reward for a good deed was to be murdered.

Teaching was not what he thought it would be either. The kids in his class for the majority had no interest in journalism. They wanted to be bloggers, tweeters and Snapchat commandos. Their cell phones were of far greater interest than him. It was all he could do to remain civil with their disrespect.

He finished the list and leaned back. *This is a fine mess,* he thought. Cole picked up the phone.

"Suzanne, can you call security and have them post a *class canceled* sign on my ten o'clock class? Thanks."

Cole decided it was a good time to go for a walk. He had no real destination in mind, but he wanted to get out and away from people. Particularly, he wanted out of #6 on his list of Nots, his office.

The air was just what he needed. The sky was blue, and in the distance, white, billowy clouds framed the buildings. The warm sun felt good on his face. With a relaxed gait, Cole began to stroll the campus. He watched students passing, reading on the heavy concrete benches, memorials to some alum or other. He thought to himself how much he would have enjoyed being a student here.

Once, a cheerful Asian girl gave him a beautiful smile and said, "Good morning!"

Other than that, he felt invisible. He passed students and staff alike with no eye contact. He offered greetings a couple of times but was ignored. They just walked on. After ten minutes or so, he found himself at Tresidder Union. Though not hungry, he entered the food court. The place was a manic swirl of activity. Chatter and laughter seemed to bounce from the walls and floor and back again.

Off to his right, he saw a Starbucks sign. Someone told him it was the first corporate coffee shop on a university campus in history. It was just what he needed.

"Welcome!" an ebony-skinned young barista with a wide smile and genuinely happy eyes greeted him. "What can I get you?" There was ascent that softly whispered of his African home.

"Mocha Venti, one hundred and ninety-degrees, please." Cole could almost feel the scalding hot cup in his hands.

"A man who knows his order!" the barista said brightly. "I like that. Your name, sir?"

"Cole." He looked at the young man's name tag. "Arthur, why are you so happy today?"

"My stomach is full, my clothes are clean, I have a job, and I am a student in the greatest university in the world. I have been blessed as no other in my village ever has."

"What are you studying?"

"Biochemistry. I will take it home and change my country."

"You are a fine young man." Cole smiled. "You, my friend, are going to do great things."

"Thank you, sir. Thank you." Arthur gave Cole a slight bow. His smile seemed to have increased in wattage by twice.

Cole moved to a small table and waited for his coffee. He watched the people around him, all blissfully ignorant of the frustration that seemed to radiate off him. A young couple, laptops open and books stacked between them, held hands across the table. For them, there was no one else in the building. Cole ached to be with Kelly. There was his contentment.

"Cole," a girl called from the end of the counter. As he reached for his coffee, she looked at him and said, "Careful, it's hot. But of course, you know that. This is Stanford." She giggled at her joke.

Cole just smiled. He took his coffee and left. He had no trouble killing the time until his appointment. It was a great day to be alive. He replayed over and over as he strolled the campus the words, "Let me introduce you to Cole Aaron Mitchell." He couldn't help smiling, which he was sure looked totally insane to the passersby.

At eleven-twenty, he made his way to the president's office.

As he approached the shiny black doors at the entrance of the building, Cole was stopped by a security guard.

"Do you have an appointment?"

"I sure do."

"ID, please."

Cole slipped the lanyard with his ID card on it and showed it to the guard.

"Thank you, have a nice day." The guard opened the door, letting Cole pass.

Another set of doors bore a sign with the president's name and title. Cole went in and introduced himself to the secretary seated at a large desk just outside a pair of large wooden doors.

"Go right in, Mr. Sage. He's expecting you."

Cole gave a quick tap on the door and opened it. His entrance disrupted what was obviously a joke among friends.

"Oh, Cole, come right in. Nice to see you," the president said, crossing the large room to meet him. "I think you know everyone."

Cole smiled widely. It was not a smile of being pleased to see familiar faces; it was the smile of the words bouncing around in his head, 'Welcome to the lynching, son.'

Cole was directed to a pair of chairs on the left side of a small coffee table facing Dean Coffiere and Mason Muller. The president sat at his desk. Cole made no effort to greet them or shake hands. This was going to get ugly, and he knew it.

"The reason I decided we should all meet is to clear the air on what seems to be a misunderstanding," the president began. "I'm sure we can get this unfortunate matter sorted out and get back to the business of education. Sound good?"

Muller and Coffiere gave their answer in unison, accompanied by smarmy smiles. Cole didn't respond.

"Now as I understand it, Mason approached you with a request to have a piece he wrote printed in The Daily. He claims you refused without even looking at it. Is that correct?" The president cocked his head slightly to the right and gazed at Cole.

"As with all great lies, there is always an element of truth to them. It is correct that I did not read his submission at our first meeting. However, what he omitted is that the decision to print or not at that point was our editor's call. His submission was read aloud to the newspaper staff, and they unanimously agreed it needed to be toned down before it would be considered for print."

"But you said you would print it over your dead body!" Muller interjected.

Cole didn't look at him.

"On what grounds did the student staff object to Dr. Muller's, what, letter, op-ed?"

"I think it best be described as an op-ed. The main grounds of their object was the racial overtones, accusing Blacks and Mexicans of killing our white students. It wasn't subtle at all, and quite offensive."

"Then who is doing it?!" Muller blurted out.

"Mason, please. Your chance is coming to express your concerns. Let me finish with Mr. Sage."

The familiar tone of the president's attempt to calm Muller down reinforced Cole's feeling of this being a, more than a little, one-sided affair.

"The thing that concerns me about all this is your hostility toward a colleague. Engaging in a shouting match in front of students and attacking them with a projectile is simply inexcusable. What say you, Mr. Cole?"

"Your friend, Mr. Muller, came to my building, into my office, into my classroom, with much the same kind of bullying behavior he has exhibited here today. I didn't go looking for him. I was pleasantly unaware of his existence until he took it upon himself to rifle through the desk of my dead TA.

"On his return trip, he interrupted my class. I was professional, as was my newspaper staff. At that point, I contacted Dean Coffiere regarding Muller's submission, notifying him it was unacceptable as it was and that we would be requesting a rewrite. Based on his blustering, I felt he should know of the situation, a move that was recommended to me by staff. The dean warned me there would be a blow-up.

"Regarding my hostility toward a colleague, Dr. Muller has been the aggressor in this incident from the beginning, demanding, bullying and throwing his weight around. On his third and final visit to my office, and I'm sure with the intention of confronting my staff about his submission, he retaliated with threats, and even after being explained policy, his response was 'Policy be damned.'

"I will only be pushed so far by a bully. My students were in full view of Muller's exhibition of bad taste and unprofessional behavior. Did I refuse to print his submission at that point? Yes, for the safety and well-being of my students. I was not about to subject them to his bullying. Did I wad up his papers? Yes. Did I throw them at him? Yes, again. The fact that it hit him in the forehead instead of my intended target was an act of providence."

"Is that it?" the president inquired.

"Pretty much."

"Mason, what have you to say?"

"Just this. This man is not qualified to teach at a university of our standing. I have a hard-won reputation on this campus. Refusing to print my requested submission is insulting. I defend every word I said. To be struck by a wad of paper in front of students is tantamount to the grossest of physical abuse. I demand my submission be published and a full apology printed in The Daily."

"Anything else?" The president sounded like a kid at the drive-thru at McDonald's.

"No."

"Dean, do you have anything to add?"

"Only that this is a dangerous precedent, and as one of the newest members of our faculty, Mr. Sage needs to be shown this kind of behavior is totally unacceptable."

"OK, so the schoolyard bully picked on the new kid. The teacher and principal take his side, and the new kid who gets tired of being bullied has to apologize. Is that it?" Cole was using all the restraint he could muster not to continue.

"I don't think I like your attitude, Mr. Sage. This was intended to be a teaching moment for you, an effort behind closed doors to show you the way things are done in academia to settle unpleasant situations."

"A sort of hazing. I see."

"Nothing of the sort!"

Cole hit a nerve.

"If you are unhappy with the way we do things—"

"You people live in a bubble of make-believe. There is a real world out there beyond these gates. Muller here would get his ass kicked on a regular basis until he learned he was just a posturing bully. Dean, you are protecting your pal, I get it. It's a perk of power. But you," Cole pointed at the president, "you are a pencil pusher, fundraiser and PR man. You have no clue how to deal with people or conflict. So here's how I look at it.

"You do not deserve an apology, Muller. And I stand by my refusal to print that disgusting attack on two different races and its call to vigilantism. That means we are at a complete impasse. Therefore, you leave me no choice but to resign my position, effective immediately. After this little soiree, I wouldn't work here if you doubled the salary."

Cole stood and walked out of the big wooden door. He left it open for anyone outside to see the three men seated on the other side with their mouths agape.

As he passed through the exit door, he bid the security guard a good afternoon. He made his way back to his office. His gait was quick and more confident than it was when he left the building earlier.

"Suzanne, do you have one of those copy paper boxes?"

"Sure do. How was the meeting?"

"About what I expected," Cole replied, going into this office.

"Hi, Mr. Sage?" a female voice came from behind him.

Cole turned to see Jody Zhuan. "Hey, there. What's up?"

"That's kind of what we wanted to ask you." From around the corner, the rest of the newspaper staff appeared.

"Where'd you guys come from?"

"We've been in the conference room the whole time," Mitch replied.

"We've come to a decision. Please don't get mad," Chloe De Leon, the only Hispanic on staff, stated.

"I think I'm about out of mad for today." Cole smiled.

Jody took the floor. "If you make us print the piece Dr. Muller submitted, we will go on strike. There will be no paper."

"That is a bold decision. You know it means you would receive no credit for the course, probably."

"We talked about that," a normally quiet boy said. "Doesn't matter. It's the principle. It is our paper, and we don't like what he wrote, and we reject the ideas and sentiment it represents."

"Is that why you stood up to that ass, uh, jerk?" Mitch asked in self-censorship.

"It is indeed. I am very proud of you all." Cole leaned back against the front of his desk, reminding himself for an instant of his old friend and mentor, Mic Brennan. "I just left a meeting with Dr. Muller, Dean Coffiere, and the President of the University. They demanded I apologize to Muller and print his letter."

"Oh, hell no!" Mitch blurted out.

"You wouldn't, would you?" Jody pleaded. "It is not what you have been teaching us at all."

"No, I couldn't. I wouldn't and certainly shouldn't. I resigned."

"You quit over it?" one of the students asked in disbelief.

"Hey, what is a person worth if they don't stand up for what they believe?"

"What will happen to the class?"

"One thing I have learned in my life is that everyone is expendable. There will be a class, and after you graduate, there will be no one who'll know I was here."

"Did you do that for us?" Chloe asked.

"I guess I did. I'm at the end of my career. You guys are at the beginning. I hope you will take this incident with you and teach these principles wherever you end up."

As if in one movement, the six members of the class rushed into the room for a massive group hug with Cole at its center.

Chapter 12

The small apartment Cole rented when he first started teaching at the university seemed drab and melancholy. What he thought of as bright and cheery in the beginning no longer felt like home. There was no feeling or smell of Kelly. She was truly part of him now, and the idea of separate living spaces was quite foreign.

He placed the box of what little possessions he took from his office on the kitchen table. He got a Coke Zero from the refrigerator and found a box of crackers in the cupboard.

Facing Kelly right now just wasn't in the cards. As much as he wanted to see and talk to her, he dreaded telling her he failed. He pulled out a chair and popped the top of the soda. *I guess you can't teach an old dog new tricks after all,* he thought. He munched a few crackers and sipped at the soda as he role-played, telling Kelly he was no longer a journalism instructor at Stanford.

It was no use. The walls seemed to be closing in. He put the crackers back, crushed the soda can, and left the apartment. He played the radio loud and tried to sing, but he was in too much of a funk for that.

The site of Lombard Street brought a smile to his face. Even though Kelly was house sitting, it was home. She was there, and their shared bed was there. Cole chuckled at the thought of standing up to the dean and president of a major university but was afraid to tell his wife he quit a job he, in all honesty, hated.

He pulled into the steep, twisted driveway and got out of the car.

Cole opened the front door. The house was quiet. He went to the kitchen. No Kelly. Down the hall, he could hear singing. He stood for a minute, just enjoying the sound of Kelly's voice. He didn't know the song; it didn't matter. It was her heart rejoicing. Now he would wipe that away.

"Kelly!" he called as if he just arrived.

"Back here!" she replied.

Cole made his way back to the bedroom.

"Hello, Mr. Sage. How is my handsome husband?"

"I have had better days. What do you want first, the bad news or the bad news? Where's Jenny?"

"Ben picked her up an hour ago. Said he wanted some father-daughter time before they bring the baby home. He took her for ice cream and to see some girly Disney movie."

"Oh, that's nice," Cole said with little emotion.

"This sounds like we need to move to the couch."

As she moved toward Cole, she reached out her arms. "But first a hug." She put her arms around his neck and laid her head on his chest. "Better?"

"Lots. Nothing seems to matter much with you in my arms."

She kissed him on the cheek, "Come on. This could lead to a lot of not talking."

"Would that be so bad?" Cole asked coyly.

"Later."

In the living room, Kelly tucked up in the corner of the couch. She picked up one of the decorative pillows on the couch and wrapped her arms around it.

Cole first took a seat on the couch but moved to the easy chair so he could turn it to be face to face with Kelly.

"I got a call today from my cousin Georgia, in Orvin," Cole began. "My aunt Lottie has had a stroke. A bad one. She is in a coma and is completely paralyzed. I'm sure she is not going to last long."

"I'm sorry," Kelly said softly. "Kind of puts a damper on the excitement of the morning."

"She's lived a full life. Eighty-whatever, she's had a pretty good run. I hope in some little way I helped make the last few years happy for her."

"How is Georgia doing?"

"As you might expect, they are so close. Surprisingly, she said Ernie was taking it really hard."

"The hell you say!" Kelly tried to lighten the mood a bit using Ernie's favorite response.

Cole smiled broadly. "I don't know why, but I really love that goofy guy. Sounds silly, but I really miss him sometimes."

"We should go for a visit." Nodding in approval of her own suggestion. "Maybe this summer?"

"Well, we could do it sooner." Cole sat a little straighter in his chair. "That is the other bad news."

Kelly didn't say anything, but Cole noticed she hugged the pillow a little tighter.

"This whole thing about printing that guy's letter? It turned into a political firestorm. The dean is his Army buddy, the president wants to keep the dean happy, and I picked the side of right. I sided with the kids wanting it toned down."

"That sounds like the right thing to me. It is their paper, right?"

"Yeah, but that's not the whole story. So, this morning Muller comes to the class again, yelling at me for talking to the dean about his interrupting my class. I guess I wasn't in the mood for his foolishness, and, well, he made me…no, I got really mad. There, I take responsibility. He pushed all my buttons. So I reached in my briefcase, got the paper he wrote, wadded it up and threw it at him."

"You didn't!" Kelly exclaimed, putting her hand over her mouth.

"Yeah, and I said we would print it over my dead body. The problem is, I was aiming at his chest but hit him square in the forehead." Cole grimaced.

Kelly burst into laughter. Not the reaction Cole expected.

"What? Are you in junior high? That's hilarious!" Kelly continued to laugh. The combination of fatigue and shock at Cole's actions struck her funny bone, and she got hopelessly tickled, unable to stop laughing. Finally able to regain her composure, she wiped her eyes and looked up at Cole's dour expression and collapsed in hysterics again.

"Oh, come on!" Kelly said, gasping for breath. "You hit him with a wad of paper! Did they send you to the principal?"

Seeing the complete foolishness in his behavior, Cole began to laugh, too. The release of emotions, from the baby, Lottie, and his quitting, overcame Cole. He laughed and coughed, then laughed some more. Tears rolled down his cheeks and looking at Kelly rolling on the couch set him off again. Like laughing at a fart at a funeral, the release was unstoppable.

Kelly looked up from where she buried her face in the pillow. Her cheeks were bright red. She wiped tears from her eyes and said, "I am so sorry. I don't know what came over me. Please finish your story."

"I hate to spoil the fun," Cole replied.

"Please, continue."

The fear of telling Kelly the events of the morning seemed to have faded with their laughter. "The long and short of it is I was called to the president's office. The dean and Muller were both there. I don't know what came over me. I just will not be bullied." Cole cleared his throat. "The newspaper business has been my life's work. It is sacred to me. I refused to print the piece Muller wrote. They all insisted I do. Push came to shove, and I quit."

"Good for you."

"What?"

"I said, good for you. How dare they try and browbeat you into going against the very principles you are trying to instill in the kids? Good for you!"

"I quit my job, Kelly," Cole repeated, still not certain she understood.

"I heard you. You hated it anyway."

"I never said that!"

"You didn't have to. I love you, and believe it or not, I understand you, sometimes better than you know yourself. The signs were everywhere. Especially in your lack of enthusiasm and excitement about what you were doing. Do you realize you almost never talked work?"

"I didn't?"

"See?"

"So, now what?" Cole asked earnestly.

"What do you mean? You told me a long time ago. You're going to write the George Sage story!"

"Just like that?"

"Just like that. Now go pick a movie, and I'll get dinner. We need a distraction." The twinkle in Kelly's eye was a sign she was up to something good.

Cole went to the bathroom and splashed his face in cold water. When he returned, he flipped through a stack of DVDs he pulled a week before. He wanted to watch something then as well but couldn't decide what and gave up on the idea. Now he was rejuvenated and scanned the twelve titles with enthusiasm.

"This should do it!" Cole announced, slipping the disc into the machine.

"So should this!" Kelly stood under the arch into the living room holding two cartons of ice cream, Double Chocolate Brownie, the other Pralines 'n Cream, each with a spoon shoved into the middle.

"Who are you, and what have you done with my bride?" Cole grinned from ear to ear.

"You don't have to eat it all, but for once let's eat all we want." Kelly handed the Chocolate Brownie to Cole, along with a napkin. "So what's on the bill for tonight?"

"It has been such a weird day, why not end it with drama, laughter, and romance?"

"Oh no, not Drew Barrymore again."

"No, *Defending Your Life*. Your favorite."

Chapter 13

Breakfast was abnormally quiet. Cole toasted and ate an onion bagel with cream cheese and sipped his mocha. Kelly stood looking out the kitchen window, her back to Cole as she drank her Green Monster smoothie.

"Well," Cole finally broke the silence, "I played a million scenarios through my head before going to Stanford. I have to admit, this one was not among them."

"It's just not fair." Kelly's voice quaked with emotion. "You have so much to offer. They'll be sorry." Her tone turned angry.

"You know how there are menus with so much stuff on them you can't decide what you want? Then there are menus that are one sheet printed in the office and nothing sounds good? That's me, lost in the big menu. There are so many choices out there. My spot will be filled by Monday. You, my love, see me on the one-sheet menu as filet mignon and ravioli. You're just a little prejudiced to think I'm on a one-sheet menu."

"You're the *only* thing on the menu as far as I'm concerned!" Kelly spun about, wiped the tears from her cheeks with both hands and stepped across to where Cole sat, then squeezed him around the neck and kissed the top of his head.

"You know, I've been thinking about what you said about writing the book. Now just might be the time."

"Where are the journals?"

"Still in my grandfather's old steamer trunk, stowed away with the rest of my stuff in the storage unit. What if I got them out and actually did it?"

"That's what writers do, you know: write."

"Good thing we didn't buy a house," Cole said, changing the subject.

"Better thing you didn't sell yours. How long are those people leasing it for?"

"A year, renewable. Or not. Would you want to live near the Marina?"

"It's a lovely home. Your stuff all fits, I have nothing left. Seems a good fit. When did you sign the lease?"

"August."

"OK, so May, June, July. Three months left, give or take." Kelly sat at the table next to Cole. "Now, about the book."

"Is it a silly idea? I mean, were you just -"

"Why would you say that?"

"I don't know, maybe it's the overall feeling of doom I've had since yesterday." Cole chuckled. "Excluding the baby, of course."

"Of course. Remember how excited you got reading those journals? How they led you to Lottie and Georgia? They changed your life. They answered questions you'd had your whole life. The little bits and pieces I read were incredible. Imagine what you could do with them, perhaps turn them into a novel."

"I don't know. I've never done a lot of fiction. You think it would sell as non-fiction?"

"What I know is you could turn them into something amazing," Kelly assured.

"Like I said, I've been thinking about it a lot lately. But Georgia's call *really* got me thinking about it. The genealogy of it all, you know? I thought I would dedicate it to little Cole. Something for me to leave behind, you know."

"Oh, Cole, that's a wonderful idea. You have to write it!"

"Well, it seems I'll have the time!" Cole laughed.

The cell phone on the table rang out with a snippet of Nilsson's *Coconut*. *'Called the doctor, woke him up. I said Doctor, Called the doctor, woke him up. I said Doctor'*.

It repeated twice before Kelly said, "Good morning, sweetie. How's mama and baby?"

"Doing great! The baby takes after his grandfather, he sleeps like a log." Ben chuckled. "I thought I would touch base. Everything good on your end?"

"We have some kind of big news. Would it be OK if we dropped over in a while?"

"I know better than to ask what it is. Sure, that would be great. I'm sure Erin would like a do-over, this time with hair and make-up done. We should be home in about an hour. They're doing an exam now, and I did the release paperwork a little while ago."

"How about we see you around noon, and I'll bring lunch? Turkey, pepper jack and avocado for Erin, roast beef and provolone for you, and tuna for Jenny. Right?"

"Always. Love you, see you soon."

"What do I get?" Cole asked with a grin.

"Me."

* * *

"Why don't we swing by the storage place on our way? You can pick up the journals."

"They are probably buried."

"What's your hesitation? I get the feeling you're half-scared to do this book."

Cole didn't look at her, just kept driving. "You know, it has been a dream of mine to write a book for several years now, kind of my fantasy swan song. I fantasize it is a raging success. I like that dream. I'd hate to see it crash and burn."

"I don't think I've ever seen this side of you. You are really afraid to fail."

"I don't think I'd call it afraid; petrified, maybe." Cole looked at Kelly and grinned. "Wouldn't it be cool if it was a success?"

"You really are a worrywart."

"I was thinking," Cole said reflectively, "what would you think about going to Orvin?"

"Why? The baby was just born. Erin will need my help."

"Really? Are you sure you just want to help? I don't mean tomorrow. Next week. I would like to see Lottie before, you know…" Cole's voice trailed off.

"Let's feel it out. See how she feels, what she thinks about us going." Kelly sounded less than enthused.

The storage unit was stuffed. Cole felt an odd wave of melancholy come over him. *Is this what he has come to?* he thought. Sitting in this half-lit storage unit, his only possessions look tired and worn. Kind of like him. He smiled at the thought.

It took Cole nearly an hour of shuffling boxes, moving furniture and restacking things to finally uncover the old steamer trunk. It was nearly to the far corner and was buried under a huge stack of moving boxes, behind a dresser.

"Found it!" Cole yelled from the back of the storage space.

Twisting and turning, he heaved the heavy trunk over the top of the first pile of boxes. When Cole finally worked his way through the winding trail between furniture and boxes, he was covered with dust.

"This thing seemed lighter when I put it in there!" Cole said, slipping the trunk into the back of the car. It took another five minutes to bring enough order to the space to bring down the roll-up door.

"I've always wondered why you drive an old Volvo station wagon," Kelly said as Cole slammed the back of the car.

"That's easy. A guy at the Chronicle was selling it when I first came to town. I had the same year

Volvo back in Chicago. Not a wagon, and a different color, but I loved it. This was cheap and it ran good, so I grabbed it. What a weird thing to bring up now. Anything else you've been wondering about?" Cole teased as he attached the padlock on the door.

"When did you know you loved me?"

"That's easy, too." Cole got in the car and started the engine. "When you were all dirty and splattered with paint."

"Be serious."

"I am. It was love at first…" Cole hesitated. "I can't think of a clever replacement for sight. You were so beautiful, even dirty. I fell hard. On top of that, you came all the way to Oklahoma to help me with the farmhouse."

"In Orvin?"

"Yep. So you see, I wasn't smitten by your style. It was the real you."

"That is so romantic. I wish I believed you." Kelly grinned and leaned over and kissed Cole's cheek.

"How about you?"

"I've fallen for you so many times, I really don't know."

"What does that mean exactly?" Cole was baffled once again by Kelly's thought process.

"I loved the way as a writer you find it hard to say what you feel out loud. I loved the way you respected my faith and moral code. I loved the way you were such a gentleman when I came to Orvin to work on the farm. I loved the way you comforted me when my house burned and I lost everything. You see, each thing seemed to overshadow the last. You are so many parts that the whole is what I love."

They drove around the end of the building in silence and headed for the gate. Cole waved at the manager as he passed the window of the office.

Cole ran in to pick up the order of five sandwiches and large potato salad Kelly called in. Sunshine Deli was a bright, blinding yellow inside, and the walls were covered with all kinds of hippie looking mantra posters, but their food was hard to beat.

"Order for Sage."

"Runnin' just a tad behind. It'll be ready in just a bit," responded Forrest, the owner of the shop. He was a bearded man in a hand-woven green, yellow, and red cap. He was much older than he was pretending to be.

Cole took a seat in a wicker chair next to a flower pot full of leafy plants. He glanced around. A voice with a thick German accent from long ago popped into his head.

Are you a boy or are you a girl?

As a high school kid, Cole and his friends would sneak off campus to a place called Freddy's Meat market. It was run by a German immigrant who fought as a fighter pilot in World War II, on the German side.

What would old Freddy think of this place? Cole thought.

The old German was famous for giving the longhairs of the sixties a hard time, and on occasion, if they gave him any guff, he threw them out. The element of leaving a closed campus combined with the best sandwiches he ever ate made for a lunch that left the young Cole feeling exhilarated for the rest of the day.

For the last fifty years, Cole held Freddy's sandwiches up as the gold standard everything else is compared to. Sunshine Deli was good, but Freddy's being a ten, this deli was a seven-point-eight, maybe on a good day an eight.

Cole smiled to himself. He remembered taking Ellie, his high school sweetie, to Freddy's in his sixty-three VW bug. Walking into the small, simply-lit place was like being part of a secret society all your friends belonged to. If he could only do it one more time.

The tinkling of the bell over the front door snapped Cole from his thoughts. A grungy looking guy with a holey Ramones T-shirt, baggy jeans, and flip-flops wandered in the door. His eyes were barely visible behind his long, untrimmed bangs. He stood for a few seconds staring at Cole, then the menu on the wall behind the counter.

Freddy would have loved this guy, Cole thought.

A young woman was at the far end of the counter, busily putting together what looked like a large order. Markee, Forrest's wife, life partner, significant other or whatever label fit, worked mid-counter, hopefully on Cole's order.

"Can I help you?" Forrest asked.

"Not unless you're a shrink." The newcomer laughed, exposing a missing front tooth. "Just a second."

He looked around the room again and spotted what he was looking for, the restroom. As he passed

Cole, the stench made him wince. As he made his way along the counter, he craned his neck to see over. His trip to the restroom was a short one.

Could he have actually washed his hands? Cole wondered.

Cole watched as he passed the tables between the restroom and the counter. He seemed to be picking up speed. As he got to the end of the counter where the young woman worked on the large order, he stepped behind the counter and grabbed one of the boxes being filled with bags of sandwiches and made a dash for the front door.

In an instant, Cole was filled with anger at the thief's bold attempt at snatch and run. Without a thought, Cole stuck his leg out just as the man got to him. His size eleven cross trainer did the trick and sent the man, sandwiches, and box flying across the floor.

Forrest hopped the counter like an Olympic high jumper and added to the thief's problems with a violent non-pacifistic kick to the ribs.

"Son of a bitch, steal my sandwiches, will you?" He kicked him again. "Markee, call the police!"

She was already on her cell. Forrest looked as if he was about to let the would-be thief have it again.

"Whoa there, buddy, I think he's had enough," Cole said, standing. He thought he better intercede before the angry owner found himself in trouble, too.

"You move, I'll give you worse!" Forrest shouted.

The man curled defensively in the fetal position. Forrest went to the door and turned the knob, locking them all in. The man on the floor lay motionless.

"Your order's ready," Markee said to Cole as she moved to the register.

Trying to step on neither man nor sandwiches, Cole made his way to the counter.

"No charge today," Forrest announced over his shoulder. "We got this. Thanks for your help."

"Are you sure? That's really not necessary. Looks like you lost a lot of today's profits already."

"I'll add it to the claim for the insurance company." Forrest laughed. "I'm not all capitalist!"

"I see that," Cole said, looking down at the guy on the floor.

Cole turned and slid a sandwich over to where the thief laid whimpering. "Better eat one; you're going to get really hungry before this is settled." Cole looked over at Forrest and flashed him a peace sign. Forrest just nodded.

Markee pushed two brown bags across the counter. Cole picked up the bags and gave them a slight up and down lift in acknowledgment of their weight.

"Sure glad you're not vegetarians," Cole said, smiling as he stuffed twenty dollars in the tip jar.

"Who says we're not?" Markee replied.

Forrest unlocked the door, and Cole made his way out.

"Next time," the owner said behind him.

Cole heard the lock click behind him.

"That took a while," Kelly said as Cole got in the car. "What took so long?"

Cole related the story of the great sandwich heist. He was not amused and showed his disgust in his telling of the story.

"If they were to build a fence around the whole Bay Area, it would make a great lunatic asylum. Every day, it's something. Everywhere we go, there's some shouting match or a madman howling at the sky. Clerks in stores are sullen and angry. You don't dare ask a question. What is wrong with these people? I've had enough of this craziness to last me a long time." Cole's frustration was leaving him nearly sputtering.

"I'm beginning to see what you mean. Maybe it is time to leave." Kelly reached over and took Cole's hand. "I think I'm ready. But is it any different somewhere else, or is the whole world crazy?"

"I sure hope not."

Chapter 14

The loud chorus of *Takin' Care of Business* from his phone alerted Cole to Randy Callen calling.

"Better get that," Kelly said as Cole loaded the large recycled biodegradable brown bag of food from the back seat.

"I'm trying," Cole said patiently.

"Yo. Hey, Randy. I'm in the car. I'll put you on speaker. No swearing, Kelly's in the car."

"Very funny."

"Hi, Randy!" Kelly said.

"Oh, gee, you were serious." Randy laughed. "Hey, I heard a nasty rumor that's going around you punched a history teacher and got fired."

"Heard and nasty are the only two words in that sentence that are accurate."

"You want to explain?"

"Sure, over dinner." Cole turned to Kelly. "Is that OK?"

"Sure."

"Randy? How about six? Your choice."

"Really?" Randy sounded delighted.

"Yeah, but you're buying. I'm unemployed, remember?"

"In that case, it's Angelino's."

"Angelino's, it is. See you at six." Cole disconnected.

"What a treat," Kelly said. "You won't really make him pay, will you?"

"That's another easy one. Of course not."

When they got to Ben and Erin's, Kelly ran straight to the door and left Cole to get the lunch.

"Hi, Grandma!" Jenny squealed, opening the door.

"What are you doing home from school, young lady?"

"Daddy said I could play hooky."

"Did he, now?"

"Hi, Mom, come on in," Ben called in welcome.

"I'm fine, thanks," Cole said jokingly.

"Grandpa, what'd you bring me?"

"Lunch! Are you hungry?"

"Tuna?"

"Of course. Where's Mom?"

"Bedroom."

"OK. Want to set the table?" Cole asked, making his way to the kitchen.

"Sure." Jenny ran to the cupboard.

Down the hall, Cole could hear voices coming from the bedroom.

"There you are!" Erin smiled widely.

Kelly was standing next to the bed, looking down at her new grandson. Erin was in a purple silk robe that gave her complexion and her hair a lovely glow.

"Well, you look like royalty." Cole came and approached the bed and gave Erin a kiss on the cheek.

"So what's this big news?" she asked.

Kelly looked over at Cole and said, "Can't we eat first? I'm starving." It was an obvious stall.

"Yeah, I'm famished," Ben said, picking up the signal.

"I'll get you a tray," Kelly offered.

"No, I think I'll sit in the big recliner in the family room. That way, you guys can eat at the table and I won't miss anything."

Jenny prepared a lovely third-grade style table with napkins, glasses, and spoons. Lunch went quickly, and the conversation was light. As everyone wadded up their sandwich wrappers and Kelly stacked the plates, Cole knew the time to let the cat out of the bag was near.

"So what is this big news Ben was so quickly hushed up about?" Erin gave Cole a knowing smile.

"We need to talk to you guys about a couple of things." Cole stood. He walked over to the ottoman in front of the couch and pulled it up close to Erin. "First, I have left Stanford. We'll keep it light. Let's just say it wasn't a good fit. My idea, not theirs."

"That's no great surprise. I could tell for a long time you weren't happy there." Erin nodded as if to give her approval.

"Kudos for giving it a shot," Ben added.

Cole looked over at Kelly. "That went better than expected."

"I have decided to write a book. I want to turn your great-grandfather's journals I found in Oklahoma into a novel. It has been itching at me for a couple of years. I think it's now or never."

"I love it!" Erin exclaimed. "It's about time."

"Well, two out of three…" Cole said to Kelly.

"Why do I think there's a wow finish you don't think we'll like?" Erin said without smiling.

"Therein lies the source of my concern." Cole looked at her for a long moment. "My aunt Lottie has had a stroke. She's probably not long for this world."

"Then you need to go see her," Erin insisted. "Don't worry about us."

"But Kelly is worried you'll need her help with the baby and all."

"Oh, that's so sweet, but Ben has taken two weeks off, and after that, I'll be up and running around no problem. Probably sooner; I feel terrific. Jenny is a great help. She even changed the baby last night." Erin looked over her shoulder at a grinning Jenny. "Really, we've done this before, you know." Erin smiled sweetly.

"What if we were to stay there a while?"

"What's a while? You're not moving, are you?"

"No, no nothing like that, I don't think. But we need a break from the city, some peace, and quiet. Kelly being attacked was the last straw for me. She's only got a few weeks before her housesitting is finished. My place is leased until August. So it seems like a nice combination of a honeymoon road trip, writing get-away, and I'm sad to say, probably a funeral."

"Mom, you're awfully quiet," Ben said, turning to his mother.

"We are going to build a life together. The idea for Cole writing the book is quite exciting to me. I want to be here if you need me, but frankly, it sounds like I would just be in the way. I get it. Since my houseboat burned, I really haven't felt at home anywhere. I need this, Ben. I need for Cole and me to strike out and see what our lives together are going to hold. We need each other, and we need to find a place we are both happy."

"Sounds like you know your mind. To be truthful, this hasn't been the best fit for us either. Maybe we all need a change." Ben gave a grimaced smile.

"Are you still thinking about that job in Texas?"

"No, that's long gone, but there are lots of opportunities if a person is open to them. I would love to do a year or two in Europe. France, maybe. How would you feel about that?" Ben replied.

"If it makes you happy, I'm happy." But Kelly's heart wasn't in her reply. "You know, I got pretty resigned about you going to Houston. If I'm going to fly to Texas to see you, I might as well fly to France. The blessing there is I would way prefer France."

"Erin, what do you think of all this?" Cole asked.

"Now that you have Kelly, I won't feel so protective. I know you'll be OK. As far as France goes, I made Ben pass on Texas. I think it is his turn. It will be good for Jenny. Maybe we can get you guys to come over, too?"

"That's the beauty of being retired, I guess. You can go wherever you want. I can write anywhere. Who knows, I may have a couple of books in me."

"Speaking of books, you mentioned you want to have a kind of genealogy angle on it. Have you ever thought of doing a DNA test as part of the research?" Ben asked.

"Yeah, Ben and I have. I've been watching a show on TV about finding lost relatives. Oh, and another one that traces famous people's family tree. It is fascinating." Erin paused. "I was thinking of having mine done. You know everybody on Mama's side of the family is gone. I really don't know much of anything about her family tree."

"I met her grandparents when I was really young, like junior high. But they died when I was in high school. I think you should do it. Let's both do it."

Cole was getting excited about the idea. "So, how does it work? What do you do?"

"Basically, they send you a kit, you spit in a sample jar and add preserving medium and send it back. In about six weeks, they send you the results." Ben sounded like he researched the process already.

"Tell you what, Erin, I'll pay for your kit if you want to do it. Early birthday present," Cole offered.

"Mr. Practical! Thanks. OK, I'll get you one for your birthday, too, since we haven't celebrated yet."

"That's my fault. So, Ben, you want to do one, too?" Kelly offered.

"Does it have to be my birthday present?"

"No! But since you now have an heir to the Mitchell name, you should have an official tree. I have lots of stuff on my dad's family, he did it years ago, but it would be fun to see how far back you can go."

"Well, to keep this going, I guess I need to buy one for you, too! Then I'm covered in both directions," Ben teased. "Say, have you thought about having your aunt's DNA done, too?"

"Lottie?" Cole replied.

"Yeah, you should have hers done, too. It might be a way of connecting to her mother's side of her family."

"That might have been a good idea before her stroke, but..."

"I got this. I'll submit a request for my 'patient' Cole Sage and have her doctor order a sample."

"Cole's your patient?" Kelly asked, always sensitive to falsehoods.

"Cole? Of course. How are you feeling, sir?"

Cole smiled and nodded at the idea. "I feel great! What a brilliant idea, Ben. What an angle for my book. I wonder how fast we can get the tests."

"Erin, what's the name of the company that's always pitching it on that show? Tree something?" Ben asked.

"I'll Google it," Erin spoke into her phone softly. "Here you are." Erin handed Ben the cell phone, and a moment later he was speaking to a representative.

"I want to order five DNA test kits, please. I sure can."

As Ben gave the person his shipping and credit card information, Cole and Kelly looked at each other.

Kelly mouthed, "That went well."

Cole winked at her. "Erin, you really think he can get Lottie's test done? I mean before..."

"Don't be so morbid, Daddy. Dr. Watson over there can pull off anything." Erin raised her eyebrows and rolled her eyes.

"OK, it cost us each five bucks extra, but we'll have the test kits in two days."

It wasn't long before the sounds of the baby crying for attention was heard. Erin slipped back to the bedroom. Jenny pulled Cole into the family room to see a puzzle she had been working on. Ben grabbed a notepad and started pumping Kelly for information on his grandparents and great grandparents.

The afternoon went by with a nice, relaxed pace. Erin napped after nursing the baby. Jenny somehow got Cole to watch *Frozen* with her for the tenth time. She sang along, and he dozed off every chance he could. Ben and Kelly shared memories of his dad and growing up. It was a sweet time for mother and son, and one Cole was sure Kelly would relive over and over.

Around five, Kelly held the baby and rocked him back to sleep after changing his diaper for the first time. Cole beamed from across the room watching the two women he loved most in the world.

"I think he's out," Kelly whispered.

"You've got the magic touch," Erin replied.

"It's a grandma thing."

"If we are going to get to Angelino's by six, we better get rolling," Cole said, hating to break up the party.

"Oh, is it that late? Erin, I'm so sorry. We didn't mean to spend the day."

"It was wonderful. I slept better just knowing you were here." Erin giggled.

They bid Ben and Jenny goodbye and headed for the car.

As Jenny stood waving goodbye from the front lawn, Cole said, "You want to drive? I'll call Georgia and check on Lottie and tell her of our plan to come visit."

"Sure, that'll work." Kelly went to the driver's side and got in.

The phone only rang twice when Georgia picked up.

"Hi, Cole."

"Hey, how you doin'?"

"I'm doin'. No change in Mama to report, I'm afraid."

"The reason I'm calling is, we want to come back and see Lottie and visit you and Ernie. Would that be all right? We don't want to be in the way or intrude."

"Intrude? You kiddin'? We would love to have you. We need all the family we can get."

"I've decided to write a book about those old journals I found in the house. I want to do kind of a family tree novel. I really don't have it all sorted yet, but I thought while I was back there maybe I could do some research. Would you have time to nose around and see if you can find a house we could rent?"

"Rent?!" Georgia protested. "You got a home here. Cole, sweetie, listen to me. Mama won't be comin' home. By rights, the farmhouse is yours.

You're getting it back when Mama goes. It's all in her will."

"Shouldn't it go to you?" Cole asked in earnest.

"I don't need it. We have a lovely place of our own. Ernie has kept up the farm for Mama. It's all family."

"Well, I don't know quite what to say. Thank you, that's very generous."

"What comes around, goes around. Isn't that what they say? You set the example."

"I never expected a return."

"I know that, that's why we love you. Now shut up about it. It's settled. Come for as long as you want. Forever would suit us just fine."

"We were thinking of coming the end of next week. Oh, one last thing. I hope it's all right. If not, you tell me, all right?"

"What are you up to now?"

"Kelly's son Ben is a doctor, you know that, right? He suggested I get a DNA test done to get my family tree figured out. Then we can see how far back I can trace it. He suggested we have Lottie's done, too."

"How would that happen? She is totally unresponsive. Don't you have to spit in a thing or something?"

"Yeah, how come everybody knows how this is done except me? Wouldn't it be wonderful to get a detailed report on her mother's side of the family?"

"I would love that. But how?"

"If it's OK with you, he's going to order a sample done by a doctor, as a work-up on a patient in San Francisco."

"Who, you?" Georgia laughed.

"As a matter fact, yes, smarty pants."

"Well, I think it is a wonderful idea. Tell him to do it with my blessing."

"You're a sweetheart. I'll get back to you as soon as I can. The thing with the farm, though, we'll talk about it.

"I told you already, there ain't nothin' to talk about; it's done, and done it will stay."

"All right, all right, I give up." Cole knew he'd lost the argument. "See you in a few days. We'll be in touch. Say hi to Ernie. Give my auntie a kiss for me."

"I sure will. Love to Kelly. I can't wait to see you."

"Bye-bye."

"Sounds like that went well. How is your aunt?" Kelly asked.

"No change. It's just a matter of time." Cole sighed. "They're giving me back the farm. Lottie is leaving it to me in her will."

"Oh, my goodness." Kelly was taken aback. "That's too generous!"

"That's what I tried to tell her, but she wouldn't have it. So we are about to own a farm."

They rode in silence for several miles, Cole deep in thought, and Kelly giving him his space.

"I really don't want to live in San Francisco anymore. I came for the job. Then Erin and Ben came. We just saw how easily he could take a job somewhere else. This is a new beginning for both of us, and I want all fresh paint, you know what I mean? No strings, no anchors. I think we should sell my house in August when the tenants leave."

"Especially if the kids want to go to France. I know how Ben is; he's probably already applied." Kelly shook her head. "The times, they are a-changin', darlin'."

Chapter 15

Angelino's was a comforting sight. Inside, the smell and décor were like a hug from an old friend. At a table for four near the rear of the restaurant in a quiet alcove, Randy stood and waved.

Kelly gave Randy a hug before being seated. Cole gave Randy a wink and sat down.

"Isn't this a treat?" Randy asked with a proud smile.

"And long overdue," Kelly added.

Cole looked down at the table in front of Randy and saw bread crumbs, then glanced at the breadstick basket.

"Been here long?"

Randy looked at the bread basket. "Busted." He gave a guilty grin. "About a half-hour."

"So, did you order, too?" Cole teased.

"Nope, you're the master. I leave that to you."

The waiter came with water and an antipasto platter. Cole ordered New York Strip steaks and ravioli all round.

"I can't stand the suspense any longer. What did you do?" Randy leaned forward like a conspirator in a devious plot.

"First off, I didn't punch anybody, as tempting as it was. Second, I didn't get fired. I quit."

"Yes!" Randy exclaimed in a hushed whisper.

"The long and short of it is this guy named Muller demanded we print a racist rant about drug dealers and the students at Stanford. I refused. Called the dean to cover my tail, and they turned out to be buddies. The dean told Muller, and he came for round two. I got indignant, not taking his bullying well, wadded up his submission and threw it at him. Problem was, my aim was off, and instead of hitting him in the chest, it hit him in the forehead."

Randy pressed in delight. "Then, then…"

"I got a call from the president, calling me to a meeting. I enter his office, and Muller and the dean are already there, obviously yucking it up. The president insists I print the letter along with an apology. I refused, push came to shove, and I quit. Next subject."

"I would have given a month's salary to have seen that!" Randy didn't even try to hide his admiration for Cole.

"Well, I wasn't that crazy about how the job ended up anyway," Cole said as part-apology and part-excuse.

"I know, me neither. So now what do we do?" Randy asked excitedly.

"We? I'm not dragging you into this mess."

"Oh, come on Cole, we're a team."

"Yeah, like Abbott & Costello."

"I was thinking more like Captain America and Iron Man."

"Tell him your idea, Cole," Kelly injected, seeing the conversation getting totally derailed.

"I've been thinking about finally writing a book. I'd like to use the journals of my grandfather's I found in Oklahoma. Novelize them."

"I can format it."

"What's that mean?" Cole asked, totally confused.

"Mobi, ePub, PDF."

"OK, now in English, please."

"You'll self-publish, right?

"What do you mean?" Cole was trying to follow, but Randy was way ahead of him.

"eBooks, that's where the market is going. Paperback sales have dropped like a rock, and eBook sales have skyrocketed. You make more money, and it is way faster to get out and into the hands of your adoring readers."

"I'm with you up to adoring readers. Do you mean people can publish their own books? What about Simon and Schuster, and Time-Warner, those guys?"

"Don't need 'em. We can do it all."

"We?"

"I, then. You write it, I can do the rest. We'll need a good proofreader and cover artist. That's not a problem."

"Yeah, but the adoring readers part?"

"I'll start, or rather continue, to build an email list."

"Continue?" Cole asked suspiciously.

"Well, yeah, I started back at the Chron'. I figured you'd need it someday. You've got about ten thousand right now, but I can do way better than that. Now there is a need for it."

"And this mailing list is, like, for direct sales?" Cole was seeing the bigger picture.

"Yep. Then we let Amazon do the rest. They're the biggest booksellers on the planet, and 80% of the market or better in eBooks is all them."

"And you figure you can do all this?"

"I'm not just a pretty face, you know. Callen-Sage Publishing, Full-service eBook production and promotion."

"This is wonderful! But Randy, how do you make an income until things get rolling?" Kelly was fully focused and in total agreement with Randy.

"No problem. I can do blog design, freelance research, whatever. I don't need much. Yet."

"Oh, here it comes," Cole said sarcastically.

"I get a cut, a partner in the publishing company. You won't be the only author we represent. When you finish the book, I'm going to put you to work writing a 'How to Write' course we'll sell, too. I got this down to a well-oiled, money-making machine. I've just been waiting for you to wake up."

"Oh, Randy, this is so exciting," Kelly said.

"How long until you finish the book?" Randy pressed.

"I don't know. I haven't even started. We are going back to Orvin in a week or so. My aunt is not well, and I was going to do some research and write while we are there."

"What's Oklahoma like?"

"I really liked it. It is a really laid back lifestyle, people are wonderful, and Orvin is located where the weather is nice," Cole replied.

"Sounds nice."

"It reminded me a little of North Carolina, where my grandparents used to live," Kelly added.

"You guys have been everywhere. I've never been out of California. Unless you count a 'Gambler Special' bus to Reno once."

"Why don't you come with us?" Kelly asked excitedly. You could work on whatever you do from anywhere, right?"

"Yeah, but…"

"Yeah, but what?" Cole asked, mulling the idea.

"Where would I stay?"

"With us, silly," Kelly replied as if the answer was obvious.

"Really?"

"Sure. If you think you could stand us."

"You'd want me?"

"Randy, if Cole had a son, you're it. You and Anthony Perez are his boys!"

"I would love that. If you're sure, I mean." Randy looked at Cole for approval.

"You must keep your room clean, and no wild parties," Cole said in mock severity.

"I'll give my notice tomorrow!"

As if on cue, the waiter set Kelly's plate in front of her. Cole and Randy looked down at their plates with big smiles.

"Wow," Randy said. "I've only had the spaghetti and meatballs here."

"Stick with me, kid, we'll show you the high life!" Cole said in his best Humphrey Bogart impression.

The trio laughed.

"Shall we say the blessing?" Kelly said, more of a statement than a request.

Randy looked at Cole.

"It's what we do," Cole said with a smile and nodded.

"Let's join hands." Kelly reached for Randy's misshapen hand without hesitation. Cole grabbed the other. "Heavenly father, bless this plan. Bless Randy as he puts his skills and knowledge to work for our mutual success. Thank you, Father, for such a wonderful friend. Please bless Erin, Ben, and baby Cole. Thank you for this glorious meal. Amen."

"Amen," Randy said softly.

When Randy arrived home an hour later, he stood for a long time in the middle of the studio apartment. Wall by wall, item by item, he took in the sole content of his twenty-four years. After subtracting what was in the small furnished apartment when he moved in, there was little that actually belonged to him.

He moved over to the cheap, particle board entertainment center. Sitting alone on one of three empty shelves was a small tarnished metal picture frame holding a fading photograph. Randy picked up the frame and looked at the three people in the photo. The young couple looked happy and like they had the world by the tail.

The small child in the woman's arms faced away from the camera. Try as he may, Randy could not bring up any memory of his parents other than the smiling image in the picture. He wished he could say he remembered his mother's arms or his father smile, but there was nothing.

His first memory was of the heavy breasts of a large woman who would hold him too close. He could almost feel her hand on the back of his neck as he wriggled and tried to free himself of her embrace. His heart actually would race at times when he recalled his feeling of entrapment and panic. He stayed in the home of Diana and Tom Fulford until he was four when she finally tired of his resistance to being cuddled.

The next placement didn't last long. He barely remembered the people. Shortly before the start of kindergarten, Randy was placed with Janet and Ray Moe. They were very kind to him. In the four years he lived with them, he couldn't remember Ray ever touching him. They were a troubled couple. Even as a small child, Randy sensed something wasn't right in the home. Janet tried to be the best mom she knew how to be. She baked cookies every Saturday, took him to Sunday School, picked him up from school and tried to be a mom just like her friends were with their kids.

Just before Christmas when Randy was in the fourth grade, Ray left. He overheard Janet tell her mother through her tears, "I thought having a child, a family, would bring us closer. It seems that's not what Ray wanted."

When he returned to school after Christmas vacation, Randy found himself at a new school and in a different home. The Costins were Randy's nightmare placement. It was two years of hell. There were three other foster kids in the house. Two black, one white, two boys, one girl. The girl was a toddler, one boy was a year younger than Randy, the other two years older.

The black kids were brother and sister. The older kid was mean and resented Randy. The Costins were in the foster program for the money, none of which they spent on the kids. Their clothes were too small, mended, and shabby. Randy still could recall playing at recess with the soles of his shoes flapping when he ran.

During the summer between sixth grade and junior high, Randy was assigned a new caseworker when his retired. As if by some fortunate accident, Boone, the older boy in the house, had blacked Randy's eye in a dispute over a small action figure that Randy got from a McDonald's Happy Meal he shared with the little girl.

On a surprise visit to the house, Beth, his new caseworker, asked what happened to his eye. When Randy explained Boone punched him, he thought nothing of it.

Her follow up question, "Does he hit you a lot?", was to change the course of Randy's life.

"All the time. He's kinda mean."

Randy left with Beth that day and never saw the Costins again. He spent three days in a group home. Beth's boyfriend was in charge of six boys, all about

Randy's age. One afternoon, Beth picked him up and took him to Margie Strohm's house.

It was to be the best placement of his life. Randy would stay with Miss Margie until he left for college. Margie was not married. She was a high school English teacher. In her care, Randy discovered books, classical music, black and white movies with subtitles, and the unconditional love of a lovely woman who was just as in need of love and companionship as he was.

Margie passed away while Randy was in college. Those years in her care, he forgot what it was to feel utterly alone. When her brother called him to break the news of her death, Randy cried for the first time in years. He recalled burying his face in his dorm room pillow and screaming in pain as if his insides were being torn out. He was out of the system and totally alone.

He gently placed the picture back on the shelf. "We're moving again," he said softly. "I have a good feeling about this time. I feel like this time it's not temporary. This time, I've been adopted. I have a family. They want me."

Randy fell asleep lying on the couch, looking back at the picture on the shelf. He felt a complete sense of belonging.

Chapter 16

"It seems that plans are being pushed along by divine design," Kelly said as Cole entered the kitchen.

"That's always good, right?"

"I got an email from Russ while you were in the shower."

"Russ?" Cole wasn't placing the name.

"Stegner, the man who owns the shower you're using."

"Oh, that Russ. Uh oh, you don't sound happy." Cole grimaced.

"It seems he has decided to come back a month early. He'll be here in ten days."

"So, we are right on schedule. What's the problem?"

"I don't know. I like this place."

"Three million, it's yours!"

"Speaking of housing," Kelly said, ignoring Cole's attempt at humor, "have you given notice on your apartment yet?"

"Yes, ma'am. That's the beauty of a month-to-month rental." Cole scrunched up his face in a gruff imitation of his landlord and growled, "First of the month is Tuesday. Be out by the weekend so I can get somebody in there."

"So, in ten days we're homeless." Kelly was not pleased.

"We do have a place to stay; we just have to get there. Speaking of which, look at this." Cole laid out the map he was holding. "We have two routes we can take: north through Colorado, or south through New Mexico. They are both the same travel time. What do you think? Which shall we take?"

"We're driving?"

"Sure. It will take a couple or three days depending on the number of stops."

"You really think that's best? I mean, we could fly and rent a car."

"First off, we'd have to ship the trunk. Don't you think it would be a total waste of money to rent a car for a month or two when we have two perfectly good cars? Besides, think of the sites we could see driving."

"I suppose. So when do we leave?"

"Next Wednesday. Midweek, less traffic, cheaper hotel rates."

"You have really thought this through. What about Randy? Is he coming with us?"

"I talked to him yesterday. He's given his two-week notice, so he'll be leaving a week later."

"Then it seems we're all set! Orvin, here we come!"

* * *

The trip to Orvin took three days. The trip took them through Sacramento, Reno, Winnemucca, Elko, Salt Lake City, Laramie, Fort Collins, Denver, Dodge City and finally Orvin. Hour after hour, Cole and Kelly talked, sang along with Cole's carefully programmed "road music", and even listened to an audiobook. They consulted the *Diners, Drive-Ins and Dives* handbook and loved some of the places and hated others. The motels were clean, and the roads were good. They arrived in Orvin with no parts missing and no bones broken, still in love and ready to get off the road.

The pass-through town held a familiar comfort that he was no longer on the road but amongst friends. As they approached the farm, Cole could feel his excitement rise.

Ernie's house looked just the same, yet it was different. Perhaps it was Georgia's touches. There was a lot more green in the pasture, then Cole realized the two properties were now equally green and lush with pasture grass. Along the fence dividing the two places, three cows grazed peacefully.

That is new, Cole thought.

In the distance, Cole could see Georgia standing on the porch.

"Is that Georgia?" Kelly asked.

"Sure looks like it. I can't wait for you two to meet."

As he turned up the drive, Cole rolled down the window and began to wave. Georgia returned Cole's wave, stepped down the porch steps, and made her way to the end of the walk.

Cole was out of the car and moving toward Georgia without saying a word. The two cousins embraced, and Georgia gave Cole a big kiss on each cheek.

"Welcome home," Georgia said with both hands clutching Cole's shoulders.

"It looks beautiful."

"Ernie's pet project."

"Hi," Kelly said, joining the pair.

"Kelly! You are even prettier than in your pictures. Welcome back to Orvin. I understand you were here once before."

"Yes, I came out to help Cole when he was fixing up the place. But it sure didn't look this beautiful," Kelly exclaimed.

"Ahh, thank you. It was a labor of love." Georgia moved to give Kelly a hug.

"Well, come on in. I've been cleaning the place up. Mama tried, but she had a hard time keeping it up. I sure do hope you like what we've done with the place."

"How is she doing?" Kelly asked.

"No change, really."

"I am sorry."

"She had a good life. She's ready to meet the Lord. Thanks to this guy, she lived the last three years in happiness and contentment I don't think she ever felt in her whole life."

"Shall we go in?" Cole said, uncomfortable with the credit for his aunt's happiness.

"Oh, Cole, this lovely!" Kelly was the first one through the door.

"Wow, this doesn't look a thing like I remembered." Cole stood inside the front door, taking in the furnishings, new paint, and refinished wainscoting.

"So you like it?" Georgia fairly beamed.

"Oh, Georgia, it is so beautiful. Did Ernie do all this?"

"With a lot of my nagging," Georgia said, moving toward the kitchen. "I cleared out the fridge. I picked up a few things at the store I thought would get you started. Nothing worse than coming home to an empty fridge after a long trip."

"You are so sweet. That is so thoughtful." Kelly entered the kitchen. "It's all so perfect. I can hardly remember how it looked before. It's like a whole new house."

"I thought I did a pretty nice job," Cole said in mock protest. "I even had a beautiful unpaid assistant who kept me on task."

"Yeah, he was always sneaking off reading those journals," Kelly teased.

Georgia turned and faced Kelly and Cole. "I want you to be completely at home. Feel free to move things around. It is your home now. We all know Mama will never come home." Georgia looked down at the floor. "She really loved this place, Cole."

Cole moved across the floor and embraced his cousin. She wept softly into his shoulder. Kelly slipped out of the kitchen to give Georgia a time to grieve. Standing on the front porch, she looked across the finely manicured lawn. The last time she stood in this spot, it was a barren stretch of dead weeds and dirt.

Enormous hydrangea blooms of deep blue now bordered the sides of the lawn.

"I think I'm going to like it here." Kelly took a deep breath, the smell of the newly mowed grass bringing a smile to her lips.

"Oh, and Georgia, a kid who has worked with me for several years is coming, too. I hope you don't mind. He'll be out in about a week. We've kind of adopted him."

"Then he's family, too."

Over the next few days, they did move a few pieces of furniture. Cole claimed the living room and its familiar bookcases for his study. Lottie decorated the bookshelves with knickknacks and small picture frames of people he didn't know. They were carefully boxed up, the journals from George Sage's trunk were arranged on the shelves in much the same way as they were when Cole first read them.

Kelly stocked the kitchen and bathroom. Within a few days, it was as if they lived there for years. The room that would be Randy's was re-worked to give it a more masculine feel. Gone were the crocheted doilies on the dresser and nightstand. The pink bedspread was replaced with an earth tone quilt she found in the closet. Cole helped move a table from the back porch they were sure Randy would need to set up his computer.

Randy arrived on the twelfth day of their stay. He drove large chunks of the trip straight through. He told of sleeping to "recharge" in truck stops and rest stops along the highway. The back of his car was packed with all manner of electronic and computer gear. He gave up his apartment in Palo Alto. So, the total content of his life was packed into his SUV.

The first day after his arrival, he slept and napped for most of the day. The second was dedicated to unpacking and setting up his room. There was lots of space since the room hadn't been occupied since Lottie took possession of the farm. The bed was against the far wall. The library table that once sat in the entrance of the house was now against the opposite wall and made a perfect work station for all of Randy's monitors and computer equipment.

He turned out to be a pretty pleasant housemate. He worked most of the day in his room. The door was always open, and he seemed delighted when Kelly would stick her head in the door with offers of milk and cookies or an afternoon snack.

One the third day after his arrival, Cole ventured upstairs and pronounced, "It's time for the official tour of this Metropolis you've moved to!"

"I think we need to get some lunch while we're out," Kelly suggested when Randy and Cole hit the bottom of the stairs.

"Big Pete's?" Cole asked.

"I think he's ready." Kelly smiled.

"Randy, me lad, you are in for one of life's rare pleasures, a gastronomical feast for both eyes and palate."

"Sounds like my kind of place! Let's do it."

Cole drove around Orvin, pointing out the high points, such as they are, the bank, post office, courthouse, and even Radio Shack. Randy was quick to let him know he preferred Amazon for his electronic needs.

"Here we are!" Cole exclaimed, pulling into the gravel parking lot.

"Big Pete's Cafeteria Style Deep Pit Barbecue?" Randy asked.

"Home of my close personal friends, Betty and Pete Cranfill, who are quite possibly two of the best cooks on the planet."

Cole opened the door, letting Kelly and Randy enter the restaurant.

"Oh, would you looky here!" Betty called across the restaurant. "As I live and breathe, Cole Sage and his lovely lady! Pete, get out here!"

Four years ago, Betty was a very large woman; now she was at least a hundred pounds lighter, maybe more. Her hair was streaked with a few more strands of silver and white, but the smile was just as big and welcoming.

"Who is this hottie I see before me?" Cole asked, throwing his arms around a whole lot less Betty than before.

"The Queen of the quadruple bypass, stomach staple!" Betty laughed heartily.

"You look beautiful!" Kelly said in delight. "You were beautiful before, but you look amazing!"

"Nice recovery, pretty lady." Betty turned, giving Kelly a big hug. "And who is this handsome devil?"

"This, my dear lady, is our very good friend Randy Callen. Randy, meet the one and only Betty Cranfill."

"Oh, stop it, Cole. Nice to meet you, Randy." Betty threw out her hand.

Randy shook her hand and gave Betty a friendly smile. "It is a delight to be here. Cole and Kelly have bragged about this place for years."

"Is that Cole?" Big Pete joined the group.

"Hey, buddy! How you been?"

"Same ol', same ol'. Great to see ya. We'll talk later. I'm probably burnin' a burger." Pete turned and scooted back to the kitchen.

"Let's find you a seat." Betty moved through the dining room until she got to a booth by the window. "Look good?"

"Perfect." Cole slid into the booth.

"Can you point me to the restroom?" Randy said, looking around the restaurant.

"Bathroom's in the back corner there by the cooler."

As he made his way to the bathroom, Betty asked in a hushed tone, "What happened to that darling boy's hand?"

"Birth defect," Cole replied.

"Well, he can't help that. I was afraid he did something stupid."

"Nope, that's the way that model comes." Cole smiled. "So good to see you, Betty. I missed you. And you're cooking!"

"So, Miss Kelly, you look as pretty as ever."

"Missus," Kelly said brightly, holding up her ring finger.

"I knew he wouldn't let you get away! And now he's got the whole loaf!"

The two women laughed. Cole thought back to when Kelly came to help fix up the farm. They had only been dating a few months, and Betty was worried about Kelly's virtue. Kelly assured her she wouldn't be giving out sample slices until someone took the whole loaf. And she never did. Cole smiled.

"So what's the special today?"

"Chicken fried steak, meatloaf, and burnt end sandwich with slaw. Take your pick, it's on the house, a welcome home present!" Betty beamed.

"I'm not passing on the burnt ends!" Cole said excitedly.

"Meatloaf for me," Kelly said.

"BBQ and fries, or brown gravy and mashed?"

"Brown gravy! Comfort food heaven."

"There he is," Betty said as Randy returned to the table.

"I was going to order for you, but I want Betty to see how smart you are," Cole said.

"How's that?" Randy asked.

"The specials are meatloaf, chicken fried steak, and burnt end sandwiches."

"You mean that crispy bark stuff from the edges of brisket?"

"The very same," Betty replied.

"No brainer. Burnt ends all the way." Randy smiled up at Betty. "I wouldn't miss that for the world."

"Have I taught him well or what?" Cole asked proudly.

"Diet Coke, tea, and for you, young man?" Betty asked.

"Dr. Pepper, I believe, is the official drink of choice in these parts."

"I know you didn't learn that from Cole. You and I are gonna get along just fine." Betty turned and headed for the kitchen.

"This is so cool," Randy began. "I can't believe I'm here."

"Pretty crazy, huh?"

"You've been so busy getting set up, I haven't asked about your departure from Stanford." Cole leaned forward a bit.

"Not much to tell. I told my supervisor my family was moving to Oklahoma. She gave me a glowing letter of recommendation, so that was cool."

"That should open some doors," Kelly said reassuringly.

"I hope so. I haven't been able to line up anything. I figured I could get some freelance research assignment, computer security work, or something by now."

"You've only been here three days," Cole said dismissively.

"But I've been looking two and a half weeks."

Betty returned to the table, interrupting Randy's thought. She slid into the booth next to Randy.

"So what does a fella like you do to keep body and soul together, Randy?"

"Anything computer. I was Cole's research guy for several years. I do computer security, build websites, blogs, just about anything, really," Randy replied.

"But can you fix one?" Betty asked.

"I can even build 'em," Randy said proudly.

"Mine's kerblewy. What's it cost to fix one?"

"For you? Nothing. I'll be happy to take a look."

"Oh, that's not fair. I'll pay whatever it takes. But you are a sweetheart. You know the guy who fixed computers around here moved to Tulsa. We've been without someone for a couple years. We have to drive into Enid or Stillwater. Who's got time for that?"

"OK, I'll see what I can do. Where is it?"

"In the office, can you take a look after you eat?"

"Sure."

"Order up!" came Pete's call from the kitchen.

"That would be me." Betty left the table.

Cole gave Randy a knowing look. "You thinkin' what I'm thinkin'?"

"What do you suppose the rent is around here?" Randy pondered.

"About a fifth of the Bay Area," Cole answered.

"What are you saying?" Kelly asked.

"Randy's Computer Repair," Randy and Cole said almost simultaneously.

Lunch was a mixture of "oohs and ahhs" over the food and the frantic planning of a business that wasn't even imagined an hour before. Cole asked what was required and if Randy brought everything he needed. Kelly played devil's advocate in the beginning but was quickly converted to an enthusiastic supporter of the idea.

Very little space would be necessary, a workbench and shelves for computers coming and going. A nice front desk and a possible display area should he expand into selling computers.

The greatest expense would be a sign. Randy was confident his savings would be more than enough for a first and last month's rent, as well as for paint and materials to build counters and shelves. The sign would have to be carefully put out for bids. Cole assured him he could help if needed.

"Don't worry about your blog. I can do postings and work on the email list in the downtime," Randy assured Cole.

"Say, Betty," Cole said as she passed their table, "do you know of any empty shop space around town that wouldn't be too expensive?"

"How big? That's a dumb question. There are dozens of empty storefronts. A lot of the old-timers shut up shop, and nobody bothers to start up a new business. I mean, when was the last time you had a pair of shoes repaired or rented a DVD?"

"That's sad," Kelly said.

"The big stores, Walmart, Target and all them out by the highway, are killing the little guys downtown. But that's progress, right?" She took her coffee pot and moved to the next table.

"There you go. So it comes down to location," Cole offered. "You all done?"

"I'm stuffed," Kelly groaned.

"That was incredible," Randy said with a contented smile.

Cole slid out of the booth and stood.

"Where you think you're goin'?" Betty asked, coming back to the booth. "We got fresh rice pudding."

"I got no place to put it," Cole said, "unless I rub it on my arm.

"Oh, me either, Betty, I'm about to burst. Nobody makes meatloaf like Pete."

"How about you?" Betty asked Randy.

"I'm full up. But that sandwich was incredible."

"I'll send some home with you. An hour from now, you'll be peekin' in the fridge for somethin'."

Before they could get to the door, Betty came from the kitchen with a brown paper bag. "Now don't you spoil my masterpiece here by eating it cold," Betty instructed. "How long you here for this time?"

"We're not really sure. Couple weeks? A month? We're homeless at the moment."

"Forever would be too short for me. I think you should make your new life together here in Orvin. You got history here."

"Let's take a look at that computer of yours," Randy said, sensing Cole's discomfort.

While Randy did his magic in the office, Cole and Kelly visited with Betty between customers.

The look on Randy's face when he reappeared was one of triumph and satisfaction. "All done. I think that will keep you up and running for a while. No more online poker! You picked up a couple of pretty nasty viruses. All cleaned up. You were lucky we didn't lose anything this time."

"You are an angel. What do I owe you?"

"Not a thing. You bought lunch, I fixed the computer, the perfect arrangement," Randy said.

"I think that job is worth two lunches. And I won't take no for an answer!"

"Agreed." Randy knew there was no arguing with his new friend.

"I really do wish you guys would settle here for good," Betty said.

"We'll be around for a while. We'll fill you in on the details when you're not so busy," Cole said.

Betty hugged Kelly, then Randy to his surprise, and patted Cole on the cheek. "So, glad to have you home again."

"Nice to be back."

As they drove from the parking lot, Kelly said, "Say, Randy hasn't seen the sandwich shop yet. We should drive by."

"Just no food," Cole agreed.

As they drove across town to Ernie's Sandwich shop, they passed several for rent signs, and even more empty storefront spaces. None seemed right for a computer repair shop.

All the spots were full in front of Ernie's Sandwich shop, so they parked next door. As they got out of the car, Cole exclaimed, "Look at this!"

The space adjoining the sandwich shop was dark. There was no sign, and it was certainly vacant.

"What do you suppose was in here?" Cole asked, putting his hands against the window to get a better look.

"I don't think anything," Randy replied.

"I hate to be a Debbie Downer, but opening a store is a big commitment. Are you ready to put down roots and live here? I love the idea, but when we leave, are you going to stay?"

Cole looked at Kelly like she'd just poured sand on top of the birthday cake. "We're just -"

"Maybe," Randy said. "Besides, you guys are all I have, no one else. I can't expect Cole to keep dragging me along everywhere. Besides, when he retires, I'm really going to be on my own. So yeah, maybe, if this worked out, it could be just the thing."

"Hey, what do you think you're doing?" a gruff voice shouted.

The group turned to see Ernie with a big, goofy grin on his face.

"Hey, buddy!" Cole responded. "What's the deal here?"

"A guy was going to put in a video game store, then decided it was too small. It's a weird space. Partially cut out of mine and the dry cleaner. Why?"

"I was thinking of opening a computer repair shop."

"The hell you say. The landlord would probably give it to you. It's an eyesore, been empty from day one. Offer him five hundred a month. I bet my best sandwich he takes it."

"You think so?" Cole asked in amazement.

"Absolutely. Want to see inside? I got a key. There's some stuff in the back. You rent the place, you can have it. The game guy bought a front counter and just left it in there."

"Yeah, let's have a look," Randy said excitedly, looking first at Cole, then Kelly.

By sundown, the lease was signed. Four hundred and fifty a month, first month free, one-year lease, no deposit. Randy Callen was in business, nine hundred square feet of his own domain. No boss, no deadlines, and most of all no one to answer to for his success or failure but himself.

Cole helped him with building shelves, Kelly painted, and Ernie kept the coffee and soda coming. It only took three days to get the place ready. The tile floor wouldn't have been Randy's first choice, but it was free. The sign was ordered, the license was paid for, and an ad was taken out in the Orvin Observer.

From the first day, there was a stream of virus-infected, dead hard drive, old operating system, fried motherboard, drivers missing, towers, laptops, and Apple computers. Randy researched repair costs in the neighboring towns, the closest a thirty-minute drive each way, and increased it by ten percent. He was fast, friendly and reasonable. The referrals and word of mouth kept the phone ringing, and for the first three weeks, he was afraid the space would be too small.

The time in Orvin inspired Cole to dig into the writing of *The Sage Saga*, as he referred to it. Kelly volunteered at the hospital three days a week. They found a church to attend, and Kelly helped out on Saturday getting the small church ready for Sunday services. By the end of their first month in Orvin, anyone would have thought they were lifelong residents.

Chapter 17

The electronic buzzer sounded with the opening of the door. Randy looked up at the pass-thru from the workbench to the reception area. A young woman about his age was holding a computer tower and looking around the room. She looked completely lost. As she moved toward the counter.

"Be with you in a second!" Randy called.

"No hurry," she replied, moving to set the tower on the counter.

Randy glanced up. He really tried not to, but then he glanced up again. Then again, she was so pretty, he thought.

He nervously ran his hand through his hair, pulled at his collar, and dusted the miniature dust bunnies from inside a computer case off the front of his shirt.

"What can I do for you today?" Randy tried to be as cheerful as his nerves would let him.

"This thing is on the fritz again. I don't know if it's something dumb I've done or if we've got one of those bacterias -"

"Viruses?" Randy injected.

"Yeah, viruses." She looked down. Randy hoped he didn't embarrass her. "Or if it is just all tuckered out. Anyway, can you take a look and see if it is worth salvaging?"

"That's the name of the game around here." Randy smiled. He just loved the way she talked. Casual, but shy, relaxed and funny, but all business. "If you've got a minute, I can hook her up and see what's going on." He hoped she had the rest of the day.

"That would be great."

"Pull up a stool, and I'll get things all plugged in."

"You're new around here, aren't you?" she asked.

"Yes, does it show?"

"Well, you just don't sound Orvin."

"Is that bad?" Randy asked, hoping it was good.

"Neither one. You just kind of, well, sound different. Where are you from?"

"California."

"That's kinda backward," she said with the slightest of smiles.

"How do you mean?" Randy asked as he continued to plug in a monitor and keyboard to her tower.

"Well, way back when, it was the Okies who went to California, not the other way 'round."

Randy chuckled. "You're right. That's funny."

As he finished connecting the computer, Randy turned and looked at the girl sitting at his counter. Her dark, nearly black, brown hair was straight, just below her shoulders and shined almost to the point of sparkling. Her big blue eyes seemed to hold a kind of sadness when she didn't know he was looking. Then when their eyes met, they brightened, like they wanted to wink at him. Randy never saw that in the San Francisco girls he met.

"I'm Randy, by the way."

The girl looked at him for a long moment, and then she gave him the most charming smile he ever received. "I'm Brooke. Nice to meet you, Randy the Computer Guy."

She giggled at her giving him a nickname. The whole room seemed to sparkle with the sound of her voice and the brightness of her smile.

Randy was speechless.

"Looks dead to me," Brooke said after a long moment.

Randy looked at the monitor. "I haven't turned it on yet."

"Shows what a dummy I am. I should buy one of the *Computers for Dummies* books."

"You wouldn't believe how many people think there is something wrong with their computers when it turns out they kicked the power cord out of the wall." Randy grinned. "I'm sure that's not your problem, though. Let's see."

As he reached for the power button, he glanced at Brooke. She was watching him like he was about to open the secrets of the universe.

Randy hoped the whirring of fans and the sound of the computer booting up would cover the sound of his heart beating. He knew Brooke couldn't possibly hear it, but he was thankful for the white noise just the same.

"They both looked at the monitor. In the middle of the screen in a small box were the words,

Windows 98 Has Crashed
I am the Blue Screen of
Death
No One Can Hear You Scream!

"I didn't want to mention that, for fear you'd think I was crazy," Brooke said softly.

"Here's the thing. I see a couple of problems. First off, your system is seriously infected with a virus or twelve. Number two, what year is this?"

"Two thousand seventeen," Brooke said with a frown.

"Oh, good, I thought I went back in time," Randy teased. "Windows 98? That's problem number two. How old were you when you got this, two?"

If anyone was watching out the window, they would think Randy just told the funniest joke in the world. "It's not mine, silly. It's from my daddy's office."

"I hope he's not a doctor."

His comment brought another burst of laughter from his lovely customer. "No, he owns the lumber yard 'cross town. "You're a funny one, you are. Can you fix it?"

"Oh, sure. Does he run the business on this computer? It might be a couple of days."

"I do, kinda. I'm the bookkeeper. Am I in trouble?"

"Is everything, I mean bookkeeping-wise, on this machine?" Randy feared the response.

"Well, sure, where else would I keep it?" Brooke seemed to panic a bit.

"When a machine is this corrupted, we usually scrape the hard drive clean, reinstall Windows and Office and start fresh. But if you don't have a backup of your files, it's a bit harder."

"And so?" Brooke pressed.

"So, it is going to require several days to get it up and running again."

"Will it cost more than seven hundred dollars? That's all I have saved up."

"Oh my word, no!" Randy said reassuringly. "I thought you said it was from your dad's office. Computer repairs are an office expense," Randy fished for why she would be paying for the repair.

"But I work on it, so I broke it. I don't want him thinking I can't do the job without huge messes." She was nearly in tears.

There was a soft, childlike quality to Brooke's concern for her job and the consequences of her not performing to her expectations. Even more so was a fear of failing her father and his reaction.

"Hey, it's not your fault. Viruses are everywhere. Do you send and receive email? You ever get them from people you don't know?"

"Yeah."

"Could have been from them. Your dad can write it off as a business expense. It happens all the time. You've just got a real whammer-jammer stack of viruses on top of each other. How long has it been acting up?"

"I don't know exactly. Year, year and a half, maybe."

Randy nearly choked. "That long. Why didn't you get it fixed sooner?"

"I was scared, I guess."

"Have no fear, Randy the Computer Guy is here. I'll get it fixed up for you. With your permission, I'll update your Windows and Office software while I'm at it." Randy felt his confidence fairly bursting out of his chest. If he could only figure out a way to ask her out, he could die a happy man.

"So, how much?"

"I won't really know until I get in it. But it shouldn't be much." Randy assured her. He knew he would make the cost as little as possible without it seeming suspicious. He would happily do it for free just to see her again.

"Under five hundred?" Brooke was still fearing the worst.

"For that, I could get you a new machine. We're talking maybe two at the very, very most. Besides, you get my new customer discount."

"You just opened. Everybody's a new customer." Brooke stiffened. "You pullin' my leg?"

"OK, you'll get my prettiest-customer-I've-had-so-far discount. Better?" Randy tried his best to be charming.

"Now I know you're havin' a joke on me." She sounded offended.

"Not at all." Randy gave her his best smile. "You are absolutely the prettiest girl to walk in these doors so far. Probably will be for a long time." Randy was not about to have her leave mad. Did he come on too strong? he wondered. He was baffled, though. Why the weird reaction to a compliment?

"You're just a slick talkin' San Fran Cisco smoothie having a laugh at my expense." Brooke was getting madder.

"No, I swear, I'm really sorry if I said something wrong. I can't believe I even had the guts to say that to you. As a matter of fact, I was trying to think of a way to ask you out, but I didn't want you to think I was some kind of player who hits on his customers." Randy felt his chances with Brooke slipping away.

"Now, in English for this country girl, please." Brooke's tone softened.

"Which part?" Randy answered slowly as he tried to rewind the conversation and think of what he could have said wrong.

"The part about hittin' your customers."

Randy smiled wide with relief. "I just meant I didn't want you to think I was some ladies man who flirted a lot and asked out every girl he sees. I guess my California was showing again. I was just trying to let you know I think you are special."

"Then, yes!'

"Yes?"

"Yes, I'll go out with you. I was hopin' we'd get better acquainted. Thank you for askin'."

Randy could feel his face turning red. He never in his life met a girl this pretty and had her say yes.

"Oh, and Randy. You can stop favoring your hand. I saw it right off. It's nothing to be embarrassed about or ashamed of. It's just different." Brooke whirled around and ran for the door.

"Wait! I don't have your number! You don't have a…" His voice faded off. "Receipt," he said, almost a whisper.

It was Thursday afternoon before Randy completed work on Brooke's computer. Having no phone number, there was no way to let her know it was done. Their date was left completely up in the air as well. As he rebooted the machine for one final check, he was struck with an idea. He'd deliver it.

Orvin couldn't have more than a couple of lumber yards. Brooke did say it was across town.

He looked out the window and saw the owner of the pool supply store down the way walking across the parking lot.

"Hey, Chuck."

"Hey there, California. What's goin' on?"

"Can you tell me where the lumber yard is across town?"

"Palmer's? Sure can. Get on Grant out there and follow yer nose. You'll run right into it." Chuck pointed. "Whatcha buildin'?"

"I have to deliver a computer."

"You didn't deliver mine!"

"Chuck, you're two doors down," Randy said with a frown.

"I'm just sayin'."

Chapter 18

Palmer Lumber was easy to find. Nothing, it seemed in Orvin, was more than a few minutes apart. The lumber yard was neat, the office building and store were painted a barn red with white trim. Large flatbed trucks were parked neatly behind a chain link fence.

Randy parked in front and retrieved the tower from his back seat. The bell tinkled as he struggled to get the front door open.

A man in a blue Palmer Lumber work shirt with a severe overbite named Paul greeted Randy.

"'Fraid we don't fix those."

"Good thing I do, then." Randy gave Paul a friendly smile. "Is Brooke in?"

"Sure is. She just ran an order back to the yard boss. Her office is over there. I take it that's for her."

"Bingo."

"Go ahead and take 'er back. You gonna hook it up?"

"All part of the service," Randy said, heading for the door marked 'Office'.

The office was neat in a frantic, lived in kind of way. There were two desks. The larger was obviously the owner's domain. The smaller desk that faced the wall next to the door showed feminine signs of occupation. A bouquet of fresh cut flowers sat brightly on the corner of the desk.

Randy set the tower down on the desk and looked around. The printer sat on a small table halfway between the two desks. On the wall next to Mr. Palmer's desk were about a dozen framed photos. A large, taxidermy deer head with a massive rack of antlers was mounted behind the desk; beneath it were wall to wall bookcases, stuffed with catalogs of suppliers.

Randy moved to look at the pictures. An old black and white shot showed the early days of the lumber yard. There were three fading hunting pictures with what Randy assumed was Mr. Palmer and a huge elk, a bear, and a whole bunch of ducks.

Quite the hunter, Randy thought.

Then a row of pictures of a little girl from about kindergarten up through high school graduation. It was unmistakably Brooke. The odd thing was, she was wearing the thickest glasses Randy had ever seen. Big, round, heavy rims, so thick they made her eyes look huge behind them. To further Randy's surprise, the poor child was cursed with the most crooked buck teeth imaginable. Her teeth stuck out so far, she couldn't close her lips around them. Around junior high, he guessed, she began wearing braces. Sometime in high school, she began to close her lips for pictures. In what must be her senior portrait, she wore a big beautiful smile. The thick glasses remained. The frames were less heavy but no more attractive.

Having lived the hellish life of a kid with a deformed hand, Randy could clearly imagine the teasing and bullying Brooke must have gone through. The photos explained a lot about her reaction to his flirting.

The scars are deep, he thought.

"Oh, please don't look at those!" Brooke raced into the room, grabbed Randy's wrist and pulled him toward her desk. "Please."

"I think they're kinda cute. The evolution of a butterfly."

"That's not funny." Brooke reached up and grabbed the thick glasses off her face.

"I'm not trying to be funny. You should see some of mine as a kid!" Randy could see the pictures were a sensitive subject and decided to let it go at that. "Hey, you left the other day without giving me a phone number. So, I played a little bit of Sherlock Holmes and decided I would deliver your computer to you."

"That's very nice, but I could have come and got it." Brooke squinted and frowned. It was obvious she could barely see.

"Too late. Let's get it hooked up, what do you say?" he said cheerfully. "And Brooke, put your glasses back on. I like them."

"It goes here." Brooke pointed at a jumble of cords dangling behind her desk.

"Where does the tower sit?" Randy asked.

"Here." There was a place just under the desk with a rectangular impression in the carpet.

"We'll have you up and running in no time."

It only took a couple of minutes to get the computer hooked back up and connected to the

Internet. Randy gave Brooke a quick tour of the new features on the machine.

"I took the liberty of putting my email in your address book," Randy said hesitantly.

"That's nice," Brooke said softly. "Randy, I'm sorry I acted so weird about the pictures over there. I hate them. I think my dad just leaves them up to annoy me. I've asked him a hundred times to take them down."

"Maybe he's proud of you," Randy offered.

"Maybe not." Brooke's response let Randy know he was wrong.

"How 'bout this? I promise not to look at them again."

"Why are you so nice to me?" Brooke asked, looking Randy right in the face.

"Because I like you. I think you are special. I think you're pretty, and I want you to like me."

"Nobody ever was nice to me before. I guess I'm suspicious."

"I can't imagine. But that all changes here and now. We haven't decided on when to go on our date."

"Soon."

"Friday night?"

"Sooner." Brooke gave Randy a beautiful smile.

"Well, how about tonight?"

"Perfect." Brooke reached down and took a Post-it note from her desk. She wrote something and handed it to Randy.

"Seven o'clock?"

"Sooner." Broke giggled.

"Six?"

"Perfect."

"I better get back to the shop, or I won't have any money to spend on you!"

"Oh, what do I owe you?"

"Nothing." Randy smiled. "On account."

"On account?" Brooke asked.

"On account of I think we're going to be good friends."

Brooke's expression went from delight to terror in a heartbeat. Randy turned to see a man in a pair of jeans and a blue striped oxford cloth shirt enter the office.

"Can I help you?" the man asked sternly.

"I'm taking care of things." Brooke looked from Randy to the man now less than six feet away.

"I wasn't talking to you. I was talking to him. What do you need?"

"I was returning the computer."

"Why?"

"Dad, I said I'm taking care of this." Brooke's voice quaked with emotion.

"Find something to do."

"I'm Randy Callen. I own Randy's Computer Service." Randy extended his left hand.

"Around here, a man shakes with his right hand."

Randy raised his right hand, showing the man his birth defect. "Thought you'd prefer shaking the hand with fingers," Randy said unapologetically.

"I'm Barry Palmer. I'm the owner, though at times you wouldn't think so." Palmer shot an angry look at Brooke, who was still standing in front of her desk. He made no effort to shake hands. "So what was wrong with the computer?"

"It was near to the point of not being functional, due to viruses and malware. Brooke will be all set to go now."

"My daughter has a way of messing things up real good. What did this little mistake cost me?"

"First of all, she had nothing to do with the problem. Whoever sold you this machine failed to provide you with the minimal level of anti-virus protection, let alone today's level of attack."

"I paid twelve hundred dollars for that machine!" Palmer said indignantly.

"Then you got screwed. It's worth about four hundred." Randy didn't like Barry Palmer or the way he treated his daughter, and it gave him great satisfaction making him look stupid.

"So are you paid up? How much am I getting reamed?"

"Yeah, Brooke was kind enough to take care of me."

"I bet she was. How much?" Palmer pressed.

"Fifty dollars. No parts. Just labor."

"Then you're done here." Palmer turned and went to his desk.

"Not quite." Randy looked toward Brooke. The look in her eyes said for him not to mention their date. "If you have any questions, give me a call." Randy winked at Brooke with the eye facing away from her father.

Brooke looked down and said, "I'll do that."

"Thanks for your business." Randy smiled and moved for the door.

Before Randy was out of the room, he heard Barry Palmer bark at Brooke, "Next time we need something repaired, you leave it to me, you understand?"

Randy made his way to the front door of the store. Paul, the man who greeted him when he arrived, was standing just outside the door, smoking.

"He's a hard man," Paul offered.

"Is that what you call it in Oklahoma? In California, we have another name for it."

"I bet it ain't polite, neither."

"You got that right. I'll see you around." Randy chuckled as he made his way to his car.

"Little advice?"

Randy turned. "Yeah?"

"Don't let him scare you off. Brooke's the closest thing to an angel here on Earth. I could tell she likes you a lot by the way she lit up when she saw you in the office. She needs a nice fella. You just make sure if you take an interest in her, you do right by her. You understand?"

"That was my intention," Randy said firmly.

"Then things will work out just fine." Paul flicked his cigarette hard across the parking lot and went inside.

At five o'clock, Randy locked the front door of the shop. He raced home to shower and change clothes. Music played in the car, but he didn't hear it.

The Post-it note Brooke gave him, now wrinkled and smeared, was stuck to the dashboard.

The directions seemed easy enough. 2416 Broken Arrow Drive. The thing that excited Randy the most, though, was the seven digits of her phone number. He glanced down at the yellow square of paper for the fiftieth time and grinned.

Kelly was sitting on the porch when Randy arrived home. She waved as he pulled up to the house.

"Welcome home!" Kelly offered.

"I got a date!" Randy shouted back excitedly.

Kelly jumped to her feet. "Tell all!"

"She came in the shop, and I fixed her computer. She's really nice. Kind of shy. Very pretty. We are going out tonight. I pick her up at six!"

"Wow, Casanova, you don't waste any time."

"I delivered the computer this afternoon."

"To her house?" Kelly asked, showing surprise. "I didn't know you delivered."

"I don't. I took it to the lumber yard her family owns," Randy explained, reaching the top step onto the porch. "It actually is a company computer."

"But you delivered it?"

"Well, yeah."

"So where are you taking her?" Kelly asked, changing the subject.

"I don't know."

"And you pick her up in forty-five minutes?"

"I know, I know, but she's different. We'll talk about it."

"You're right, your choices are so limited. Use the 'new guy in town card'. She'll take mercy on you. I hope! But no Big Pete's, you hear me?"

"I only know three places: Ernie's, The Dairy Queen, and Big Pete's." Randy laughed.

"Where you goin'?" Cole asked, coming out on the porch.

"Randy's got a date."

"Cool, take her to Big Pete's."

"You handle this. I've got to get ready." Randy high-fived Kelly as he made his way in the house.

"Big Pete's, really?" Kelly grimaced.

"I like it. I took you there," Cole replied defensively.

"It wasn't our first date!"

In less than ten minutes, Randy was showered, changed and back out the door.

"Wish me luck!" he called as he went out the door.

According to the GPS on his phone, Brooke's house was about twelve minutes away. That gave him plenty of time. He would make a quick stop at the florist for a bouquet of fresh flowers.

Bouquet in the front seat and the mixtape of MP3s he made that afternoon softly playing, Randy was ready to pick up his date with five minutes to spare.

One last-minute review. Randy looked in the rearview mirror. "Hair, check. Shaved, check." He put his hand to his mouth and exhaled. "Breath, needs a mint."

Randy took a pack of breath mints from his shirt pocket and popped one in his mouth. "Flowers, check. Tunes, check." He heaved a big sigh. "Here we go."

As Randy pulled back into traffic, he hoped he would make a good impression. It was a long time, almost a year since he had been on a real date. The San Francisco dating ritual was coffee first, then lunch if you were lucky, then dinner or a movie. His luck with the women of the City by the Bay was lunch at best, coffee at worst. Even worse, though, was getting stood up for coffee.

He was skipping two steps and going straight to dinner, he thought. "That's a good sign," Randy said to himself. "This is going to be good. Don't screw it up." Randy's self-talk was helping calm his nerves.

"Turn left onto Broken Arrow Drive in five hundred feet." The sexy female voice of the GPS signaled the final approach.

"Thank you, Sonia," Randy said to the voice as he slowed looking for his turn.

He put his foot to the brake and slowed to a near stop. Just ahead on the sidewalk was a dark-haired girl. Brooke! What was she doing out here? he questioned. Rolling forward slowly, he came to a stop across from her.

"Brooke?"

She waved with an odd jerking motion. Randy stopped the car.

"Everything OK?"

Without a word, she ran across the street and to the passenger side of the car. Randy fumbled clumsily for the door lock. The door flew open, and before Randy could move, Brooke jumped into the car and sat on the flowers.

"Hi," Brooke said softly, not looking at Randy. "Can we go?"

"Sure," Randy answered as the car accelerated. "What a surprise. I didn't think you'd come out to meet me." Randy's voice was jovial, and his remark was lighthearted.

"Are you mad?"

"Of course not. Why would I be?"

"It's kind of weird, maybe?"

"It's nice to have someone anxious to see me! So, since I'm the new guy in town, I thought maybe you could pick where we go to dinner. I only know three places, and none is worthy of a first date."

"Can you pull over for a second?"

Oh, God, she's going to throw up! Randy thought as he pulled to the curb. In a quick motion, Brooke opened the door and slid out of the car.

Turning, she said, "Oh Randy, I smashed your beautiful flowers!"

"Actually, you smashed your flowers. Do you like them?"

Brooke gently lifted the bouquet and held them to her breast. "I love them. No one has ever brought me flowers before."

"Then hold on a second, and we'll do this right." Randy opened his door and hopped out of the car. He rounded the back of the car and came to where she stood.

"Here," Randy said, taking the flowers. He hid them behind his back. "Hi, Brooke, are you ready to go?"

Brooke looked at him quizzically, then realized they were starting over. "Yes, do I look all right?"

"You look beautiful! Here, these are for you." Randy brought the flowers from around his back and offered them to Brooke.

"Oh, they are beautiful!" She smiled as if in complete surprise.

"Well, shall we go?" Randy asked.

"Let's!" Brooke said brightly.

All resettled, flowers in her lap instead of under her, the car pulled from the curb.

"So, since I'm the new guy in town, I thought maybe you could pick where we go to dinner. I only know three places, and none is worthy of a first date," Randy repeated, with no sign of irony.

"Oh, goodness." Brooke frowned. "Let me think a second. Here, turn at the next street."

Randy did as instructed. If he had any nerves before, they were completely obliterated by the strange start of his date. He tried not to be obvious, but he kept looking at the beautiful girl sitting beside him. How did he get so lucky?

"OK, this is kind of weird," Brooke began, "but, have you ever been to Big Pete's Barbeque?"

"As a matter of fact -"

"Oh, good! It is my favorite, and my dad won't take me there anymore," Brooke said with delight. "He and my mama used to go all the time, but since she died, he, well, he stopped going."

"Big Pete's, it is!"

As they drove, Brooke gave a running commentary on the sites and wonders of Orvin. The businesses, landmarks, and places that held special memories. Randy was thrilled she was opening up. The tour took the strain off the drive and relieved him of having to keep the conversation going.

"I have to warn you, Betty and her husband Pete have known me since I was little. So it might be kind of embarrassing, the stuff she might say, so please, just kind of ignore her? Please?"

"I'll do my best." Randy could hardly contain himself. It was no telling what Betty might do or call out to Pete through the kitchen pass-thru.

As the gravel crunched and the car came to a halt, Brooke reached over and took Randy's arm. "Thank you so much."

"For what?"

"For asking me out, for bringing me here, for being so wonderful. I don't know, everything!"

"It's me who should be thanking you. You have made my year in one week!" Randy was grinning so hard, he was worried about what he looked like. "Shall we?"

Randy leapt from the car and raced around to open Brooke's door. As she slipped out of the car, Randy could hardly breathe. He felt like he was going out with a movie star. Brooke held the flowers close to her. She reached out and took Randy's arm.

"I could eat a horse!" Brooke said excitedly.

"Hmmm, not sure they serve those," Randy teased. "Do you want to leave those in the car?" Randy asked, pointing at the flowers.

"Oh, please no. Is it OK?"

"Brooke, anything you want is all right with me."

The door to the restaurant barely closed behind them when Randy saw Betty making her way toward them. She held her hands together like she was in prayer and pressed them to her lips.

"Oh, my blessed Redeemer! I have seen a miracle today!" Betty moved toward them so fast, Randy wondered if she would be able to stop without running into them. "I don't know who to hug first!"

Brooke looked up at Randy with a puzzled expression.

"Come here, you!" Betty threw her arms around Brooke and gave her a hug. "Could you be any more beautiful?" She released Brooke and turned to Randy. "Come here, you!" Randy was the recipient of a hug that nearly cracked a rib.

Betty stepped back, one hand holding Brooke's left hand, and the other holding Randy's right.

"I'm not sure how I feel about this now that I think about it. I think I'm mad at you Brookie for stealing my new boyfriend!" Betty teased.

"You two know each other?" Brooke asked in total confusion.

"This handsome bugger fixed my computer!"

"You rat!" Brooke said. "You've been here before."

"I am doin' nip-ups at the sight of you two together. How long has this been goin' on?"

"First date," Randy said, trying to get Betty to back off a bit. To his relief, she got the hint.

"Well then, the best seat in the house for the lady with the beautiful flowers and her new beau." Betty turned and yelled to the kitchen, "Hey Pete, get a load of this! Our baby has got a fella!"

Brooke's cheek blushed in a deep hue. Randy hoped his cheeks weren't as red as they felt. "Do you have horse on the menu?" Randy asked, trying to stop the interrogation.

"What?" Betty asked in a mix of shock and offense.

"Brooke said she was hungry for horse."

"I said I could eat a horse! That's different," Brooke replied, not getting the joke.

"You never know around here." Randy winked at Betty.

As they walked to their seat, it seemed everybody in the place smiled their way. Randy was so proud, he didn't know what to do. So he just smiled back and walked on.

The corner booth by the window was situated in a way where they were almost hidden from the admiring eyes of the other patrons. They took a seat, and Brooke placed her flowers in the center of the table.

"I know you don't need a menu," Betty teased Brooke. "What about you?"

"I'll have what she's having," Randy said without hesitation.

"Comin' right up."

"That wasn't so bad." Randy smiled.

"Not for you," Brooke whispered. "I think everybody I know in the world is sitting in this place."

"I can't think of anywhere else I'd rather be, then."

"I'm sorry about before," Brooke said as if she had been waiting for the chance to speak.

"Before?"

"About not being at home when you came to pick me up. I'm sorry. It must seem weird."

"I just thought you…"

"Don't try to be nice. It was weird. Look, I need you to understand something if we should happen to see each other again."

Randy's heart sank. He may have skipped a few steps in the dating ritual, but he thought another date was almost a sure thing. "If?"

"My dad is very difficult."

Randy thought about responding but decided silence was the best idea.

"The reason I was walking," Brooke looked down at the flowers on the table and ran her fingers gently along a petal, "he didn't want me going out. He didn't want me to see you. So I left."

"I don't know what to say."

"You got a preview at the yard office. I didn't want you walking in on that buzz saw again. It wouldn't be fair."

"Don't worry about me. What about you? I mean, how bad does he get?"

"You mean does he hit me? He has never touched me."

"Tell me about your mom. What was she like?" Randy was very uncomfortable with Brooke's verbal and emotional abuse. He needed to talk about something different. He really needed time to know how to deal with Brooke's situation.

"She was very sweet. I miss her every day."

"How long has she been gone?"

"She died when I was twelve. So, almost ten years." Brooke nodded. "Pneumonia. I had been sick, really sick with croup. She caught a bad cold from me. It turned into pneumonia. So, it was my fault she died."

"That's not true. Sickness is what people die from. No one is to blame. She nursed you, she loved you. You can't blame yourself for her death any more than you can -"

"Dad says it is my fault," Brooke cut him off. "He always reminds me every time I get a cold or the flu or anything." She was the victim of her father's anger and bitterness at losing his wife, and it grieved Randy to hear her lay it open.

"Two racks of Pete's finest!" Betty stood at the end of the table with two huge platters. "The Brooke Special, extra sauce, fries, no coleslaw. Root beer coming right up! That OK with you, sir?" Betty turned and scurried back toward the kitchen without an answer.

Randy laughed. "No, I would like..." he answered mockingly.

For the next three hours, Randy and Brooke ate, talked, laughed, questioned, answered, and got to know each other. To both their surprise, Betty left them alone.

Randy spoke openly about the pain, abuse, and loneliness of years in foster care. He answered any and every question Brooke put to him. He found he could be open with her about his deepest insecurities. They talked at length about his deformed hand.

At one point, Brooke gently took his hand and touched each little nubby finger. Then she pressed her lips to the top of his hand. As he sat motionless, Randy realized he couldn't remember ever in his life anyone touching his hand. He fought back tears.

There was a kindness and compassion in this girl of a kind Randy never knew. She carried years of hurt, insults, verbal abuse and distance from her father. Her lack of confidence would from time to time rear its head. Randy would try to immediately inject something positive about her. He found it difficult not to mention her beauty, but he fought back the urge and would tell her how charming she was, how smart she must be to do all the books for the lumber yard. As they learned more about each other, Randy drew from what he learned to show the value he saw in her, thereby rebuilding her broken self-esteem.

Even though they lived in the same house, shared meals, spent their days at work and nights in front of the television together, Brooke and her father lived in two very different worlds.

In the evening, Brooke would retire early and read. Her favorites were stories of famous people in history, tales of faraway places and time travel. Her books took her to times and worlds where her heroes and heroines lived, loved, and found their happily ever after. For those minutes before sleep, she saw beauty in the world.

"So kids, I can give you the keys if you want to stick around, but I'm headin' for home in fifteen minutes." Betty smiled and rested her hand on Randy's shoulder.

"Oh geez, it's nearly ten!" Randy looked up at Betty and gave her an embarrassed grin.

"It's a wonderful thing to find someone you can really talk to. Me and ol' Pete have been at it for years. And you know what? He never gets tired of listening to me."

"I've been talking my head off, Betty. I didn't see how late it was."

"Angel, it made my heart sing to see you two enjoying each other's company. I hope you'll come back soon and do it again."

"I hope so, too," Randy replied. "Think we should?" Randy smiled at Brooke.

"Tomorrow?"

They all laughed, but Randy could have burst into song.

The drive home was a little less chatty. A strange tension seemed to crackle like electricity in the car.

"Brooke, is it going to be OK when you get home?" Randy asked as they turned up Broken Arrow Drive.

"Sure. It takes him a while to get riled up. I'll be in bed before he can get a chance." She gave a nervous giggle. "That's it there, with the Palmer truck in the drive."

Randy spun a U-turn and parked in front of the house.

"Can I walk you to the door?"

"I would like that." Brooke smiled sweetly.

Randy went around the front of the car this time, smiling all the way through the windshield. He opened the door and reached in for Brooke's hand.

"I have had the most wonderful time, Randy. Do you think we'll do it again?"

"Unless your dad shoots me in the next couple minutes."

"Stop it!" Brooke whispered. "Can we?"

"I can't think of a thing in the world I would love more."

As they stepped onto the front porch, Brooke stopped and faced Randy. "I've been dreaming about this all night."

"Getting home?" Randy joked nervously.

"No, this." Brooke went on her tiptoes and kissed Randy's lips.

The porch light turned on. "I guess I won't be getting seconds."

Brooke kissed her fingertips and gently touched Randy's lips. "Goodnight."

Randy couldn't stand it; he wrapped his arm around Brooke's waist and kissed her deeply. "Goodnight."

Chapter 19

Most of Cole's morning errands were completed. With a bag of yellow notepads and a bottle of Liquid Plumber from the hardware store in hand, Cole made his way to the car. He would swing by and see Lottie on his way home.

He felt he should visit more than he did, but his heart just wasn't in it. The frail ashen brown form that lay still and silent in the dimly lit room wasn't his sassy, vibrant aunt. Cole believed in the soul. It was the essence of a human being. In his life as a journalist, he faced people from all walks of life, all levels of society. One thing was constant, their soul. Some possessed a spirit of joy, and their essence transcended their situation. Others, from the moment you entered their presence, projected a soul of dark, uncaring evil.

Lottie was a woman whose soul was wholly given over to the God she held so dear. The light she gave the world rose above her station in life and shone on everyone she met. They were left knowing the essence of this little woman was a source of good.

Now she lay in a sleep, a coma that robbed her of speech, movement, and life. The first time he saw her in the convalescent hospital, he felt as if her spirit had flown. The shell he would visit no longer housed the essence of the woman he loved.

As he tossed the bags in the back seat of the car, Cole's cell phone rang.

"Hello?" The bright sunlight made it hard to see the Caller ID.

There was no sound for several seconds, then a voice Cole didn't recognize said, "Cole?"

"Yep," Cole said, getting in the car.

"Mama's gone." It was then Cole recognized the voice.

"Oh, Georgia." A lump came up in Cole's throat. "Where are you?"

"I'm with her."

"I was on my way. I'll be there in a couple of minutes."

"Thank you."

The room was nearly dark. The blankets and coverlet were pulled up and neatly folded back just under Lottie's chin. She really didn't look much different than on Cole's other visits. This time, though, she looked more relaxed, and there was a look of peace about her.

Georgia stood silently by the window. The curtain was drawn, but she faced it. Ernie sat in a chair with his head down.

Cole didn't want to break the silence, so he stood quietly by the bedside.

After a minute, Ernie looked up and said, "Thanks for coming."

Georgia turned and smiled. "She's gone, Cole. It is such a strange feeling. I knew since the stroke she would never be normal again, never came out of the coma, really. But this, this is really..." Her voice trailed off.

Cole moved to where she stood and gave Georgia a hug. "Well, as they say in church, 'to be absent from the body is to be present with the Lord', isn't that right?"

"That's right."

"Then good for her. Even though we'll miss her, she's got what she lived for."

Cole stayed for another few minutes. When the attendants came to take Lottie to the mortuary, he encouraged Ernie and Georgia to leave as well and let the two men do their job.

* * *

The warm May wind blew warm across the small cemetery. The white casket was already in place under the green canopy. The scalloped flaps snapped in the breeze. The bouquet of white carnations Cole and Kelly sent was draped over the casket.

Patiently standing at the front of the canopy was the officiating pastor. The Reverend Lucas White was nearly as tall as he was round. He wore a broad smile as he welcomed the small group of mourners to the site. His shiny bald head already showed the signs of perspiration.

Georgia and Ernie lead the way. A group of six ladies from the church followed. Randy Callen, who asked if it would be all right if he attended, came next, walking beside Kelly, and Cole took up the rear.

Glancing around, Cole realized this would be the total of those at the service.

That's OK, he thought. *I hate a room full of people who come to funerals out of obligation.* These are the people who cared about Lottie. Here in the sunshine and green grass and tall cottonwood trees, they were observing her "Going Home" celebration.

Today, there would be no mournful hymns, no sentimental eulogies of the wonderful woman whose earthly vessel lay before them. This service would be a celebration of Lottie Thompson joining hands with Jesus and walking into heaven.

As the group took their seats, Pastor White took his place in front of the casket.

"What a beautiful day to go to heaven!" he exclaimed. "Sister Lottie is in the presence of the Lord this morning. That's all right, it's OK to be jealous."

There were giggles and soft chuckles from the group. Ernie, for some reason, found it funnier than anyone else.

"I didn't know Miss Lottie for as long as some of you. Sister Stewart, you know what I'm talkin' about, you were there when I was born. But it doesn't matter. Her love of her Savior made us family from our first meeting. I always wanted to tell her one more time how much she blessed me with her wonderful spirit. I did a couple of times, but in typical Lottie fashion, she waved me off. 'Aw, go on, now,' she said. But I meant it.

"You know, some see the accumulation of days as a thing to fear. Not our Lottie. No, sir, she was counting the days until she would see Jesus face to face."

The old ladies from church punctuated the pastor's remarks with "Amen," "Yes, sir", "Glory," and "That's right."

While the pastor was talking, a young man of about eighteen slipped up to the side of the group and stood with his head bowed.

"Those of you who know me know how I love to sing. Some of you wish I didn't!"

The group laughed, and one lady said, "Help us, Lord!", which was met with goodhearted laughter.

Cole looked around the group and was pleased everyone one was smiling. Especially Ernie. He was like a kid at his first circus. His eyes sparkled, and he leaned toward the pastor with anticipation of the next thing he would say about his mother-in-law.

"You know, today when there is so much talk about the races, and racism, and all those other 'isms', I want y'all to look at the people sitting here lovin' on Miss Lottie. Now, I wasn't gonna say nothin', but my heart is bursting at the testimony of this child of God we are here to wish bon voyage.

"Now, first off we got her son-in-law, Ernie. He may have some pretty nappy hair, but he's not black." The pastor looked at Ernie and winked. "I know how much Sister Lottie loved him because she told me so, how she couldn't have picked a better man for her only child."

Tears were now streaming down Ernie's big sunburned face. They were tears of love and pride at the pastor's words.

"And looky here," White pointed at Cole, "now here is some truth. This man is Sister Lottie's blood kin."

The old ladies seemed to gasp softly all at once.

"If you don't know our brother Cole, he was his auntie's pride and joy. She loved to tell the story of how he found her and Georgia and brought them to Orvin. He didn't think twice about their color. He was kin, they were part of his blood, and he loved them. I don't mean to embarrass him, but as a total stranger, I want you to know, Mr. Sage, you are what we all strive to be. God bless you real good, brother."

There were calls of "That's right" and "Bless your heart", and several of the old ladies got up and gave Cole pats on the back and a couple of hugs around the neck. Kelly reached over and took Cole's hand.

"And while we are handing out bouquets, I got a word for this lady right here." Pastor White looked at Georgia with a big, love-filled smile. "This young lady took care of her mama for many a year, was there for her through it all. She is a daughter I would be proud to call my own. Miss Georgia, you know, I am sure you know how proud of you your mama was. Speaking for all the folks at Greater Love, our church has been mightily blessed since you and your mama joined us. You are part of our forever family, and we love you."

Georgia raised her handkerchief to her face and for the first time shed a tear. Ernie put his big arm around her and drew her close.

"Now one thing, though, we got to get ol' Ernie here in a pew more often. Just sayin'. I supposed everybody's wondering who this handsome young man is standing over there."

The old ladies all smiled brightly.

"That's my boy, Matthew. He is going to sing Lottie's favorite hymn. If you feel so led, feel free to join in."

Matthew moved to the spot vacated by his father when he stepped to the last chair in the front row and sat down.

"The first time I met Sister Lottie, she came to me after service and told me the song I sang that morning was her favorite. I never forgot the nice things she said to me. She was a fine, fine lady. So, this is for her."

The young man began to sing in a strong, clear tenor. "I come to the garden alone, when the dew is still on the roses, and the voice I hear falling on my ear the Son of God discloses." When he got to the chorus, the entire old lady row stood as one and began to sing, "And He walks with me, and He talks with me, and He tells me I am his own. And the joy we share as we tarry there, none other has ever known."

Moments later, the assembled group all stood. It seemed Georgia's beautiful alto rose above Matthew and the rest of the group to the song's conclusion. At the last note, the group all applauded and spontaneously began to hug each other.

"Now, I haven't been doin' a lot of scripture reading today. Matter of fact, I didn't even bring my Bible. I think we already know where Miss Lottie is and what we need to do to make sure we join her in Glory, in the sweet by and by."

"Yes, Lord! Thank you, Jesus!" came from the old ladies of the Greater Love Church of God in Christ.

"But I would be remiss if I didn't quote one scripture. Second Corinthians 5:8 tells us, 'We are of good courage, I say, and are willing rather to be absent from the body, and to be at home with the Lord.' So, we aren't going to stay to watch that pretty white box be lowered in the ground. That earthly vessel we knew and loved as Mrs. Lottie Thompson is no longer needed because today she is walking the streets of glory! Amen? Amen."

Pastor White went to Georgia and gave her a big hug, then turned to Ernie and did the same. He moved to where Kelly and Cole stood and shook Cole's hand, then pulled him into a hug.

"Who is this lovely lady?"

"This is my wife, Kelly. And that handsome young man is our family friend, Randy Callen."

"Thank you for making the trip all the way from California." With that, the pastor moved to greet and thank his flock for coming.

As they made their way to the car, Randy said, "Is that what a funeral is like? I've never been to one before."

"That was the perfect place to start, then. It wasn't your usual service, but you know, that's what I want mine to be like. It was indeed a celebration of Lottie's love and life." Cole patted Randy on the shoulder.

Chapter 20

"Hi, Erin!"

"Hi, Dad. You sound like you're in the next room. Great connection this time."

"I'm downtown. We went to lunch at Ernie's Deli. Better cell service here. How's my grandson?"

"Ornery, just like his namesake." Erin laughed. "Have you got your DNA results back? I got mine today! I am so excited."

"What's it say?" Cole was as excited as Erin to finally see the results.

"Oh no, not until you get yours. It wouldn't be fair. I will tell you this, there are a couple of surprises."

"You are a wicked child," Cole said in his best Irish accent.

"It's hereditary," Erin teased. "Now I have proof! I won't keep you. Be on the lookout. Ben got his yesterday, but don't tell Kelly. The big reveal is going to be fun."

"I'll check my email as soon as I get home."

"Can you do Skype or Facetime there?"

"Randy brought enough stuff to equip the Pentagon. I'm sure we can. We may have to do it from a café or something, though."

"Call me as soon as you get your results!"

"Will do. Bye, love to all." Cole disconnected.

"We need to go home," Cole said.

"I still have to get groceries," Kelly protested.

"We can get them later."

"What's going on?"

"The DNA results! Erin got hers back today. I want to check and see if I got mine."

"All right, Let's go." Kelly was less than enthusiastic about cutting her trip to town short but couldn't bear making Cole wait.

Kelly was forced to remind Cole to slow down three times on the way back home. As he turned off the engine in the driveway, he jumped from the car and headed for the door.

"Hey, did you forget something?" Kelly called behind him.

"No, I'll unload in a minute," Cole called back.

"Never mind, I'll do it." Kelly shook her head and looked at the two plastic bags from the hardware store.

In the middle of several unimportant emails and a healthy serving of spam was just what Cole was hoping for.

The email from *Tree of Life* bore the subject line "Your DNA Results!"

Dear Mr. Sage,

Find attached the link for your Tree of Life DNA test results. We hope it will open the door for you to connect with family connected by a common genetic link. We have added a list of people who share your DNA.

Please take a moment to watch the short tutorial so that you will be able to get the most out of your test results. Attached to this message you will find a ten dollar gift certificate, for a friend or family member who would like to purchase a DNA test kit of their own.

If you have any questions our friendly, helpful staff will be happy to help guide you on your journey of discovery!

Tree of Life Genealogy, Inc.

Without hesitation, Cole clicked on the blue hyperlink. Moments later, he was looking at a small green and yellow chart.

Great Britain	40%
Ireland	26%
Western Europe	21%
Scandinavia	8%

"I guess you're what they mean when they say, 'a white man,'" Kelly said, looking over Cole's shoulder.

"That's me, the Wonder Bread Kid."

"Here," Cole stood. "See if yours has come in."

"You think?" Kelly got so caught up in Cole's excitement, she all but forgot she did a test, too. "Here we go!"

A similar page to Cole's appeared on the screen. "What do I do now?"

"Scroll down."

"There it is! OK, let's see, Western Europe 43%, Great Britain 28%, Eastern Europe 11%, Iberian Peninsula 8%, Finland/Northwest Russia 8%, and

Scandinavia 2%. Isn't that fascinating? Who knew?" Kelly leaned back and reflected on the chart in the center of the screen.

"I gotta call Erin," Cole said excitedly.

Kelly reached out and put her hand on Cole's hand that held his phone. "Sweetheart, I know you are excited about all this." She paused. "This is exciting and all, but you always knew your background. Be careful with Erin. This is a whole new world for her."

"What are you saying?"

"I'm saying sometimes you speak before you think. This is a new connection to her mother. Just be a good listener. That's all."

"Am I that bad?" Cole asked defensively.

"I didn't say anything about being bad. I am just saying be sensitive."

"I'll put you on speaker."

Cole punched in Erin's number and waited. "Did you get your results?" Erin asked, coming on the line.

"Hi, yes, I got it. So, tell me what did you learn?" Cole asked.

"You first. I'm dying to hear."

Cole read the numbers from the chart. "No big surprises. You?"

"Well, since Mama never talked about family history…" Erin seemed to be tasting her words before she continued. "If we had done these tests without having ever met, would it have led me to you?"

Cole glanced at Kelly before he answered. "I don't know, sweetheart. That's a 'what if' we'll never know the answer to. I may have never done a DNA test without Ben, you know?"

"I guess you're right."

"So?"

"So, Father dear, here are my results! Italy 40%, Germany 16%, Great Britain 22% Iberian Peninsula – I had to Google that – 8%, Ireland 14%. So, if I understand this right, Mom was Italian and German. Germany is in Western Europe, so some of that comes from you, too, right?"

"Makes sense to me. Your mom's grandma was always cooking Italian. You know, I don't think we ever paid much attention to that stuff. Funny, huh?"

"When your tree has roots, there is no reason to dig," Erin said.

"Heavy. Is that original, or did you get that out of a fortune cookie?"

"Fortune cookie?!" Erin laughed. "Seriously, if you know who you are, there is no reason to question your origins. That's why you found your grandfather's journals so important, right?"

"I guess so. You are very special, Erin." Cole paused. "So, where do we go from here?"

"Go on *Tree of Life*. See if you have any DNA matches. Then you can start building your family tree. Dad…" It was Erin's turn to pause. "Will you do mom's, too? I mean, will you show her as, well, I don't know, a spouse or something? Along with Kelly, of course."

Cole looked at Kelly. She smiled and nodded.

"Sure, that's a great idea. Boy, some future genealogist is going to freak out when he sees the intertwining branch of our tree!"

Erin laughed merrily. "This is so important to me. I am so thankful you are taking this journey, too. I love you."

"I love you, too. I think I'll get to work!"

"Me, too. I have some time before the baby wakes up and Jenny gets home. Good luck!"

"Talk soon." Cole hit the red symbol on his phone to end the call.

"How'd I do?"

"Perfect. I hope I didn't hurt your feelings," Kelly said, leaning forward and kissing Cole on the cheek.

"Nope. Sometimes I just need a little guidance. I love you." Cole stood and moved to the living room. "I think I'll see what I can find on the genealogy web page. You never know, I could be a descendant of the King of England!"

As Cole waited for the computer to boot up, he flipped through his notes for the next chapter of his book.

The website was divided into two main sections, family trees, and DNA. From his work on the journals, there were enough names and dates to start a pretty good chunk of his father's lineage. His mother's side of the family was all written down in the massive family Bible that set for years on a stand in the dining room of his parents' home. It was in storage in San Francisco, so it would have to wait.

As he began to add names and a few dates, little apples appeared in the corner of each entry. This whole process was so foreign to Cole, he was hesitant to click one on for fear of losing what he entered. Curiosity finally got the better of him, and he clicked the little red apple.

A window popped up, and there was someone else's work on his tree. His heart raced thinking he found a relative until he realized there are millions of people using the site and the farthest cousin on his tree related only by marriage could be entering data to the site.

As he followed the path of his paternal grandmother, a whole world of names of ancestors he knew nothing of began to appear. Along with their names were their birthplace, sites of their death, and the years they lived. Their children and grandchildren were listed, and Cole could see the sheer volume of information would soon overwhelm him.

It was then he made the decision to concentrate solely on the most direct of his relatives. Parents, grandparents, and their children only back as far as his great-great grandparents to start. Still, the number of people descended from one couple was astounding. Like a funnel in a gas can, the width of descendants narrowed until it seemed he was the only one left.

The little apples appeared next to the names of all the children of George and Alma Sage except Effie. Most of the information was not new. It was nice to have the exact birth and death dates for Will, Grace, and Albert. Most of the information on their children was well documented in his grandfather's journals.

Cole spent quite a while working through each of his great aunts and uncles, adding them and their children to his ever-growing family tree. Cole forced himself not to click on the clues that would carry him back to past generations. He needed to stick with just George and Alma on down.

It struck Cole that any link to George and Mattie were missing. That meant Lottie and Georgia were something Cole himself would be adding to the Sage family tree. He wished for a moment Lottie could see her name, and that of her sister, getting added to the branches of this odd and varied family history.

The methodical way he worked on each clue and added the information gave Cole a sense of pride and accomplishment. This process was far from his normal way of doing research, and the bug really bit him hard. The urge to go get an afternoon snack was pulling him hard toward the kitchen, but looking at his great aunt Gertie's little red apple drew him strongly. She was the last of the children, and the one he knew the least about.

The hint window popped open, and to Cole's delight, there were three children, two girls and one boy, Monroe. One of the girls, recorded only as Little Mary, died at five years old. The other girl, Neva, married a man named John Jackson who was born in Springfield, Illinois and died in Nova Scotia. They had three girls. The information stopped there. Nothing was entered for the girls.

Cole stared at the screen for a long moment at the names, Francis, Margaret, and Polly. His blood was in their veins. They shared common DNA, yet they are lost to the family history. It could mean their descendants haven't recorded their information. They could have died, married and moved far away from Nova Scotia; never married, which was unlikely, or any number of things that made them the last record of their family.

Cole looked at the apple on the name Monroe, the male child of the family, and clicked. It took a moment for him to realize there were hints and data from several sources under Monroe's name. The first hint he opened was for a different person. The locations and names of his parents were not correct, so Cole clicked the ignore button.

The next tab was the right person. Gertrude "Gertie" Sage and her husband, Cornwallis E. Jenkins, were the parents of Monroe C. Jenkins, born August 12, 1906, in Chicago. He married Ophelia Ann Starkey on July 18, 1926. They had one son, Harry, born December 22, 1928. Monroe died March 22, 1955, in Cleveland.

He was young, Cole thought.

Opening the box for Harry, he found he was married twice and had three children. The person who entered the information on Harry and his family left sidebar notes on each member. Harry died of cirrhosis of the liver at fifty-two. His first wife divorced him after a year. His second wife died at eighty-three. They were married until his death. Their oldest child, a girl named Constance, died at twelve of multiple sclerosis. The middle child, a son named Kevin, died in Vietnam.

The youngest, Keith, was married at eighteen when his girlfriend got pregnant. She was sixteen. Their daughter was named Patty. Apart from her birth date, which was three months before Cole's, there was no other information. In a bracketed entry was the town, Brookfield.

"That's just outside Chicago," Cole said aloud. "I wonder if I can find her."

Chapter 21

Cole stared at the monitor. The little beige button that said *Contact Your Match* loomed so largely over his emotions, he found it hard to click it. The cursor hovered over the button; Cole's inner conversation wasn't allowing him to take the plunge.

"Whatcha doin'?" Kelly called from the door. "Ready for a snack?"

Kelly's voice startled Cole, and he clicked the button when he jumped.

"I scare you?" Kelly laughed. "You about jumped out of your chair."

"No, no. I was just sitting here, trying to decide whether to contact a cousin I found on Tree of Life."

"You didn't tell me. What's the story?"

"I don't know much. Do you remember my great aunt in the journals who moved to Chicago and was never heard from again? Her family is showing up on my family tree. This woman, I'm guessing, is my generation. Do I want to open this can of worms?"

"Why not? Finding Lottie and Georgia has certainly worked out."

"Yeah, but…"

"Go ahead. What have you got to lose?"

"You're right. You're always right," Cole teased. "Here goes."

As Cole began to type a message, Kelly retreated to the kitchen. "Snack?" she called back.

"In a few minutes!"

Dear Patty,

It seems we are cousins. I'm new to this genealogy stuff, but your family seems to be closely connected to mine. I would love to chat with you and hopefully learn more about your great-grandmother and my great-aunt, Gertie Sage Jenkins.

Your cousin,
Cole Sage

"That sounds dorky," Cole muttered as he hit send.

On the corner of the page was an information box. The last time Patty Jenkins logged in was in 2009. Cole got a sinking feeling she was never going to see his note! What a waste of time. He reached over and picked up the phone.

"Randy's Computer Repair. Randy speaking."

"Hey, that sounds great. Did you write it? There's a real ring to it," Cole teased.

"Funny guy. What's up?"

"Brush up your super-sleuth skills. I need to get a phone number."

"Nice. I was kind of zoning out," Randy said.

"Not busy?"

"Not today. So, who are you looking for?"

"A woman named Patty, or maybe Patricia Jenkins. Last address Brookfield, Illinois, maybe."

"Anything else?"

Cole gave him the birthdate on *Tree of Life*. Randy didn't answer. Cole could hear him clicking away on the keyboard as music played in the background.

"Patty Ann Jenkins, 20010 Parkline Drive, Joliet, Illinois. Think that could be her? She's fifty-eight, right? There are two others, but one is like eighty, and the other is a college student. That's it. At least in the Land of Lincoln."

Randy gave Cole the phone number.

"So, how was your date?"

"Nice. Really nice."

"Where'd you go?"

"She picked the place." Randy couldn't help grinning.

"And?"

"Big Pete's."

"My kind of girl! Tell me about her."

"She's really nice. Very pretty. She's got some self-esteem issues. She is really insecure." Randy said with slight concern.

"How do you mean?"

"I casually told her she was pretty, and she thought I was making fun of her. It was totally weird. But she lightened up, and we seemed to have something."

"When did you meet her?"

"Monday," Randy replied.

"Cool. Where did you meet her?"

"She came in the shop."

"Two weeks and you're already fraternizing with the customers. Did you at least fix her computer?"

"Funny, yeah, and I delivered it. Her family owns a lumber yard across town. Palmer's, do you know it?"

"I think so," Cole said. "I bought some two by fours or something there when I was here fixing up the farm."

"So will there be another date?" Cole almost didn't ask but figured if he didn't, Randy might need a nudge.

"Yep," Randy said proudly.

"Nice job! So when's your date?"

"Yesterday. I took her to lunch. I think she likes me."

"And you didn't say anything?" Cole pressed.

"Well, with Lottie's funeral, I don't know, there just was the right moment."

"That's OK, way to go. So, did you make plans to see her again?"

"Sure did. Saturday night, dinner and a movie."

"Smooth." Cole heard the buzzer in the shop. "Looks like you have a customer. See you later."

"See ya."

"Hey, Kelly, Randy's got a girl!" Cole shouted the news toward the kitchen.

In a heartbeat, Kelly was standing in the doorway. "I know." Like a proud mother hen, Kelly strutted back to the kitchen, happily singing, "This place is turning out OK for our boy, tra, la, la. It's turning out OK."

"Why am I always the last to know everything?"

There was no answer. Kelly was back in the kitchen, singing merrily.

Cole looked down at the number he scribbled on a torn sheet of paper next to his keyboard. He punched in the number and waited. The phone on the other end rang several times, and Cole was about to hang up when someone answered. A TV was blasting a commercial for cat food in the background, meow, meow, meow.

"Hello." The voice was slightly husky and showed signs of being annoyed.

"Hi, my name is Cole Sage. Is this Patty?"

"Who is it?"

"Cole Sage. I believe we may be related. Your name came up on *Tree of Life*, the genealogy page. Is this Patty Jenkins?" Cole was already wishing he could hang up.

"Nobody's called me Patty in a long time."

"Sorry."

"No problem." Her tone lightened. "I go by Pat now, but Patty's fine, too. What can I do for you, Mister…hold on, let me turn this racket down." The television sounds went silent. "There, that's better. So what can I do for you, Mr. Cole?"

"Cole's my first name, a common mistake. We are related through a distant relative. Your great-great-grandmother and my great-grandfather were brother and sister."

"Is that so?"

"It seems to be. Like I said, I found you on *Tree of Life*."

"On what?" Patty asked.

"The genealogy page. You haven't logged on in a while."

"Oh, yeah. Yeah, the family tree thing."

"Right. I just thought I would call and introduce myself. I don't have any family. I was an only child, and everybody seems to have died. I was pretty surprised to find you, to tell the truth."

"Nice to meet you, cousin," Patty said, relaxing a bit more. "So where do you live?"

For a moment, Cole felt maybe he should be a little guarded with his information, but then he paused and said, "Oklahoma at the moment."

"You don't sound like you come from there." Patty's statement seemed almost like an accusation. "You always lived there?"

"Actually, I was born and raised in California, then after college, I lived in Chicago for years."

"That close? We could have met, then. So what do you do, Cole?"

"I'm a writer. I worked in newspapers for years."

"That so? So why Oklahoma? I have family here."

"Family? I thought you said you didn't have any family?"

It dawned on Cole that Patty was as guarded as he was trying to be. After all, he was a total stranger calling up, claiming to be family.

I see why she'd be suspicious, he thought.

"I am the last of the Sage line, it would seem. I inherited a farm, actually a house on a small plot of ground. My aunt died last week."

"Sorry to hear that, Patty interjected.

"So, I came to be with my cousin and her husband."

"You lost me," Patty interrupted. "Your aunt died? And you're visiting your cousin? That's not the end of the line. What's your game?"

"No game. Let me start over."

Cole told her of inheriting the farm, finding the notebooks and discovering Lottie and Georgia.

"That's very generous of you to just give a stranger a farm. You must be well off." Patty gave a slight teasing laugh.

"I'm certainly not rich. But I get by. They needed a home, Lottie was older than me, and it just seemed the right thing to do. Now that she's gone, her daughter has given it back to me. Kind of a roundabout set of circumstances, I guess." Cole was responding to Patty's warmer, friendly attitude. "So tell me about you."

"What do you want to know?"

"The usual stuff, married, kids, job, hobbies, anything. Anything that will help me get to know you," Cole said with genuine interest.

"Why?"

"Why what?"

"Why do you need to know that stuff? Forgive me if I sound a bit standoffish, but I don't know you. Now you want to know all about me." Her warmth was gone.

"You know," Cole hesitated before he continued, "maybe this was a mistake. Sorry I bothered you."

Before he could hang up, Patty said, "Hey now, don't get all huffy. I'm a single woman living alone, and I'm careful who I give out personal information to. Never bothered to marry. Had my share of fellas. No kids, I hate kids. No pets, don't like them either. I've worked a lot of jobs, mostly waitressing. I got knocked up senior year of high school, dropped out, miscarried, didn't go back. I live in a shitty fleabag apartment with my old man Ricardo. He's on disability. How's that?"

"That's fine. Thanks for your time." Cole hung up before she could say anything else.

He didn't notice Kelly standing in the doorway until she spoke. "That didn't sound like it went well."

"She sounded like three packs a day and a chip on her shoulder as big as a toaster." Cole chuckled. "Good grief! That long lost should have stayed long lost!"

"Are you going to tell Georgia?"

Cole shrugged. "No point, really. Someday. Maybe."

"So are you going to try and get some writing done?"

"I think I've goofed off enough, don't you?"

"I didn't say anything; just curious what the rest of the afternoon held."

"Bored?" Cole asked.

"A bit. But it's OK. I'll do some laundry or maybe, just maybe, catch up on my soaps!" Kelly said with a wicked grin.

"I'll go buy some Bon Bons and join you!"

Kelly crossed the room and gave Cole a kiss. "I love you, Cole Sage."

"I love you more, I'm sure."

"Now get to work!" Kelly made her way to the doorway. "I know what you're thinking, and the answer is no." Kelly winked at him. "But I'm free tonight."

Cole did go to work. For the next three days, he worked into the evenings on his book. The journals told such a strong story, he found sewing together a narrative to be a pleasure. The novelization of his family history gave him an even clearer, deeper understanding of where he came from.

He made every effort not to editorialize, to stay true to the text of the journals, only adding description and occasional background to the story. What he was producing was a picture of America in the first half of the twentieth century. The struggles, prejudices, and the tragedy that befell the nation.

The constant thread in the story was the resilience of George, his paternal grandfather. Cole struggled at the first reading of the journals with George's alcoholism, and the incredible waste of potential of this charismatic character. This time around, he saw deeper meaning in the conflicts within his grandfather. The old axiom "There but by the grace of God go I" took on a more personal meaning. This was a cautionary tale, a warning, a signpost that with every entry seemed to call out, "Beware!"

Cole sat one afternoon when Kelly went to town and examined his own life. The shadow of the man he wrote about colored and influenced him to his very marrow. Though he never really knew him, the influence on Cole's father, the shaping of his character, world view and personal ethics impacted Cole in ways he was still coming to grips with.

The hostility, though seldom spoken of, his mother carried for her father-in-law, too, impacted Cole's make up. As he sat bringing up memories of his adolescence and the sometimes harsh discipline and instruction he received from his parents, he wondered if they could have read these same journals, if his life would have been different. Had his parents approached the life of George Sage with this information, how would they have been different? As he wondered, Cole wept.

He wept for years lost with his grandfather. He wept for the estrangement of his grandfather from the son he loved. He wept for his mother's unflinching hatred of her father-in-law. But most of all, he wept for George. The pain he carried, the loss he endured for so many years must have been unbearable.

The book, now nearly completed, was so personal on so many levels, Cole found himself struggling with the idea of throwing it out to the world. Was it able to convey the love, fear, pain, and loss he felt for the family he wrote about? Could it heal other families? As he reviewed the notes and journal entries for the last few chapters, he felt a melancholy knowing this journey would soon be over.

That night when he lay waiting for sleep, Cole breathed a prayer that his words would be a source of inspiration and reflection for those who would read it.

* * *

"Kelly, can you get the door?"

"I'm getting in the shower!" came the voice from the top of the stairs.

Cole pulled the pan from the stove and made his way to the door.

"Mr. Sage?" asked a man of about sixty.

"That's me."

"Then this is for you!" He handed Cole an unmarked white envelope. "You've been served."

Cole turned the envelope in his hand. "What's this for?"

"None of my beeswax. I just get twenty bucks to drive out and give it to you. Don't shoot the messenger. Have a nice evening." The man turned and returned to his car.

"Thanks," Cole said sarcastically.

He slapped his palm several times with the envelope on his way back to the kitchen. He took a seat at the kitchen table, opened the envelope and began to read.

"What?" Cole said in anger. "You've got to be kidding me!"

The envelope contained documents pertaining to a lawsuit filed by Patricia Jenkins, claiming, in part, that she was the oldest living relative of George Sage and as such, was the sole heir of his estate. After a couple paragraphs of boilerplate, it also demanded the farm be vacated by any and all occupants. Cole folded the documents, placed them back in the envelope, and threw it sailing across the room.

A hundred thoughts pinballed around in his head. The longer he sat, the angrier he got. He tried to understand how she could have the nerve to claim an inheritance. Her side of the family, and his great-aunt Gertie in particular abandoned the family in Orvin more than a hundred years ago. Different scenarios played out in his head, some bordering on hysteria. Just as Cole thought of a defense, another idea would shove its way into his thoughts, erasing the previous plan.

"Dinner ready?" Kelly asked from the archway into the kitchen. Taking one look at Cole's face, she asked, "What's wrong with you?"

"You are not going to believe it!" Cole snapped.

"Do I need to go out and come back in?"

"No, no, I'm sorry. We're, I'm being sued...well, Georgia and I."

"For what?" Kelly asked in disbelief.

"That cousin I found on the genealogy page thing. She's claiming she's the rightful heir to the farm."

"Is that true? Is she?" Kelly frowned and moved to a chair at the table.

"Technically? I guess, but morally no." Cole gave a disgusted sigh. "Her great-great-grandmother left here for Chicago before World War I and pretty much cut all ties with Orvin. If I hadn't tried to reach out in some kind of misplaced familial kindness, she wouldn't even know this place exists! She didn't even recognize the Sage name, for heaven's sake."

"So what are you going to do? I have an old friend in San Francisco who's a really good lawyer."

"I have just the guy for this. And he'll owe me," Cole said as if speaking to himself. "Too late tonight. I'll call in the morning."

"I'm not going to say it will be OK, because I don't have a real good feeling about this. I'm so sorry."

"Yeah, me either. Well, at least Lottie died owning the family place."

"That's right. When will you tell Georgia?"

"Let me see what ol' C.W. Langhorne has to say."

"Who?"

"He's the guy who found me and got this whole ball rolling. I'll give him a call in the morning."

"Then that's settled. Now, where did you leave dinner?"

* * *

"Would you lay still?!" Kelly said in exasperation.

"I can't sleep," Cole grumbled. "I'm getting up."

"What time is it?"

"Three-fifteen."

Chapter 22

Cole awoke from a fitful night angry.

Randy was in the kitchen making breakfast when Cole went downstairs.

"Are you able to scan a document for me?" Cole ran his fingers through his hair. The look Randy gave him forced him to change the question. "Dumb question. Will you scan a document for me?

"Good morning to you, too. Did you sleep under the bed or on it?"

"I don't think I slept."

"What's going on?" Randy asked, flipping his eggs.

"It seems my wonderful new cousin I found is suing to take the farm."

"You're kidding!"

"I wish I was. I got served papers last night. I need to send the copies to a lawyer."

"If you have the number, I can fax them quicker," Randy suggested.

"I'm sure I have it somewhere."

"If not, we can Google it. When are you calling them?"

"What time is it?"

"Eight-thirty."

"Nine o' one."

It only took Randy a couple of minutes to fax the papers to C.W. Langhorne's office. At exactly one minute after nine, Cole rang the office.

"Law offices of C.W. Langhorne."

"This is Cole Sage. Is Mr. Langhorne in?"

"Well, there's a blast from the past!" the receptionist exclaimed.

"Nice of you to remember. Is Mr. Langhorne available?"

"Nope, he's married." The receptionist giggled.

Cole didn't respond. He patiently waited until the woman realized he was in no mood for her clever comebacks.

"I'll put you through," she said after several seconds.

"Mr. Sage, this *is* a surprise. How may I be of service?"

"We have a problem."

"Not one that can't be addressed, I'm sure." Langhorne recognized from Cole's tone and the use of "we" that this was not going to be pleasant.

"It seems I am not the last of the Sage descendants, as you previously thought. A cousin, three months older than me from the Chicago area, is suing me for the Oklahoma property I inherited."

"Indeed, it does sound like we, or should I say I, have a problem. How is it this cousin, man, woman came to the realization they stand to inherit?"

"Woman, Patty Jenkins. She popped up on the *Tree of Life* genealogy website after I did a DNA test. I called her to make a connection with a relative. Since, as you know, I didn't think I had any."

"And so how is it she came to know about the farm?"

"That's on me," Cole said, realizing he was the root of the problem.

"Hold on one second, Mr. Sage."

Through the muffled sound of the handset being covered with Langhorne's hand, Cole could hear the voice of the receptionist.

"Mr. Sage, you are a dream client," Langhorne said, coming back on the line. "I have the fax here you sent of the papers you were served. Thank you so much. Bear with me a moment, and I'll have a look."

Cole sat listening to the sound of papers flipping. Langhorne placed the phone on the desk as he read. The occasional humph of discovery made Cole a bit more relaxed.

"Alrighty, Mr. Sage. It seems there is cause for a bit of concern. I will contact Ms. Jenkins' legal representation and see what their position is, flesh out this somewhat limited document. Give me your number there in San Francisco, and I'll get right back to you."

"I'm in Orvin, living for the moment at the farm," Cole offered before giving the attorney his number.

"Is that a fact? I thought we signed that property over to your aunt?" Langhorne questioned.

"She passed."

"My condolences." Langhorne took a pause. "I rarely find myself in this kind of situation, Mr. Sage. That is to say, I pride myself on my thoroughness, my tenacity, and my bloodhoundedness. Seldom have I ever made such a blunder. This is entirely my fault. I bear the responsibility for correcting it. If there is any way humanly possible to stop this woman from gaining possession of the property, it will be done. You have my word."

"There is plenty of blame to go around," Cole responded. "If I'd have kept my big mouth shut and my curiosity under control, she would have been none the wiser and we wouldn't be having this conversation. So, don't beat yourself up too bad. I really do appreciate your offer."

"I won't be getting much sleep until this is settled. I don't want you to worry about the cost either. This is my mistake, and I'll clean it up. And of course, there will be no fee."

"That is very generous. I have faith you'll figure this out. Best of luck."

"I don't believe in luck. I believe in good old Oklahoma bullheadedness."

"Thank you, Mr. Langhorne."

"I'll not leave you hangin' either. I'll keep you in the loop. Talk soon."

Cole turned to face Kelly and Randy's gaze.

"Well?" they said, almost in unison.

"Well, it doesn't sound good. Langhorne is taking full responsibility for the mistake on his part. He'll do all the legal stuff gratis, but to what end? If she's the oldest, she is the next in line to inherit, not me. Pretty cut and dried, the way I see it."

"A white flag already?" Kelly wasn't smiling.

"I deal in facts, not misguided what-ifs."

"Is this guy any good?" Randy asked.

Cole shrugged. "His pride is wounded. That's a pretty good motivator. But the law's the law. That's where he better be good."

"I have a shop to open. This is gonna work out." Randy stood and made his way for the door. "You got a plan B?" Randy turned as he reached the door and gave Cole a grin.

"Do I ever?" Cole shrugged.

The front door closed with a heavy thud. Kelly got up and poured another cup of coffee.

"Do you have a plan B?" Kelly asked, sitting back down at the table.

"I still have my place in San Francisco, but I can't bear the thought of going back to the Bay Area. Driving here, I felt such a sense of release, knowing we cut all ties there."

"What about the kids?"

"You know as well as I do their days there are numbered. Ben's already been offered an incredible job in Texas. How long can Erin hold off his career opportunities? You heard what he said about Europe. That's a done deal. It's not if; it's when."

"I guess if I'm being honest, I know that. Sometimes you surprise me."

"How's that?" Cole was taken back by the comment.

"You're a very romantic, sentimental guy. Then you can be a razor-sharp pragmatist. That is two very strange sides of the same coin."

"Hot or cold. Right or wrong. I calls 'em like I sees 'em." Cole laughed, and it felt good to have a bit of comic release.

Cole spent the afternoon working on his book. The first draft was nearing completion. As he reviewed his notes and re-read several journals, a sense of loss overcame him. He was really beginning to feel the old farm was home. Since he'd returned, he felt it more and more. Before the lawsuit, he was trying to work up the guts to ask Kelly if she would consider living here on a permanent basis.

Thank goodness I didn't include that to my list of stupid mistakes, he thought.

There was a heavy-handed knocking on the front door. Cole could hear Kelly walking around upstairs, so he didn't bother calling her to get it.

"Hey, Ernie, what's up?" Cole asked as he opened the door.

"You want to go for a ride? I need to pick up some stuff at the farm supply."

"Sure, I need a break. What are you doing home this time of day?"

"That's kind of why I want you to go with me, so we can have a talk."

The serious nature of Ernie's answer concerned him. There was no smile, no smart remarks, just the request for company.

"Let me tell Kelly I'm leaving." Cole left the door open and went to the foot of the stairs. "Hey, Kelly!" Cole shouted.

"Yeah?" she answered, leaning over the rail.

"I'm going to take a ride with Ernie. I need a bit of a break. It will be good to get out."

"Hi, Ernie!" Kelly called down.

"Hi, yourself!" Ernie responded.

"See you in a bit," Cole called back, moving toward the front door.

The two men made pointless conversation until they got in the truck. Ernie backed all the way out of the drive before he spoke again.

"Is there something we need to know about the farm, Cole?" Ernie's voice showed a blend of hurt and anger.

"As a matter of fact, there is. I was going to come over to see you guys this evening when you got home." Cole's words sounded shallow.

"Yeah. What's goin' on?"

"It seems I'm not the only Sage left."

"The hell you say," Ernie blurted out. "What do you mean?"

"The long and short of it is, I've been doing some family tree stuff. I found a cousin on the Internet. She's three months older than me. I was being friendly and trying to make a connection, and like an idiot, I told her about inheriting the farm and giving it to Lottie, and how you guys...you know the rest. Anyway, she sued me to get the farm, claiming that by being the oldest, it should go to her."

"Just like that?"

"I got served yesterday afternoon, late. How'd you know?" Cole questioned.

"This fella came in the deli this morning just as we were opening. I think he was out in the parking lot, waiting." Ernie's voice trailed off.

"And?" Cole pressed.

"And he served my ass. Georgia, too. Both of us are called as witnesses."

Cole sat speechless. Ernie tapped his fingertips on the steering wheel, not saying a word.

"You gonna lose the place?" Ernie finally said.

Cole thought for a moment before answering, "I don't know. That's the truth. I called the lawyer who found me this morning. He promised to do everything he could, but…"

"Damnation, Cole, that just ain't right."

"It just might be. The lawyer, Mr. Langhorne, says it didn't look real good. The law is the law, you know."

"Still don't make it right."

"What if he found her in the first place like he should have? We wouldn't be having this conversation. She would have inherited, moved in, lost it to taxes, sold it, who knows. I would never have entered the picture. That's how it *should* have worked."

"Still ain't right. She damn sure better not live there. I'll make her seven levels of hell miserable." Ernie's anger was boiling up.

"No, you won't. You're a good guy. Besides, Georgia wouldn't let you." Cole laughed, trying to ease the frustration they both felt. "Hey, you missed your turn. The farm supply is that way."

"I didn't really need to go. That was to get you out of the house." Ernie laughed. "You hungry?"

"Do bananas have seeds?" Cole replied.

"Do what?"

"Never mind. I'm always hungry."

"Good, now you can explain all this to Georgia."

At the deli, Ernie made Cole a sandwich that would certainly spoil his dinner, but that didn't stop him from finishing it off. It didn't take long to explain matters to Georgia because she read the documents they were served with. She was not as vocal about her disapproval of the situation as Ernie, but Cole sensed her anger nonetheless.

"I'll run you back as soon as I get a couple of things cleaned up in the back if you don't mind," Ernie said to Cole as he finished his soda and chatted with Georgia.

Cole stood. "I'll help. Defray the cost of my sandwich."

"The hell you say! Sit down. It's not a gift if you work it off. You can do that when you come beggin'."

"That'll be the day." Georgia laughed.

"I think I'll run next door and see Randy. I haven't been back since he officially opened. Give me a yell when you're ready. No hurry."

"Looks like he's doing a pretty good business. What a nice kid." Georgia smiled as Cole moved to the door.

Wanting to peek in without Randy seeing him, Cole moved just past the divider wall and looked in the shop. Standing at the counter was a shapely young woman with black hair. She was stylishly dressed, leaning at the counter, and not seeming to be in a hurry to go anywhere. Randy smiled at her and at one point patted her hand.

The bell tinkled as Cole entered the shop. Randy stood a bit straighter and looked as if his hand was in the cookie jar.

"Hey, my computer doesn't work!" Cole bellowed. "I thought you said you fixed it?!"

The girl whirled around with fire in her eyes. Cole laughed.

"Very funny!" Randy said, shaking his head.

The girl was absolutely beautiful. Her dark hair framed a fair-skinned face with stunning blue eyes. She still didn't smile.

"Brooke, this is Cole Sage. He thinks he's a comedian."

A big smile broke out across Brooke's face. It only enhanced her loveliness.

"I've heard all about you, Mr. Sage," Brooke said pleasantly.

"Maybe I should go out and come in again," Cole said, wishing he hadn't tried to be funny.

As he approached the counter, Brooke extended her hands and they shook. "That was almost funny," Brooke said with a deadpan expression. Cole was put in his place, and he loved it.

"Ernie came and got me, then fed me a sandwich."

"Brooke brought me lunch," Randy announced proudly.

Cole unintentionally looked at the clock on the wall; three-thirty. "How nice."

"Homemade lasagna." Randy smiled.

"We had some left from last night, and I remembered Randy said he liked Italian. He told me about you and your wife taking him to a wonderful place in San Francisco. I've always wanted to go to San Francisco." Brooke's desire to make a good impression was speeding up her normal rate of speech by double.

Cole looked at Randy and saw a whole different person than the one he thought he knew. His total infatuation with the dark-haired young woman made him somehow more handsome. Cole always thought he was a good looking kid. This was different; he was now a handsome man, showing off his girl. There was a proud familiar feeling and swelling in Cole's pride.

This is an important moment, Cole thought, *savor it.*

For a moment, Cole thought back to when he introduced Ellie, Erin's mother, to his boss Mick Brennan at the Chicago Sentential so many years ago. He remembered how the old newspaper man crushed him when he said Ellie was too good for him. Cole vowed not to make the same dreadful kind of comment, even in jest.

"Randy, I don't know how you managed to find the prettiest girl in town, but I think she's a winner." Cole gave Brooke a knowing wink. "And you, young lady, I hope you realize what a great guy my protégé is. If he should do anything out of line, though, you let me know and I'll sic Ernie next door on him!"

Brooke blushed at his attention. "I don't think that will be necessary, Mr. Sage." Brooke returned his wink with a mischievous smile.

"Please call me Cole. It makes me feel younger."

"Deal. Cole."

"I have interrupted enough. I just wanted to say hi. I wasn't expecting such a lovely introduction. See you later, Randy. Brooke, I hope we'll get to see you out at the farm sometime."

"I would love to meet your wife. Randy says she's wonderful."

"Certainly more than I deserve."

"I doubt that," Brooke said softly.

Cole made his way to the door and back to the deli. He couldn't wait to get home and tell Kelly about Brooke.

Chapter 23

"Let's go for a walk," Kelly greeted Cole at the front door.

"Where to?"

"I don't know. How about back to the pond? Let's get those folding camp chairs while we're at it."

"I've got some very cool news."

"Tell me when I get back. I'll grab us some water."

Cole went to the covered porch on the back of the house where the two bright blue nylon slipcovers sat in the corner. He stood for a moment looking out of the screened porch at the land that lay behind the house. Thanks to Ernie's generosity with his sprinkler system, the alfalfa was a lush green.

I really do love this place, he thought.

His memory took him back to the day Ernie helped him round up hundreds of tumbleweeds and burn them in a pit he dug with his backhoe. The ground was hard, dry and neglected, all except for the green oasis that was the pond.

He smiled remembering Kelly's reaction to his learning noodling. Cole thought the idea of catching catfish barehanded was a strange backwoods spectacle. He never expected to see Kelly running back to the house in horror after Ernie slammed one of the huge fish in the head with a hammer to kill it. They were just really getting to know each other then. A faint smile crossed his lips as he realized he loved her even back then.

"Ready?"

"Yeah, all set."

"Whatcha lookin' at?" Kelly asked as she moved next to him.

"I was just admiring our farm. I never thought I'd ever hear you ask to go back to the pond."

"I'm good so long as you don't stick your arm down some poor fish's throat!" She laughed.

"It didn't stop you from eating a plate full, as I recall."

"Oh, it was sooo good!" Kelly said, admitting her fondness for the crispy fried catfish. "I still think it's barbaric to club the fish to death."

"Lesson learned. Next time, I'll shoot them," Cole teased.

"Let's go, can we? So what is this big news?"

"I met Randy's girlfriend!" Cole said excitedly.

"And?"

"She's a nine, maybe a ten," Cole said with a proud grin.

"Sexist!" Kelly teased. "What was she like?"

As they walked, Cole told her of Brooke and the way Randy looked and acted around her. Kelly was delighted with the report. As they walked, Kelly began humming a tune Cole recognized but couldn't name. They walked along, each in their thoughts about Randy finally finding somebody.

The alfalfa smelled sweet, and small yellow butterflies fluttered around them as they walked along the edge of the field. A large section of fence that bordered Ernie's property was removed, making it easier to plow and irrigate.

Finally, Kelly broke the spell of her joyful humming and Cole's thoughts. "It still amazes me that Ernie is willing to farm both these pieces of ground," she said as they passed the opening in the fence.

"He gets all the crops he plants, alfalfa, watermelons, corn, whatever. He loves to farm, and this side pays for the seeds, fertilizer, gas for the tractor, all that stuff. So his half is all profit. Cool, huh?"

"I guess so. You certainly wouldn't be able to do anything with it," she said knowingly.

"Lottie couldn't have either. Ernie makes a few bucks, we get a picture-perfect farm. He wouldn't do it if he didn't want to. Everybody wins."

To their surprise, the tall grass around the pond was mowed and almost looked park-like. There were two lounge chairs on the bank and a small table between them.

"Looks like somebody else had the same idea," Kelly said cheerfully.

"This has Georgia written all over it. Want to use theirs or ours?"

"Theirs are less work," Kelly said, taking a seat. "This is lovely."

The pond sparkled like diamonds in the late afternoon sun. The occasional bird landed on the far side to bathe, eat a bug, and enjoy the water.

"This is nice," Cole said. "What made you think to come out here?"

"I need to talk to you. I thought this might make a good place to relax and have a chat."

"Nothing bad, I hope. I think I've met my limit for the month."

"No, I just want to feel near you when I share some news with you. Ben called while you were gone. He has accepted the position in France."

"I can't say I'm surprised. I would if I were him. What about Erin?"

"It kind of sounded like Erin encouraged him this time," Kelly stated.

"Does that make you mad?" Cole sensed a bit of tension in her voice.

"Not exactly. I guess I'm just a little upset to think of them leaving. We are so used to going over for dinner, birthdays, holidays, it is going to be hard."

"The only thing is, you've had them for nearly ten years. I've really only had them since coming to San Francisco. I'm trying to put up a good front, but I can't stand the thought of them leaving. But I also know things in this life change. The difference is, this time I have you. Without you, I think I would really be lost."

"You really don't want to go back to California, do you?"

"No. You?"

"I have nothing except you. So where I go and live is going to be something we decide together. My only other real connection will be in France."

"Would you consider staying here?"

"Asked the man who is being sued for the property."

"For a moment, I forgot."

"I'm so sorry, sweetheart. You're really worried about losing it, aren't you?"

"Doesn't look good. You know, I don't owe much on my house in San Francisco. We can buy just about anywhere with the equity."

"Do you want to go back to Chicago?" Kelly questioned.

"No." Cole was surprised by the question. "Did I answer too soon? As much as I'm a Chicagoan at heart, I don't think I would want to deal with that cold anymore."

"Thank goodness," Kelly said in relief.

"What about you? Do you want to go back to Sausalito?"

"It was fun, but it was B.C."

"B.C.?"

"Before Cole." Kelly gave Cole a big grin. "I was fine while it lasted, and it did wonders for my self-esteem and processing my grief after Peter's death. But that is behind me now, Cole Mine."

A large fish splashed the water as it leapt to grab at a dragonfly just above the water.

"Then here we sit. Two places we don't want to go back to, and a million to choose from."

"Then there is the elephant sitting between us neither one wants to talk about. You asked me if I would want to stay here. It is really hard to think about when everything is so uncertain."

"I kind of hate to even talk about it, for fear it will happen," Cole admitted.

"That's kind of an ostrich approach," Kelly replied. "I heard somebody say once when an ostrich sticks its head in the ground, it leaves itself open to get kicked in the butt."

"I feel totally helpless. I know Langhorne is working on it, but when was the last time we heard from him? There is no one I can fight face to face. No bad guy to go after. I can't even get help from the cops this time around."

"Says who?"

"What do you mean?" Cole asked, totally baffled by Kelly's response.

"For being so smart, sometimes you can be so dumb. Where does this woman live?"

"Outside Chicago."

"What if she is the 'bad guy'? Not just someone suing you, but actually a bad person? Like on the TV shows when they bring up what a creep the defendant is."

"I don't think that works in a civil suit."

"Who knows? But it is something, right? What would you do if you were still there?"

"Drive over and see her," Cole responded.

"Oh, come on, Cole. Wouldn't you call your friend Tom Harris, the detective?"

Cole suddenly felt like a complete fool. "How stupid. Of course. What is wrong with me?"

"Too close to the problem, I'd say," Kelly said, stroking Cole's wounded ego.

Cole dug in his pocket and pulled out his phone. "Look at that! Three bars." He punched in a number.

"I thought you died!" the voice that answered said sarcastically.

"Hi, Tom. Go ahead, let me have it. I have no excuse." Cole waited for his friend Tom Harris to continue scolding him. When he didn't, Cole continued. "You busy?"

"I'm standing over the 306th dead body so far this year. I've got hostile witnesses and even hostile-er family and friends. No, I've got nothing going on. What's up with you?"

"I almost don't want to ask."

"Another six months, I'll have *another* three or four hundred. What do you need? It will be a nice distraction."

"I'll fill you in with the details later, but I need a background check on a relative."

"Is Erin in trouble?" Harris laughed. "I thought you didn't have any relatives? That's why you inherited that place in Oklahoma."

"Me either, but it seems I have a cousin in the Chicago area. Patty, maybe Patricia, Jenkins, fifty-eight. She's suing me. Claims the farm should be hers. I would kind of like to know who I'm dealing with, you know?"

"Got it. I'll see what I can do. I have to get Al Capone here processed and to the morgue. He shot three people before they put him away." Harris said something to someone in the background, but Cole couldn't make it out. "I'll see what I can dig up when I get back to the office. Where are you? School, home? What?"

"Orvin, at the farm."

"You're kidding. What the hell are you doing there?" Harris was not amused.

"Part of the long story. I promise to give you the complete blow by blow when you're free."

"You bet you will. I can't wait to hear this one!"

"Take care. We'll talk later." Cole tapped a button and laid the phone on his lap.

"See, that wasn't so hard," Kelly said.

"Yet." Cole gave her a defeated look. "Can you imagine the guff I'm going to have to take from Harris?"

"Ah, poor baby. You guys and your macho, I-can't-lose competitiveness." Kelly chuckled.

"Is that what you think? I lost?" Cole shot back.

"No. I didn't mean...I was just...I didn't mean to make you mad. I was teasing," Kelly said defensively.

"Sorry I snapped at you. It's just kind of humiliating that Stanford didn't work out."

"Humiliating? You quit; you didn't get fired. You stood up for your principles, right? It didn't help that they changed the game plan *after* you took the job. That's a pretty crappy thing to do. I just meant guys always are trying to one-up each other and-"

"And women don't?"

"Well, yeah, of course, women are horrible about the keeping-up-with-the-Joneses kind of thing. Are you really bothered by leaving the university?"

Kelly could see there were issues they should have addressed a month ago.

"Sometimes I think maybe I could have handled it better, that's all. I'm so sorry if I embarrassed you in front of your friends."

"Seriously? You are the last person who could ever embarrass me, ever." Kelly swung her legs around on the lounge chair. "You are my everything. I am so proud of who you are, your character, wisdom, and strength. Don't ever think standing your ground or some stupid job could make me think any less of you." She leaned across the narrow space between the chairs and put her arms around Cole's neck and kissed him.

When they returned to the house, they found Randy sitting on the porch. "There you are!" he called out as they rounded the corner of the house.

"Hi!" Kelly waved. "We were back at the pond."

"The pond! I forgot all about that. I couldn't figure out where you could go out here without the car."

"No worries, Dad, we are OK," Cole teased, mounting the stairs.

"I hear Cole met your girlfriend," Kelly said, sitting in the chair next to Randy.

"I'm not sure she's my girlfriend, but he met Brooke at the shop."

"Brooke. That's pretty. I hear the pretty name goes with a really pretty girl." Kelly was enjoying seeing Randy color up a bit.

"She is beyond beautiful, Kelly. But best of all, she doesn't even know it. She is so sweet and down to Earth. I really like her. I hope I don't screw it up."

"Screw it up? What on Earth makes you say that?" Kelly's tone became one of concern.

"Her mom died when she was younger, and her dad raised her. He is a pretty intense guy. I met him when I delivered her computer. He was a total jerk. Then when we went on our date, she left the house to get away from him because he hassled her about going out with me. Weird deal."

"What does she say?"

"Nothing, really. But you can tell his verbal and mental abuse has taken a toll. She's terrified of making him mad. But she's so sweet, I just don't get how anybody could…" Randy's voice faded into his thoughts.

Kelly looked over at Cole for support. None was forthcoming. "You should bring her over for dinner some night."

"That's what Cole said."

"See, I have some pretty good ideas sometimes," Cole said, sticking his chin in the air mockingly.

"We would love to have her for dinner. And I'll fix whatever you want."

"What if I barbecue something? She loves barbecue," Randy said, showing real interest in the idea.

"I can make a salad and some beans, and cornbread."

"And I can eat everything you're talking about," Cole joked. "Did you say cornbread? Have we been in

Oklahoma too long? Since when do you make cornbread?"

"I have skills you have yet to be dazzled by, Mr. Sage."

"So when can we do it?" Randy asked excitedly.

"Whenever you want," Cole and Kelly said, almost simultaneously.

"This is going to be really cool. How about tomorrow?"

"Can't we do it sooner?" Cole teased.

"Yeah, too soon."

"Tomorrow would be fine. Let me know as soon as you confirm," Kelly said.

Randy took his phone off the arm of the chair, stood and went into the house without responding.

"Ah, the wonder of young love." Cole smiled. "I remember when I first took you out. I felt that age or younger."

"I must say, you were, and are a spectacular date. I thought romance and chivalry were dead until I met you."

"Why, thank you, Mrs. Sage."

"You are quite welcome, Mr. Sage."

"She said yes!" Randy exclaimed, bounding back through the screen door. "I'll be back. I have to go buy some meat! Do you need anything?" He didn't wait for an answer. He ran down the steps and to his car.

"I hope you don't need anything," Cole said.

"Not a thing." Kelly's reply covered more than groceries.

Chapter 24

"Mr. Sage? This is Sarah Connors. Remember me?"

"I sure do. It's been a while. How are you?"

"I'm doing well. I understand you are back in Orvin to write a book."

Is this a friendly call or a Nosey Rosy poking around for gossip? Cole thought.

"Yes, that's right. You probably saw the article in the paper when I was here before about finding my grandfather's journals in an old trunk. I've decided to write a book based on his journals, and where better to do it than Orvin?" *There, that should satisfy her curiosity,* he thought.

"Isn't that wonderful! I think I have found something that might be of interest to you. The Chamber of Commerce has begun work on putting together an Orvin Museum. Nothing huge, you understand. The library has donated two large rooms where we will be able to display things. Anyway, we have been asking the community for donations for the exhibits. Connie Westmoreland's kids were kind enough to donate all the old notebooks and diaries of her grandfather, Doctor Lambert."

"I know that name," Cole interrupted. "He's mentioned several times in the journals."

"Well, there you go! I was right. They date back to the turn of the century. The last one, not this one." Sarah laughed merrily at her joke.

"How many are there?"

"Oh, a big ol' box full. But why I called you, there are these little black books, kind of like you would carry in your pocket. I was flipping through some of the old, old ones, and I saw reference to a bunch of Sages. I figured they were kin of yours. I mean, there was only one Sage family in town, right?"

"Absolutely," Cole said, his heart starting to race. "It would be amazing to get to see them. They could be corroborating evidence for the things in the journals."

"My thoughts exactly. I have them here at the bank if you want to swing by and pick them up."

"Ms. Westmoreland wouldn't mind?"

"Oh, heavens no. She's ninety-four, and if I'm not being indelicate, isn't all there, you know what I mean? They just put her in a home. She was trying to light a fire in her oven. She thought it was an old fashioned wood stove. So, if you kept them, no one would probably care. I don't know how we'd display them anyway. His old black bag, tools and stethoscope and all will be really nice, though."

"Sarah, dear, you have made my day! I will see you this afternoon without fail! Thank you so much for thinking of me."

"Happy to help. I'll see you later on."

"You are not going to believe this!" Cole called excitedly as he ran upstairs to find Kelly.

"You look like a kid who just got what he wanted for Christmas!" Kelly replied as Cole came into the bedroom. "What's going on?"

"A lady just called. She has the doctor notebooks from the early part of the century. My family is mentioned a bunch of times. What amazing background for the book! It can shed a more adult light on the stories George told as a boy. This is incredible. I knew magical things would happen if we came back here."

"I haven't seen you this excited since our wedding night!" Kelly teased.

"Not quite, but close." Cole laughed, then crossed the room and gave Kelly a kiss on the cheek. "I'll go get them after lunch."

"Why wait? Let's go now."

"Really? You're not busy?"

"No, I'm just puttering around. Dinner is thawing, the breakfast dishes are done, the wash is in the dryer, and you, my love, need to go to town before you blow a fuse. Speaking of which, I think I blew the one on the back porch again."

"I'll check as soon as we get back. Let's go." Cole was in the hall on his way to the stairs as he answered.

As luck would have it, the space right in front of the bank was empty.

"I'll wait here."

"Good idea, Sarah Connors is a real chatterbox. I can use you as my excuse to leave."

Before Cole could make it to the door, Sarah Connors was on the sidewalk with a big brown cardboard box.

"I knew you wouldn't be able to stand it!" Sarah said cheerfully.

"Here, let me get that," Cole said, taking the box from Sarah.

"Hi, I'm Sarah Connors," she said, approaching Kelly's window.

"Hi, Sarah. I'm Kelly."

"You broke a lot of widows', divorcees' and old maids' hearts when you landed this one." Sarah gave a jerk of her head in Cole's direction.

"I'm a lucky girl, all right." Kelly smiled at the suggestion.

"We must get together for lunch one of these days, I'd love to get to know the lady who married Orvin's most famous citizen." Sarah was almost too bubbly.

"We'll have to do that," Kelly agreed.

The trunk of the car slammed shut.

"OK, all stowed away. Thank you so much, Sarah. I am so grateful," Cole said.

"Well, I just might come to you for some help with our new museum," Sarah responded, making it clear this would be a quid pro quo arrangement.

"If I'm not totally buried in the book, we'll see what I can do." Cole quickly created a foolproof escape from any involvement in Sarah's new pet project.

"So nice to meet you, Sarah," Kelly offered as Cole got in the car. "See you soon."

The car seemed to start and back out at the same moment. Cole waved, arm out the window, and called to Sarah as the car became parallel with the sidewalk. "You're the best, Sarah! Thanks again."

"Would you like some help sorting?" Kelly asked as Cole carried the box of notebooks and files up the stairs on the porch.

"That would be great. You really want to?"

"Of course. How do we start?"

"How about by date?" Cole set the box on his work table in the living room. "I suppose by decade to start with."

"This sounds like a big pot of coffee. Mocha, mocha dear?"

"Sounds great."

An hour or so later, there were four stacks of little black leather notebooks on the table.

"It would seem the good doctor either died or retired in the forties. I guess I'll start with this stack. They are from the 1890s. That's incredible."

Cole opened the first notebook and began to flip pages. Kelly disappeared into the kitchen.

The handwriting was crisp and reasonably easy to read. Page after page, the doctor made notations and observations on the house calls he made. From time to time, Cole chuckled at the candor of Dr. Lambert's comments.

Lazy, slovenly, and looking for an excuse not to go to work. Faker. Nothing wrong here that a good bowel movement wouldn't cure. Glutton. Secret drinker.

It was the entries of a far more serious nature that gave Cole pause.

Cancer, won't be long. No hope. Syphilis, must tell Mrs. Barren, God bless her. Beyond my ability to treat.

The notes and comments gave Cole an insight into the heart of the man. After 1895, he jumped around a bit to eliminate notebooks. The forties all ended up back in the box. As did most of the thirties. He returned to the 1890s after lunch.

Cole used Post-it notes to mark pages that made reference to the Sage children. Dr. Lambert was called out when Harriet Sage miscarried a child in the spring of 1898. *She won't be carrying a child again* was written next to her name.

The next book made no references to the Sage family. Cole was about to quit for the day when a familiar name appeared in the notebook.

July 30, 1899

Message from George Sage requesting a home visit after nine pm. Family quite upset. I was sent upstairs with Mrs. Sage to their daughter Effie's room.

Effie is at least three months pregnant. She refused to name the father in front of her mother. Chester Palmer is his name. He's a teller at the bank. It seems he took advantage of her after a church social. They were seeing each other in secret.

Cole stared at the page. *Why was there nothing in the journals about this?* he thought. *Did they abort the child? No, that simply wasn't done.*

With renewed vigor, he continued reading.

November 23, 1899

My monthly visit to the Sage home. Effie looks pale. She has not seen daylight since July. She seems to be progressing nicely.

George and Harriet have hatched up a plan. Not sure how it will work. We'll see.

There was a one-line entry in December: Sage Visit 9 PM.

"Kelly! Got a second?" Cole called out.

"Be right there."

Kelly came into the room and took a seat on the sofa.

"I found something," Cole said dryly. "It seems Effie had a child."

"Effie, the old maid school teacher? Really? Boy or girl?"

"I don't know yet. Still reading, but I kind of wanted you around when I find out. I have a very strange feeling this won't end well."

Cole picked up the notebook on top of the 1900 stack. "Listen. January 29, 1900. Called to the Sage house, 3 AM. Effie bleeding. It is a month too early. I sent her to her bed for the rest of her time." Cole looked up. "She's been confined to the house since July. So, it seems she will have the baby in secret."

"Well, she certainly couldn't walk around town with a big belly. The whole town would know. Can you imagine the scandal? They, or she, would have to leave town. Who's the father? Do we know?"

"A guy who works at the bank. There has been no other mention of him. Of course, the doctor would be involved in that, wouldn't he?"

"Probably not. Keep reading," Kelly urged.

Cole ran his finger across several pages, then stopped dead. He looked up at Kelly.

"What is it?"

"February 15, 1900. 5:45 am. Effie Sage give birth to a fine baby boy." Cole stopped reading. "Kelly, that is my grandfather George Sage's birthday. Effie wasn't his sister – she was his mother! Listen to this. 'George Sage Sr. offered me one hundred dollars to falsify the birth certificate to show George and Harriet as the parents of the child. I told him to go to hell with his money. I said I would do it for Effie and nothing else. The bank teller has skipped town.'"

Cole laid the notebook gently on the table.

Since Cole took over the front room for writing, Kelly resigned herself to the stacks of journals on every flat service. The floor was frequently scattered with color-coded three by five cards, part of Cole's odd system of outlining and keeping track of quotes, dates, and thoughts that came to him while he was writing. She was allowed to discard the ones that were torn in two, even though on occasion Cole scrambled to the garbage can to try and retrieve some morsel of information he was rethinking.

Occasionally, Kelly heard a loud outburst of "Stupid machine!" and "Sage, you idiot!" Coming from the front room. These unnatural, sudden releases of frustration usually translated into his little finger hitting the cap lock on his keyboard and his random hitting of keys that reset margins, line spacing, or any number of format settings.

For the most part, though, Kelly knew when Cole went to the living room, it was a time to read, write and revise. A quiet would fall over the house, and she would find a noiseless activity to occupy her time. She tried to stay close in case his frustration with the computer grew to his inability to spell a word close enough for the Spell Check to be recognized and make suggested corrections.

She also proved a valuable resource when he was stumped for the name of an object like "that thingy that goes on the end of a stick to get cobwebs from the corners of the ceiling." Sometimes he would call out with a partial request, only to say, "I got it" before he finished. The process fascinated Kelly, and she was always eager to read the day's progress.

This afternoon, however, he was unusually quiet. She moved past the door an hour in to find him lying on the sofa with a yellow three by five card in his hand. He was so focused on it, he didn't notice her bringing him a cup of coffee. On the floor next to him was a green file card.

October 1, 1912 - I have three sisters and two brothers. I am told I had two more sisters and a brother but they died before I was born. I am the baby of the family as I am so often reminded, and I am so, by some twenty-four years. All my brothers and sisters are married except for Effie who is the oldest. She has the room next to mine. Sometimes I can hear her crying at night. I would like to see what the matter is but I would not know what to say.

* * *

"Erin, it's Dad."

"Is everything OK? You sound funny."

"Yeah, fine. I just needed to hear your voice."

"Liar, there is something wrong. What is it?" Erin tried to ease the tension in the call.

"You got me." Cole chuckled half-heartedly. "I need to ask you something. Please be honest with me."

"Of course, Dad. I would never lie to you." Erin sensed a seriousness in Cole's voice.

"When you found out I was your father," Cole paused for a long moment, "did it matter? What I mean is, you were brought up to believe one thing, and it turned out to be something else, something false, something unexpected. What was that like?"

"Well," Erin gathered her thoughts. "At first I was angry with Mom. That passed quickly. To tell you the truth from my heart of hearts? I always wished it were you. I mean, I thought it might be. You see, the way Mom talked about you, how she kept little clippings and things. The way her eyes would sparkle when she told a Cole story, I knew you were more than just an old flame. The way she looked at me when she would tell one of those stories from when you were young, she was seeing herself somehow. I know that now. What's this about, Dad?"

"A woman donated some notebooks that belonged to a doctor here in Orvin. He died in the forties sometime. He was the only doctor in town. He was the Sage family doctor. The notebooks were comments and a record of house calls. They actually made those back then!" Cole chuckled. "Anyway, it seems my great aunt is actually my great-grandmother. Effie Sage, who we thought never married and died of influenza, was actually my grandfather George Sage's mother."

"Really? That is…"

"Yeah, I was speechless, too. The thing that bothered me, bothers me, is that he never knew his beloved sister was actually his mother. Then I thought of you. What if your mom died without us reconnecting? I could have died never knowing you. You could have lived your whole life thinking some fictional oilman was your father. Worst of all, Ellie would have died with a lie on her heart. I don't know, it just kind of hit me upside the head."

"Wow. Who would have thought a family history could yield so many secrets? I guess it's all part of God's master plan somehow. So who was the father?"

"A guy named Chester Palmer. He worked at her father's bank," Cole said thoughtfully. "I have to do some digging." Cole paused. The name Palmer rang bells hard, but he couldn't place it at the moment.

"Dad?"

"Sorry, the name Palmer suddenly rang a bell. I hope I didn't interrupt anything. I don't know why, but I just needed to talk to you first. Silly, isn't it?"

"I don't think so. We are blood, you, me and Jenny. We thought for a long time we were the end of the line. With little Cole, there's four of us! The thing is, now there is the possibility of more people we are related to. Kind of exciting, don't you think?"

"I hadn't really thought of it like that. I guess I was so focused on Effie. Thanks, kiddo. As always, you see the best side of things. Talk later."

"Love you. Say hi to Kelly."

Chapter 25

Cole spent most of the morning on the front porch with his laptop. The warm sun felt good on his legs, and the wind in the alfalfa blew sweet across the yard. Kelly ran to town for groceries, and Randy was at the computer shop. A wave of melancholy swept over Cole. He loved the farm. He loved the family, and the memories it represented. Now it was to be taken away.

This time, his kind-heartedness came around to bite him. The excitement of expanding his family, finding more blood relatives, caused him to let down his normally guarded nature. At the moment, it seemed so natural.

He thought of the road his life had taken. He pondered what would have happened if Ellie died without reaching out to him. He would have certainly been fired upon Mick Brennan's death. The old editor was all that stood between him and…Cole looked out at the green field waving across the street…

And what? he thought.

Life has such a strange way of happening while we are trudging through meaningless days. His world was renewed, he was reborn, his career revitalized, and his whole trajectory shifted. One phone call, one small, pink message slip changed everything.

Erin, Ben, Jenny, and now little Cole would have lived their lives without him. All the love that has filled his life over the past few years, he would never have known. Then there was Kelly.

More than anything, she reshaped his world. He loved her with all his heart. He knew though that, deep down, there was a small corner that when he looked for it, was the memory, caress, and soul-bond left by Ellie. Nothing could ever replace what she was to him. Still, Kelly now filled his days with constant joy and companionship. As he faced growing older, he knew with the grace of God she would be there until he breathed his last.

The porch he sat on was a symbol of the past and a promise of the future. Wood, plaster, paint, and stability that will stand another hundred years. The souls of his grandfather, his great love Mattie, and their children seemed to smile with the good times this house held. Never once since he came to know this place has the pain, terror, and death it saw been a part of his life. To see Lottie, the little girl born here, being reunited with the spirit of the farm and the mother she barely knew gave Cole a deep satisfaction. Her last days were spent knowing she was home, a real home, inhabited by her biological parents. Though never bound by the legal bonds of marriage, their love before God and their children was as sacred and divine as any vowed in a church.

For a moment, his mind caressed the fond memories of discovering his family in the pages of the old journals. Within a week or two, those feelings of pride, the understanding of the prejudice and hatred that brought separation and death to this farm, would be a book. A book he hoped his small sliver of fame would put that story into the hands of people across America. A book he hoped would shine a light on the ignorance and ungodly resentment people carry for those they don't know or understand. A book he hoped would show that below the melanin of the cells we call skin, we are all human beings with the same love of our mates, children and the place we call home.

From the corner of his thoughts came the vision of a person he never met who could take it all away, an ugly, wicked old woman dressed in grey, holding out her empty palm. A faint smile crossed his lips at the image his disdain painted. The image of a woman who for personal gain would rip this farm from the family that cherished it and honored its former occupants. Cole's heart sank at the thought of the farm being sold, or worse, lived in by a person or people who held no knowledge of the Sage family of Orvin, Oklahoma.

From somewhere beyond his musings, a buzzing, humming sound interrupted his thoughts. Cole reached for his phone.

"Good afternoon," Tom Harris said.

"That tone sounds as if it won't be much longer," Cole replied.

"Bad night. Three-year-old took a 9mm bullet to the head while asleep on the couch at her grandmother's house. Kind of set the tone for the day ahead. You know, Cole, this is not what I signed up for. We've seen some evil people do some very evil deeds, but this wholesale slaughter, this war of gang on gang, black on black, teen on teen, and the carnage night after night is starting to wear me down."

"We are dinosaurs, my friend. Inhabitants of a world that no longer exists. That became very clear to me when I returned to college as an instructor. Maybe it's time to think about getting out. How many years do you have in?"

"Twenty-eight. Three more than I need to get my pension."

"Take it. Do it on a high note. You're in one piece, your mind is fairly intact." Cole chuckled. "The kids are grown, no more braces or college. It's time for you and your lovely bride to see Costa Rica like you've always talked about." Cole's sincerity surprised his friend.

"You all right? You're not dying or anything, are ya? You'd tell me if you had cancer or some other God-awful thing, right?" Harris wasn't used to such heart-to-heart communication.

"I'm fine. Honest. I was just sitting here thinking about this little farm, the people who lived and loved here. It just made me think how quick it can all be taken away."

"Well, that's kind of why I called."

"You find something on my long lost cousin?" Cole asked, not sure what to expect and bracing himself.

"They're a bad lot, Cole. The Jenkins clan was a whole basket of bad eggs. Patricia is the last of the clan, as far as I can tell. Her dad was knifed to death while doing time at Joliet. Going back two generations, there are bank robbers, loan sharks, strong arm robbery, auto theft, extortion, pandering, assault with deadly weapons, attempted murder, you name it, somebody in the family had it on their rap sheet.

"Dear, sweet Patty is a peach. Check fraud, shoplifting, public drunkenness, assaulting a police officer, battery, resisting arrest, giving false testimony, failure to identify, and the ever-popular prostitution. Get the idea? There's a lot more, but why impugn the lady's reputation?

"I'm sorry to be the bearer of bad news. Are you sure that DNA test got it right? This is more of a cesspool than a gene pool."

"What is it they say? Nurture, environment, and association? Looks like it's stronger than good genes. So, she saw an opportunity and went for it. Makes you wonder how she paid for a lawyer," Cole questioned.

"Odds are she found some storefront shyster who would wait until the place sells," Harris offered. "On a hopefully more pleasant note, how is married life?" Harris asked, changing the subject.

"It is even better than I expected. Kelly seems to understand all my faults and loves me anyway."

"So, mental illness runs in her family?" The time for serious conversation had come to an end.

"It seems from your report, my family is the one missing the honesty and sanity gene." Cole paused. "Hey, Tom, think about what I said. Enough is enough. The lawsuit aside, it feels pretty good not to have to show up somewhere every morning. I have never felt so free. Let the new guys deal with the madness."

"Not to give you too much credit for intelligent suggestions, but I have been thinking the same thing. Thanks, buddy, we'll talk later."

"See ya."

Cole hit *end call* as he looked at the name and number on the face of his phone. Then he saw his own reflection. Who was that old fart in the glass? he wondered. Cole shook his head.

The quick *honk-honk* of Kelly's BMW coming up the drive was a welcome sound. Before Cole could stand to greet her, his phone rang. It was from Palmer Lumber Company. Palmer!

He thought, *That's why that name rang a bell.*

"Hello?" Cole wasn't sure of the who or why he was getting the call.

"Sage?" The voice was forceful and not the least bit friendly.

"Who is this?" Cole demanded.

"Barry Palmer. Is my -"

"How'd you get this number?" Cole interrupted. He was in no mood to be growled at.

"Off an invoice. Is my daughter there?"

"Your daughter? Why would you call *me* to find *your* daughter?"

"She said she was going with that computer guy to your house for dinner."

"It's one-thirty. That's a bit early for dinner, don't you think? Is there a problem?"

"She isn't answering her phone."

"And?"

"And I don't know where she is."

The tone of the conversation was not one of concern. Cole wasn't sure what Palmer's point was in calling him.

"Did you call Randy? She is his girlfriend, not mine."

"Who?"

"The computer guy."

"He is most certainly not her boyfriend. She has no boyfriend," Palmer insisted.

"Seems to me they have been dating a while." Cole hesitated but pressed on. "Is there something you need? I mean, is there a message or…?"

"I need to know where she is. She left at lunch and hasn't returned."

"What time was that?" Cole was curious.

"Noon. When else would you go to lunch?"

"You seem awfully hot under the collar over your own daughter being a half-hour late coming back from lunch."

"She doesn't need to be lollygagging around with some repairman."

Cole could feel his anger rising. He turned to face Kelly as she got to the top of the steps.

"What's wrong?" she asked, seeing his agitated state.

Cole waved his hand and smiled. "How old is she?"

"Twenty-two. What does that matter to you?"

"It doesn't, and that's the point. She's an adult. She has a boyfriend, and they are probably looking across a table at each other and have lost track of time. Did you call the shop? A couple days ago they had lunch there."

"And just how would I get that number?" Palmer demanded harshly.

"Same way you got mine. He repaired your computer. Get the tag. Call directory assistance for computer repair. Is this an emergency?"

"Well, not an emergency. I just need to know where my daughter is."

"I would bet a hundred bucks she's with Randy, a fine young man with a growing business and a close associate of mine for almost five years. He is honest, honorable, trustworthy, a total gentleman and quite smitten by your lovely daughter, who I had the pleasure of meeting. I suggest you let her be an adult, and unless she punches in and out, which wouldn't surprise me a bit, let her enjoy this beautiful afternoon." Cole could hear Palmer huffing. "If there isn't something that is actually important, I have things to do."

"I don't know who you think -"

Cole hit the end call button and then blocked the number.

"What on Earth was that all about?" Kelly asked.

"It was Barry Palmer, Brooke's dad, calling to see if she was here."

"Why would she be here?"

"This guy is obviously some kind of control freak. She's a half-hour late getting back from lunch, and he's mad, wants to know where she is."

"She's probably with Randy."

"Evidently, she is too good to be lollygagging around town with a repairman."

"He said that?"

Cole laughed. "That poor kid. I can't imagine dealing with that kind of parent."

"Poor Randy. No wonder she has self-image issues. This really concerns me. It is his first real love, and this dad sounds like he will be nothing but trouble in their relationship."

"I can't imagine him taking any crap off him," Cole said, showing pride in Randy's backbone.

"Not at the threat of losing Brooke. No matter how big a jerk he is, he's still her dad." Kelly's concern seemed to be heartfelt.

"Gee, seems I missed a lot not raising a kid," Cole said, realizing he was out of his circle of experience.

"Ben had a girlfriend in high school whose mother was a controlling, jealous hellcat. The girl was the sweetest thing you'd ever want to meet, but she was so emotionally abused, he would actually flinch if you said her name too loud. We're loud, happy and friendly; that just didn't work for her."

"So what happened?"

"They went their separate ways when Ben got sick of the mother. Last thing I remember hearing is that she got into drugs. Self-medication. It isn't all just for the fun of the high, you know."

"How'd you get so smart?" Cole asked with a loving smile.

"Same way you did. I pay attention. Remember this little talk when you are around her. It is a hard life for a kid. She needs to see normal relationships."

"You think I can do normal?" Cole quipped.

"No, but you can do almost funny."

Cole took the bag of groceries from Kelly, and they went into the house in silence.

Chapter 26

"So what time does this shindig get started?" Cole asked, flipping a page on the new TIME magazine.

"Six. Randy will be here at five-fifteen. He said to fire up the barbecue." Kelly was at the sink rinsing a head of lettuce.

"He's not picking her up?" Cole questioned.

"She told him it would be better if she drove out. You know, Cole, that whole thing with her father really worries me. What if they should get married? What then? Is he going to make their lives miserable?"

"I hope not. Randy has a lot of talent. He can get a job anywhere. Great resume and a brilliant letter of recommendation, if I do say so myself. They might just have to put some distance between them."

"You wrote him a letter of recommendation?"

"Well, not yet, but I could."

"I've been thinking."

"Uh oh," Cole teased.

"If Brooke asks to help with the dishes or dessert or something, I've been thinking maybe I could have a little girl-to-girl chat with her."

"Bad idea. You've never met the girl. That would be prying or nosey or something you don't need to be."

"I'll just go with the flow and see what happens."

"If you screw this up or scare her off, you will drive a whale-sized wedge between us and Randy. I think your lovely nose should stay out of it."

"You are such a -" Her thought was interrupted by the ringing of the phone. "Hello. Hi, Georgia! Yep, right here, hold on."

Kelly handed Cole the phone.

"Hi, Georgia! What's goin' on?"

"I have a fella here who was asking about you. Not quite sure how he made the connection. People talk, I guess. Anyway, got a minute? He's from the local paper."

"Sure, put him on."

"Mr. Sage, my name is Ed Abernathy. I own the Orvin Observer. How you doin' today?"

"Fine. What can I do for you?"

"I was wondering if I could get together with you for a few minutes."

"I'm afraid I'm tied up today. We have company coming later, lots to do. I have a couple of minutes now. What can I help you with?"

"I really hoped we could get together."

"I'm finishing work on a book I'm writing, and I am totally focusing on that. Can we just talk now? While I'm waiting for the company?"

"I guess I can tell you what I need on the phone. Come October, I will be eighty years old. I'm thinkin' it may be time for me to slow down a bit." He paused for a response. When none was forthcoming, he continued. "I've been doing some research on you, Mr. Sage."

"I'm in trouble now."

"Looks to me that you have been runnin' with the big dogs for most of your career. You, sir, are a newspaper man's newspaperman."

"I have had a wonderful time at it, too. I get the feeling you are buttering me up."

"They were right; you're a sharp fella. I have a proposition for you, Mr. Sage." Abernathy's voice turned matter-of-fact and serious.

"No," Cole said, without a hint of humor.

"Hear me out, if you will?" Abernathy said, with more than a hint of desperation.

"Mr. Abernathy, you seem like a news dog of the old school, the kind of newspaperman they don't make anymore. I will be happy to hear you out, but I'm afraid my answer will be the same."

"I have spent the last fifty years as editor and publisher of our little paper. When I started out, we were a daily. Then we went to five days a week. Now we are a weekly. I lost my son to the Vietnam War and my wife two years ago to Alzheimer's. My daughter lives in Omaha. Last time I saw her, George W. was president. I do not want to lose my soul along with my heart, sir."

"I'm listening." Cole softened.

"I have all I need to get by. House is paid for, and Social Security will keep me in groceries and cigars." Abernathy chuckled. "The paper makes a decent income. What with grocery stores fighting each other for customers, tire shops, chiropractors and the like make up the rest of the ad sales. Regular as clockwork. We dropped the classified stuff a while back. eBay, Craigslist, and Facebook killed those. They were a pain in the ass anyway. The features and news stories come from the news services, along with anything I feel needs tellin' or sayin'."

"I'm really not lookin' for a job," Cole interjected.

"Oh, I'm not offering you a job! No, sir. I want to give you the paper. I figure you have black newspaper ink in your veins, and that's something you just don't outlive. I will step aside, you can write all the copy you want. Janell runs all the advertising and billing. Old Tom, the printer, is good for at least another ten years, and he is almost on autopilot. We are a finely tuned operation, Mr. Sage. All we need is somebody younger, smarter, and fresher to write and clip the copy. What do you say?"

"Mr. Abernathy, I am seldom at a loss for words, but you have left me speechless. This is probably the most generous offer I have ever been given."

"It's not generous at all. As a matter of fact, it is very selfish. I want the paper to go on as long as it is able. I want to die knowing the love of my life is alive and well. Until I heard you'd come to town, I had resigned to dying at my desk. I know my mind isn't what it used to be, and I think the lack of snap in the copy shows it. That, and folks keep coming in with misquotes and names circled in red." Abernathy laughed sadly.

"You know, I've been writing a book, and that has really grabbed all my spare time. I have a couple more I intend to do as well. So…"

"No need to worry about that! You can work the paper a couple of days a week, three tops, and still have time to do whatever else your heart desires. What have you got to lose? You'll have nothing invested. After I'm gone, hell, burn it to the ground if you want. I just can't bear to see it die before I do."

"Look, I am flattered and honored you would even consider me to take over your paper, but -"

"No need to answer right now. I know it's not to be entered into lightly. Take a few days, a week, as long as you need. But think it over, please. I really see you as the answer to my prayers." The old newspaperman's voice cracked with emotion.

"All right, I will talk it over with my wife. That's the way we do things around here. I'll get back to you. Thanks again."

"You won't be sorry."

"All right. We'll see." Cole pushed the *off* button on the handset. He closed the TIME and stood. "That was weird," he said, moving over to the sink to face Kelly.

"What's that?"

"Georgia put a guy on the phone who owns the Orvin paper."

"Orvin has a paper?" Kelly asked, letting slip a little condescension.

"Seems so. It's a weekly. Anyway, he offered to give it to me."

"What?"

"Yeah, he said he was eighty or was going to be, and wanted to retire. He doesn't want to close it down and said he would give it to me if I would run it at least until he dies."

"I told him I would talk to my wife."

"You have always wanted to be an editor!" Kelly said excitedly. "Can you do it? I mean, run the whole thing?"

"He says he has people to do everything except write copy, you know, the news and features."

"Are you going to do it?"

"Do you want me to?" Cole asked, a bit surprised at her reaction.

"It's your decision. I can't think of a reason for you not to if you want."

"I can think of several. One, what if we lose this place? Two, I kind of like being an author. Three, I really like not have any deadlines or schedules. Four—"

"OK, I get it. But what about the excitement of owning and operating your own paper?"

"Well, I always kind of figured I would end up the editor of a paper. That would be my last hurrah. It really thrills me that it might happen, but it kind of seems like I would be going out with a whimper, not a bang. I mean, it only comes out once a week. I don't know quite what to think."

"To be continued. Here's Randy." Kelly pointed.

Cole turned to see Randy's car coming up the drive.

A while later, Randy was admiring the coals in the barbecue grill. "Almost ready," he said to Cole.

"I'm starving. When is Brooke going to get here?"

Randy pulled his phone from his shirt pocket. "Any minute now."

"I'll go check on Kelly. Maybe there is something I can sneak to take the edge off my growling stomach."

Cole made his way into the house and found the front door standing open. Kelly was nowhere to be seen. As he approached the front door, he spotted a yellow VW Bug convertible in the drive parked behind Randy's car. Kelly and Brooke stood on the porch, chatting away.

"Welcome!" Cole said from the doorway.

"Hi," Brooke said with a smile.

"We've just been chatting." Kelly smiled. "How are the coals coming?"

"Ready to go. The chef is just about to put the steaks on. Just waiting for the guest of honor."

"Then let's get this party started." Kelly ushered Brooke through the door.

Out the back porch, Brooke saw Randy and quickened her step, leaving Cole and Kelly standing in the kitchen. She crossed the yard where Randy stood minding the grill. They couldn't hear, but they could see her kiss Randy on the cheek and give him a hug.

"This *is* promising," Kelly said.

"Should I take him the steaks?"

"Give them a moment," Kelly instructed.

The dinner was wonderful. The steaks were perfect, and everyone was stuffed. When Kelly stood to clear the table, Brooke jumped up and offered to help. Kelly winked at Cole. All was going according to plan.

With the water running and the plates stacked, Brooke spoke first. "Wash or dry?"

"Oh no, you're our guest. I can do them later. I'll just put them to soak," Kelly replied.

"OK, I'll wash," Brooke said brightly.

"You are a doll. Thanks." Kelly handed Brooke an apron.

"Randy said you guys have only been married a little while."

"Coming up on three months," Kelly said.

"That is so cool. I wish my dad would remarry."

"How long has your mom been gone, if you don't mind me asking?" Kelly saw her chance and took it.

"She died when I was in the third grade."

"That's been a few years, then. Has he seen anyone?"

"Oh, gosh, no!" Brooke said emphatically. "He has never, I mean, he won't…"

"I get it. So it's just the two of you."

"Yep, just us," Brooke said. Her tone changed to a mix of sadness and anger.

"You don't sound so happy about it."

Brooke handed Kelly a rinsed plate. "Randy hasn't told you about my dad, then."

"Is there a problem?" Kelly asked softly.

"I think he would have rather I died than my mom. We don't get along. He is smothering me to death." Brooke turned from the sink.

Kelly waited a long moment before she spoke. "You want to talk about it?"

"I have no friends. He drove them all off years ago. He demands to know where I am every minute of the day. He was creepy about it. My friends, even as junior highers, tired of it in a hurry. I was late coming back from lunch the other day with Randy, and he yelled at me for ten minutes." She wiped her cheeks with the backs of her hands. "Randy is so sweet about it. I can't believe he hasn't dumped me. What kind of girl at my age lets her dad push her around like that? Before our first date, we got into such an argument about me going out with a 'repairman', I ran from the house and Randy found me walking up the street two blocks from my house."

"Why do you think he's trying to keep such a tight grip on you?"

"Who would do the laundry, cook and clean the house? He's helpless." Brooke's anger was rising, and her voice showed her frustration. "It would be different if he was nice to me, but he treats his workers better than me."

"Have you thought about moving out? Find a little place of your own?"

"Since I was twelve! Instead of paying me, though, like a real employee, he gives me an allowance. Enough for clothes and personal items. He paid for my car, the insurance and I use a company gas card. He says I don't need anymore. If I buy too much gas, he wants to know where I've been going to use so much gas. So I have barely enough for a hamburger, let alone an apartment."

Kelly smiled, not quite sure how to continue. "I'm so sorry. Is there anything we can do to help?"

"Don't get sick of me coming over!" Brooke laughed, trying to take the focus off her father. "Don't you just love how Randy took over the barbecue? I bet Cole is the one who usually does it."

"He is a real sweet guy. He and Cole have a real special relationship. But I am the grill master around here." They both laughed.

"Please don't tell Cole about all this. I really want him to like me."

"No worries there. He thinks you are wonderful."

"Oh, stop. I know I don't offer much. I've been so sheltered, I really never have much to say."

"There is nothing wrong with that. I talk too much!"

"What are you two conspiring about?" Randy stood at the door into the kitchen.

"How to get you to bring Brooke over more often." Kelly winked at Randy, and his cheeks flushed with color. "I'll finish up in here. You guys go enjoy the sunset."

"Hey, is this a private party, or is anyone invited?" Cole asked, joining them in the room.

"Here, you dry," Kelly said, throwing Cole a kitchen towel. "They are going out to watch the sun go down.

"Well, Mata Hari," Cole said after Randy and Brooke went outside. "What did you find out?"

"I can't tell you. But I think she is pretty scared and angry at the treatment she has received growing up. A lot of resentment. But I believe our boy there will be just the thing to set her free." Kelly looked out the back window.

Randy's arm was around Brooke's shoulder as they rocked gently in the yard swing.

"I think she will be just fine." Kelly leaned over and kissed Cole on the cheek. "Now let's get these dishes done!"

Chapter 27

"How about lunch on the front porch?" Kelly called to Cole who sat staring at the computer monitor.

"Yes, please! I'm about to nod out." Cole responded, standing and stretching.

"Get the door," Kelly called as she approached the front door with a large tray.

Since they moved in, they bought a small, four place table and placed it on the front porch. Kelly and Cole found themselves eating lunch, and even dinner, outside. In the six weeks since they arrived, they have hardly missed at least one meal a day outside. Cole liked to use it for his morning mocha and read *The Oklahoman*, the state's largest daily paper. Kelly held tightly onto the tradition of writing notes and letters to family and friends. Pen in hand, she found the fresh air at the little table a wonderful afternoon respite.

Up the road, Cole watched a gold four-door Lincoln Continental coming their way. It drew his eye because apart from its enormous 1970s size, it moved like a fat man through a bake sale, slow and steady.

"Look at that, somebody with a car older than mine!" Cole joked.

"They're either a hundred years old or looking for someone," Kelly said, watching the snail-like progress as she set the tray on the table.

Cole went right to work on his bowl of fruit as he continued to watch the car. "They're looking for somebody all right, and it looks like it's us," Cole exclaimed as the car slowly turned in the driveway.

The huge car pulled up in front of the house at an odd angle, dwarfing Kelly's BMW. The windows were all tinted except the front; even so, Cole couldn't see the driver due to the reflection on the windshield.

The wide back door swung open, and Cole looked over at Kelly with a quizzical look. A shiny cowboy boot hit the gravel. A moment later, a pudgy hand grasped the top of the door. Cole heard a low groan, and the top of a gray John B. Stetson hat appeared above the door.

"Cole?" Kelly said, with a hint of a giggle in her voice.

"Mr. Sage, what a lovely place you have here! Mrs. Sage, so nice to finally get a chance to make your acquaintance." Standing at the gate at the end of the sidewalk was C.W. Langhorne. He stood, feet wide apart, hands on his wide hips, in a finely tailored Western-style suit, taking in the view of the house, the porch, and Cole and Kelly looking back at him in amazement.

Cole stood to his feet and called with an enthusiastic greeting as he moved toward the gate, "Mr. Langhorne! What a surprise! What brings you to Orvin?"

"An important client, of course." Langhorne extended his hand.

"Please, come in." Cole took a step away from the gate. "What about your driver? Would he like to come in, too? Kind of warm today."

"That would be my receptionist."

"Well, by all means, we'll invite her in." Cole jogged around to the driver's side of the car. "Hey, there! Please come in. You'll smother out here."

"Are you sure?" the receptionist asked, not wanting to break some office protocol.

"It is a long drive, and I bet a stretch of the legs, a powder room, and a tall glass of lemonade would do you a world of good." Cole smiled at the way he fell into Langhorne's pattern of speech in welcome. He opened the heavy door.

"That is very kind, Mr. Sage. I accept!"

Cole turned just in time to see Langhorne make his way up the front steps to the porch. It was like watching Humpty Dumpty mount the wall. As he reached the top step, Langhorne removed his cowboy hat, placed it over his heart and said, "It is a delight to meet you at long last, Mrs. Sage."

Kelly crossed the porch from where she stood and offered her hand to Langhorne. "The pleasure is all mine, but please call me Kelly."

Langhorne moved forward, allowing for his driver-receptionist room on the porch.

"And this is?" Kelly inquired.

"I don't think I have ever known your name," Cole added from the top step in the sudden revelation.

"Loreena. How do you do?" the receptionist said pleasantly.

"So nice to meet both of you. I've heard so much about you from Cole. Can I offer you some lunch? We just sat down, and there is plenty for all of us."

"That would be awfully nice of you, but we certainly wouldn't want to put you to any bother," Langhorne replied.

"No bother at all. I'll be back in a minute. I'll just grab some plates and a couple of glasses. Have a seat." Kelly pointed to the four chairs at the end of the porch.

"I have a feeling your drive out here is either because you've got good news or something really bad. If you would hold off until my wife gets back, I would appreciate it. In the meantime, we can just enjoy the lovely day and each other's company."

"That we shall. You know, the last time I was here was...good gracious, I don't know, but in any case, it certainly didn't look like this! You have done wonders with the place, Mr. Sage."

"Since we are out of the office, on my front porch about to have lunch, why don't you call me Cole? I think we have reached the stage in our relationship where we are farther from attorney-client and closer to friends."

"I am honored that you would see me as such, I truly am." The lawyer seemed to be genuinely moved by Cole's gesture. "I am not one to boast a long list of friends."

Cole looked at Loreena, and she was smiling and looking at her boss in a most admiring way.

"Here we are!" Kelly said, rejoining the group. As she placed the plates and glasses filled with ice in front of her guests, she continued. "This is such a pleasant surprise. We don't get much company. We know so few people here."

"So what's the news?"

"Let them settle a bit and have a bite. There's plenty of time for business," Kelly interjected.

"Thank you, Miss Kelly. I still feel like I'm flying down the highway." Langhorne nodded.

"So, how long have you worked for Mr. Langhorne?" Kelly asked Loreena.

"Truth be told, Miss Kelly, Loreena is my wife of some thirty-six years," Langhorne explained before Loreena could respond.

"Seven," Loreena said shyly.

"This visit is just full of news," Cole said in total surprise.

"I sense a story here," Kelly said in anticipation. "Tell all, where'd you meet?"

"We met at the U of O. I was in my second year, Claude was a senior."

"Another mystery solved," Cole exclaimed.

Claude Langhorne cleared his throat uncomfortably.

"We were in the library. A boy from one of my classes was making unwanted advances. He made, what you might call, a sexually inappropriate comment. Claudie was at the next table and heard the rude boy and came to my rescue. From that moment on, he has been my knight in shining armor."

"I've got to tell you, I am amazed at how you keep your private and personal life so completely separate."

"That, my friend, is in part the key to our three-decade longevity. We decided early in my practice that another woman around eight hours a day might, well…never put cake in front of a fat man. Yield not to temptation. So, I hired the prettiest girl I ever saw, and she has been my right arm ever since." Langhorne took a long sip of his lemonade.

"He is so charming. Don't you just love his humility?" Loreena giggled like a school girl.

Cole chuckled along, not knowing if she was joking or being serious.

"Now, your turn!" Loreena said, shifting the attention from herself. "Where did y'all meet?"

"You want to explain, or should I?"

"I want to hear your version," Cole answered.

"Cole's daughter, Erin, is my son Ben's wife. In an effort to create closer family ties, I invited him to a dinner party I was having. He had just moved to San Francisco, and I thought it would be nice."

"Were you dee-vorced, Cole? If I may be so bold," Loreena inquired.

"She has deceased," Kelly answered before Cole could speak. "My husband passed away as well, so we were both alone."

Cole looked at Kelly with deep love and admiration. He never imagined she would suggest Ellie had even been his wife. Her graciousness and understanding of Cole's love for the woman who filled his life for so many years of separation, misunderstanding, and longing was perhaps the most gracious gift he was ever given.

"What a beautiful thing," Loreena gushed.

"You can't even imagine," Cole said, reaching over and taking Kelly's hand.

His plate was soon empty, and Kelly filled Langhorne's empty glass. "I know my husband is about to implode waiting for the news you've brought us. Mr. Langhorne, would like to share your news?"

"Yes, dear lady, it would be my pleasure." Langhorne sat a little straighter in his chair. "The bottom line is, the case against you has been dropped. The story of how we arrived at that very pleasant occurrence is the thing of great mystery stories." Langhorne smiled wisely, like an actor about to perform a marvelous soliloquy. "It seems Patricia Maria Jenkins has been dead these eighteen years. The woman who lived as Ms. Jenkins assumed her identity and, in turn, brought suit against you was an imposter.

"Her name is Carolyn Collins. She and Ms. Jenkins attended the same high school. Though never friends, or as far as we can ascertain, they indeed didn't even know each other. There was a striking resemblance between the two. Names, places, and various incidences of their community needn't be learned or memorized because Collins lived a parallel existence. That is to say, same junior high, high school, but a completely different set of friends and acquaintances. Kind of a devil and angel in the same world.

"The real difference is that your real relative succumbed to a fast-spreading form of cancer at thirty-nine. Collins, herself no stranger to the law, saw an opportunity to escape her downward spiral of drugs and took it. According to the police, she actually carried Patty's obituary in her wallet.

"When she appeared at her old high school requesting a transcript, the resemblance, and with the additional years, no one questioned her. When she told the office ladies it was for admittance to the local community college, the office ladies were too thrilled to ask for ID. Indeed, one of the younger secretaries went so far as to say she remembered her, or rather, your cousin. She obviously didn't do the math. With the Social Security number printed on the transcript, date of birth, and location, she applied for a driver's license. She moved to a different community where no one knew her, and the rest was fairly easy.

"She, to her credit, did attend the college, went to AA and Narcotics Anonymous meetings and for a time walked the straight and narrow. But as is the case so many times, she met a man who reintroduced her to the world of drugs and drink. Crimes of various kinds followed. He was caught, convicted and sent to prison. For Ms. Collins, now firmly established as Ms. Jenkins, it was too late to turn back."

"So she lived the life of Patty Jenkins for how long?" Kelly asked.

"Near as we can tell, close to twenty years. To her mind, she *was* Patricia Jenkins."

"But what about the DNA?" Cole interrupted.

"Now that is a bit of luck. *Tree of Life* was quite cooperative when it came to Patricia Jenkin's genealogical work. That is after I became a member." Langhorne smiled wryly. "According to her profile, the real Patty did a DNA test shortly after her diagnosis. To her credit, she chose a path much different than the other members of her family. Though she never married, she became quite interested in her family tree. I have no doubt, had she lived, she would have found you, Mr. Sage, Cole."

"Bless her heart." Loreena sighed.

"So, bringing it all back around," Cole began, still not certain he was putting all the pieces together, "how did you get Collins to take a DNA test?"

"I wish I could claim some great insight here or brilliant Sherlock Holmes deduction. Truth be told, I asked her for a DNA test to buy some time while I tried to figure out some legal precedent for her not being able to claim the inheritance." Langhorne took a sip of lemonade for the dramatic effect. "She refused."

The sound of Cole's laugh would have brought a smile to a dead man. The joy, amusement, and appreciation of his good fortune brought giggles and laughter to the group. Even the staid lawyer C.W. Langhorne rocked in his chair with a boisterous laugh, seeing the irony in the story.

"So the one weak link in her case was discovered when you stalled for time!" Cole wiped his eyes. "That is the best!"

"When you received word she wouldn't do the test, what did you do?" Kelly asked, still enthralled in the story.

"I called the police and reported a suspected case of identity theft. I explained the circumstances to an officer, who by the miracle of happenstance was the arresting officer in one of Ms. Collins' legal infractions. He remembered the name Patty Jenkins quite well. It seems Miss Jenkins, nay Collins, kicked the officer in a vulnerable spot to males during her booking," Langhorne explained.

Cole began laughing again. "This is too much!"

"Officer Riem, as I recall, took great pleasure in bringing her in for questioning. Faced with the accusation, compounded with her refusal to do a DNA test, which the officer said he could compel her to do, she confessed." Langhorne interlaced his plump fingers and lay them across his ample stomach.

"As the cowboys down here say, 'You, sir, have won your spurs'." Cole put out his hand in congratulations to Langhorne.

"Thank you so much, Mr. Langhorne. You have no idea how much this means to all of us." Kelly beamed.

"Oh, I think I have a good idea, Miss Kelly. Please call me Claude."

"I shall do that."

"This is just so precious to me," Loreena said through tears of pride. "Isn't my Claudie just the most wonderful lawyer ever?"

"That he is." Cole smiled, seeing Loreena's love of her husband. "That he is."

Chapter 28

"I'm done!" Cole yelled from behind his monitor. "The book is finished!"

"It's about time!" Kelly giggled from the doorway.

"What do you mean? Three months and a couple days is incredibly fast, with all that lawsuit insanity throwing off my game," Cole said defensively.

Kelly shook her head. "I was kid-ding!"

"Let's celebrate! Want some pineapple upside down cake?"

"That sounds wonderful. But first, would you do me a favor?" Cole asked.

"Sure." Kelly went to the side of the desk. "What do you need?"

"A hug." Cole put his arms around her waist and gave her a squeeze. "Thank you for all your support and encouragement," he whispered. "I couldn't have done it as well without you."

Kelly leaned back and looked Cole in the eyes. "How come you are so wonderful?"

"Constant review and memorization of *The Laws of Attraction*? It's you. You reflect back from me."

Kelly leaned forward and gave Cole a long kiss. "Smooth talker."

"Are you guys busy?" Randy asked, coming downstairs.

"Kids!" Cole said, releasing Kelly. "Nope, just basking in the glory of having finished my book," Cole said with mock bragging.

"Cool! Congrats. Wow, that was pretty fast. How long has it been?"

"How many times have you paid the rent on the shop?"

"Three."

"Then three months and two weeks," Cole replied. "With a few minor distractions thrown in."

They all moved to the kitchen table.

"That's awesome. What's it called?" Randy asked as Cole took a seat.

"*The Sages: Saints, and Sinners.*"

"Nice," Randy said, nodding.

"You didn't come down to hear Hemmingway brag. What's up?" Kelly poked Cole good-naturedly.

"You know you guys are my family. I have no one else," Randy began with a somber tone. "Cole, you have done more for me than I can imagine any father ever did. And Kelly, you have taken me in like a member of the family. You have cared about me. You are exactly what I have dreamed a mother would be like.

"We have made a pretty great team. I have done things and been given opportunities I never could have dreamt would come to me. If it weren't for you, Cole, I'd still be sitting at *The Daily Record* doing research on local property line squabbles and removing viruses from the editor's computer he was always picking up on porn sites." Randy grinned shyly. "So, I need to tell you something."

Kelly glanced at Cole with a concerned look.

"I have asked Brooke to marry me!" Randy's smile could have lit a dark room.

"Wow!" Cole said in relief. "I thought you were moving to Vermont or dying of cancer or something! That's great!"

"Oh, Randy!" Kelly jumped up from her seat at the kitchen table and gave him a loving embrace. "That's wonderful."

"When did this all happen?" Cole asked. "You really don't waste a minute!"

"Two nights ago. You said one time, 'When you know, you know.' I know Brooke is the one." Randy's smile left his face. "I spoke with her father last night."

"How'd that go?" Kelly asked softly with great concern.

"Brooke invited me over for dinner. That probably wasn't the best way to have done it. Even though she told him I was coming for dinner, he was less than pleased. When I tried to shake hands with him as he opened the door, he just left me hangin'. That's cool, but it kind of went downhill from there.

"I knew something was up when Brooke didn't come out of the kitchen. When she finally appeared, her eyes we all red and puffy. 'Hi, Brooke," I said. She didn't look up, and I could barely hear her response. 'How much longer? I'm hungry.' Her dad was so demanding in the way he spoke to her, it made me mad. 'It will be right out,' Brooke said. 'I'll give you a hand,'

I told her. 'Men don't do kitchen stuff; that's women's work.' He is such a jerk. 'Then I'll keep her company,' I told him. When we got in the kitchen, Brooke threw her arms around me and started crying. 'I'm so scared,' she said. 'What on Earth happened?' 'He doesn't want me going out with you. He called you terrible names and made fun of your business. I defended you, and he went ballistic. What are we going to do?' 'Get you out of here, for starters. The sooner we can get married, the better.' 'Any time now!' Brooke's dad yelled from the dining room. I grabbed the salad bowl and a bowl of vegetables. Brooke brought the baked pork chops. They were stuffed, they were really good. Anyway, he was scowling like he wanted to kill me when I set the food on the table. 'I think that's everything.' Brooke's hesitant tone made it sound like an apology. 'Well, let's bless it,' her dad growled. Can you imagine that mean son of a…sorry. How dare he talk to God? I mean, I'm not much of a prayer, but I don't think I would be asking God for anything acting the way he was."

"Sometimes it is hard to understand how some people can call themselves Christians. We can't look at them as examples, though. We can only make sure we are right with God. I've seen so many people turn their back on God because of people who are Christians in name only. Their actions tell a whole other story." Kelly's words were kind, and she hoped Randy would take them to heart.

"So, I didn't hear what he said, really. I kind of said my own prayer, asking God to help me get through the evening without punching him." Randy laughed.

"I'm assuming your prayer was answered." Cole chuckled.

"Yeah, I just focused on Brooke. I tried to make eye contact as often as I could. It was tough; she didn't look up much. She's like a whipped puppy when she's around him. Finally, she spoke. I can't imagine how hard it was for her. 'Dad, we need to tell you something,' she said finally. 'You better not be pregnant!' He looked right at her, and he was so angry and cruel, he practically spit when he spoke.

"'Mr. Palmer, I love Brooke very much, and I would like her to be my wife. I've asked her to marry me, and she said yes. We would like your blessing.' I got it all out in one breath, but I did it. I glanced at Brooke, and her eyes were wide and her muscles in her jaws were pumping like crazy.

"'Like hell, you will!' He shoved his chair back and stood. 'I won't have it, you hear me?! I won't have my daughter marrying a crippled repairman! You may think it's a clever way to inherit my business, but it won't work. I will write her out of my will if she marries you!'

"'He doesn't want your stupid business! He just wants me! Just me! We are going to get married, whether you approve or not! I love Randy! He is kind, gentle and he loves me. He is everything you aren't!' Brooke suddenly became a force of nature. She was standing now, too.

"I didn't know what to say or do. I felt like a coward or a fool, or both, just sitting there, but I figured they needed to have it out."

"I am so sorry, Randy. This should be a time of happiness. Is Brooke all right?" Kelly interjected.

"Her dad stormed out and still hadn't come back when I left. We're good. I do worry about one thing. That's one of the reasons I wanted to talk to you guys."

"Do you think I can take him? I'd be happy to kick his ass for you." Cole raised a clenched fist and nodded.

"Cole! What a thing to say. I'm ashamed of you!" Kelly flared.

"Sorry. Just trying to add a little comic relief."

"Not funny."

Randy and Cole exchanged glances and both burst into laughter. "Kind of, it is," Randy said between his nervous laughter.

"Oh, you two!"

"Sorry," Cole said with a wide smile.

Kelly shook her head. "I must confess, I did envision shooting him myself for a second," Kelly said, fighting back her laughter.

"Whew," Cole said. "I'm sorry, Randy. You were saying you were worried about something?"

"Yes, please continue." Kelly wagged her index finger at Cole. "And no more from you, funny guy."

"I'm kind of worried Brooke's relationship with her dad will have left scars. I mean, is it going to carry over into our lives together? Is she going to have problems? I mean, will she...I don't know exactly what

I mean." Randy's confusion and frustration were heartfelt.

"I'm sure she has a lot of anger and hurt. Just the little time I spent with her when she came for dinner, I could see there is a lot of pain. I think talking to a family counselor would really help her. You could bring it up in your pre-marital counseling."

"What's that?"

"Most churches now have couples go through a series of meetings before they are married to discuss their lives together, any issues or differences they may have. It would be a perfect time for her to talk about her struggles with her dad. It would be the perfect setting to open the door to get some good counseling."

"I don't think she would do it at her church. Her dad's a bigwig there. How about your church? Would they take on people who don't go there?"

"I'm sure they would. It's a wonderful place. You both might like to go there."

"I'll talk to Brooke. Maybe we could go with you guys so she can see what it's like."

"That would be wonderful." Kelly smiled. "So will her dad be involved? I mean, will he be willing to give her away?"

"I don't know."

"So what can we do?" Cole asked. "My first idea was vetoed."

"Stop it!" Kelly scolded playfully. "We are here for you both. Whatever you need."

"Just accept her. Show her what normal people are like. You guys mean so much to me. I want her to love you, too." Randy gave a big sigh. "Is there any pineapple upside down cake left? I need some comfort food."

Chapter 29

In the month that followed Randy asking for Brooke's hand, he purchased a ring and they began planning for their life together. To their complete shock and amazement, her father insisted on throwing an engagement party. His attitude toward the couple changed little, but it seemed in order to save face in the community, there were certain time-honored Orvin traditions that must be observed. The couple was delighted to oblige.

Barry Palmer surprisingly went all out for his daughter's engagement party. The banquet room of Sawyer's Steak House, the home of the Orvin Rotary, was decorated with bunches of fresh flowers. The thread-worn burgundy tablecloths that met the Rotarians every Thursday at noon were replaced with new, crisp white ones with napkins to match.

The guests were met at the banquet room door by none other than Roy Sawyer. This was an occasion. Usually, the owner couldn't be pried away from his barstool with a crowbar. He warmly greeted people as they arrived and seated them for the dinner. First to arrive were Cole and Kelly, Georgia and Ernie, and a few minutes later Randy and Brooke came in. Brooke looked beautiful in a deep blue dress. She held tight to Randy's hand. It was as if she were about to identify a corpse, not be the guest of honor at her own engagement party.

Betty and Pete Cranfill from Big Pete's Cafeteria BBQ came through the door looking like they were never in a restaurant before. Truth be told, they were making a rare escape from their six days a week schedule.

Finally, Barry Palmer approached the table after chatting for several minutes with Roy Sawyer. He didn't invite anyone to the dinner.

Name cards were placed around the table. Cole at one end, Barry at the other. Kelly was to the right, and Georgia was to the left of Cole. To Barry's right was Brooke, to his left the seat was empty, perhaps in homage to his late wife. Pete and Betty were to the right of Kelly. Ernie and Randy were to the right of Georgia.

Resting in front of each guest was a dinner menu, in the form of a five by seven sheet of paper. There were two appetizers, Shrimp Cocktails or Deep Fried Artichoke Hearts. The entrees were three different steaks, T-Bone, ribeye or filet mignon, or half a barbecued chicken. The sides were baked beans, baked potato, or French fries. Below the word Drinks was printed, "You Name it!"

Until Barry was seated, the group chatted and remarked on how pretty Brooke looked. Randy seemed to glow with the compliments paid his lovely bride-to-be. Brooke smiled and nodded but scarcely said a word.

"Thank you for coming," Barry began without a smile. "This is a chance for all of us to get to know each other. An engagement is a serious step in young people's lives and shouldn't be entered into lightly. I hope you all enjoy the dinner." Barry sat down to the thanks of the various members of the party.

"Charming," Kelly whispered as the waitress began taking orders.

"Randy is given to exaggeration. But wow, this guy really makes you feel welcome." Cole poked Kelly in the ribs under the table.

If the others were aware of Barry's unfriendly demeanor, they didn't let it affect their good time. They laughed, joked, and told stories about their own engagement and teased Randy about the speed of his sealing the deal.

"When you know, you know," Randy replied several times. "I'm just lucky Brooke knew, too!" To which Brooke would smile brightly and give Randy's arm a squeeze.

Dinner was served with the efficiency of a well-drilled team. Perhaps it was that Roy was watching, or perhaps the staff was that good. In any case, the food was wonderful, and the table conversation was the fellowship of old friends. The one exception was Barry.

He ate in silence, spoke only when spoken to, and offered nothing to the festivity. From time to time, Cole caught him looking at Brooke, and occasionally Randy. Barry seemed to really be studying the people at the table. He never smiled, his eyes showed no emotion, and his expression never changed.

When the table was cleared, a large blueberry cheesecake was brought out to the delight of everyone.

"My favorite!" Brooke said to her father. He finally smiled.

While everyone ate their dessert, Randy tapped his water glass with a spoon. "I guess this is the time I say something." Randy smiled as he gathered his thoughts.

"Most of you don't know I was a foster kid most of my life. No blame, no excuses. It is who I am. When I met Cole, I was working at a small newspaper. I thought it was my dream job and I would stay there forever. Then in walks this hot shot newspaper guy from Chicago, and it changed my life forever.

"I followed him to San Francisco for the best job I could have ever dreamed of. Then, as if things couldn't get any better, Cole invited me to join him when he was hired at Stanford University. Well, all decisions aren't always the best." Randy laughed and gave Cole a big smile as he raised his eyebrows.

"Some are just flat out bad ideas!" Cole offered.

"The thing is, though, at each step Cole showed me love and respect and gave me a sense of value. So when he said he was going to Oklahoma to work on his book, my heart sank. Then Kelly did the unimaginable, she asked me to come along. So those points go to Kelly.

"You all pretty much know the rest, the shop, and meeting Brooke. What you don't know is that from the second she walked in the shop with a computer in her arms, I was in love. Brooke is the best thing that has ever happened to me. She loves me, warts and all." Randy held up his deformed hand. "That's something," Randy choked with emotion.

"Not only is Brooke the prettiest girl in Oklahoma, maybe the world, but she also has a heart that matches. I love you, Brooke. And I love all of you who love her and have included me into the extended family."

As Randy sat down, Brooke's father, Barry, stood. The room suddenly went still in uncomfortable silence.

"Since my wife died, my focus has been on business, Rotary, and church. It has not been on my daughter. The faults I saw in her were magnified through the lens of my loss and resentment. Her mannerisms and beauty just deepened my grief. She is so very much like her mother.

"Seeing the love around this table for her chosen mate, and the way you all have taken her in makes me so ashamed I nearly left earlier. Randy, I owe you a heartfelt apology for the way I have treated you and the way I have behaved toward you. I beg your forgiveness.

"Brooke, I know I have caused you years of pain. Neglect, combined with my constant criticism, has left you with a lot of anger and emotional scars. It took Randy's love for you to open my eyes to see what I have done to you.

"I can never make up for what I have done, but I want to help get you started on your lives together. As soon as you can find a piece of ground, I will build you a house. That is if you don't mind."

The table erupted in applause. Brooke and Randy grinned from ear to ear, partly in shock, but mostly in gratitude.

"So, in front of God and this company, I beg your forgiveness, and I swear I will change, starting tonight." Barry Palmer collapsed into his chair and sobbed.

Brooke moved behind her father's chair, wrapped her arms around his neck, and kissed him gently on the cheek. Whatever she said as she whispered into his ear was not heard by the people at the table. Barry raised his hand and placed it on her cheek.

The table was silent for several minutes. Kelly and Georgia both sat with eyes closed, apparently praying. Ernie played with his napkin and didn't look up. Randy looked at Cole and gave him a strained smile. Cole just nodded knowingly.

Barry wiped his eyes with his handkerchief and stood to face Brooke. They embraced and stood, gently rocking.

"I apologize," Barry said, turning to face the guests. "That's not like me, but it needed to be done."

The group unanimously spoke words of encouragement and compassion. Barry sat and took a drink of water. Brooke returned to her chair, and Randy stood and hugged her.

Without standing, Cole began to speak. "I think we have all been through a lot of emotional upheaval in the last couple of months. The loss of my beloved aunt, our farm nearly being lost to a con artist, and the friction, now dissolved within the engagement we celebrate tonight. I want to express my admiration for Barry and the fences he has begun to mend tonight. You are a man I am proud to know and hope to call a friend." Cole looked at Barry and smiled.

"I came here to say goodbye to my aunt and write a book. Part of that journey was a DNA test and hours of research on the *Living Tree* website. The book is finished, but along the way, I made some incredible discoveries, one of which I want to share with you now if that's all right."

"Can we stop you?" Ernie couldn't resist teasing. Nor could Georgia resist the slap she gave him on his thigh that was louder than she expected.

"I can always count on Ernie." Cole chuckled. The rest of the table joined in, and it was a nice way to lighten the atmosphere. "Like I was about to say, I made several discoveries on this journey into my family history.

"The most shocking, if that's the right word, was the discovery that my great aunt Effie was, in fact, my great-grandmother. It seems she was involved with a young man who worked at her father's bank. She became pregnant, and the young man did a runner.

"He went to California, but somewhere along the way his son or grandson returned to Orvin. Which one, we'll figure out later. The thing I do know is that Chester Palmer, my great-grandfather's great-great-grandson, is also here tonight. It seems that Barry is my cousin."

"The hell you say!" Ernie exclaimed.

"Say that again!" Brooke said, looking toward her dad.

Barry sat staring at Cole with a stunned expression.

Cole pulled a sheet of paper from his shirt pocket. "Chester had a son named Milton, whose son was Glenn. He had a son named John."

"My grandpa!" Brooke interrupted.

"That's right. John had a son in 1969 named Barry. And Barry had a beautiful baby girl in 1991 named Brooke."

"We're family?" Barry asked in complete amazement.

"Seems so," Cole replied with a wide grin.

"I don't know how much more good news I can take," Randy said, shaking his head.

"So are we second cousins?" Brooke asked Cole.

"I guess so," Cole said cheerfully.

"You know," Cole began, "when you are engaged to the prettiest girl in Orvin, maybe Oklahoma, there's not a whole lot a fellow needs. Thanks to Barry, you will have a home. Randy has been with me through some really dark times in my life. Even more important, he has been present, and part of, the best. Back in California, I have just about the best daughter a man could ask for. But I never was blessed with a son. So Randy's as close as I ever got."

The group chuckled. Brooke's father smiled. Randy looked down at the top of the table. Brooke reached over and patted him on the back.

"The point is," Cole said.

"Please," Ernie said.

"Hush now," Georgia scolded.

"The point is, Kelly and I have been wracking our brains for a gift idea to celebrate the engagement of these two wonderful kids. One of the things in life that always seems to eat up the lion's share of a monthly budget is the rent."

The group all voiced various responses.

"Mr. Callen, do you have a dollar?" Cole stopped and waited for a response.

"Will five do?" Randy asked.

"Here." Brooke pulled a dollar bill from her handbag.

"What now, a magic trick?" Ernie teased.

"Hush," Georgia good-naturedly scolded.

"As a matter of fact, some might call it magic. Randy and Brooke, like Barry said, in front of God and this assembled company, I hereby sell you a lot on the farm for the construction of your new home for the agreed upon amount of one dollar." Cole cleared his throat, showing signs of emotion welling up. Kelly reached over and took his hand. "Unless you don't want it."

"I don't know what to say, Cole. Between you and Mr. Palmer, the generosity is overwhelming." Randy stood.

"I do. The word is yes! Oh! You guys are the most wonderful." Brooke threw her arm around Randy's waist as she fought back tears of joy.

Cole sat down, and Kelly patted him on the arm.

* * *

A crisp fall breeze snapped at the branches of the cottonwoods. A faint wisp of steam rose from the cup that Kelly cradled in both hands. The small green and red plaid blanket across her lap clashed with her orange sweater, but it didn't matter. She was cozy and relaxed.

Cole sat facing her on the wide porch rail between two potted plants. He wore a thin blue windbreaker over a red Stanford T-shirt, the only souvenir from his stay at the university. He knew there was a conversation coming that he probably would end up compromising on, and for the first time since their marriage, he feared the outcome. He smiled at Kelly, but she could see his heart wasn't in it.

"What's up, buttercup?" she said with concern.

"My book comes out next week, Randy's engaged, Lottie's gone, and the storm of my venture into genealogy has passed. We are adrift, and I feel unsettled and a bit concerned."

"Oh, that's all," Kelly teased, trying to lighten his mood.

"No, that's not all. Now you have to go back to San Francisco to testify. That scares me. Those are nasty, violent people. They assaulted you once; they wouldn't blink at doing it again." Cole reflected before continuing. "What if we had Langhorne do a video deposition? You could stay here. No chance of some thug following you home."

"You really think that will happen?"

"No, I'm not saying it will, but it could. That's enough for me."

Kelly puffed up her cheeks and blew out an uneasy sigh.

"Then there is the whole thing of where are we going to go? After Ben's call, unless you want to move to France, we are a ship adrift."

"How do you mean?" Kelly frowned. "They are going to follow their dreams. Ben sees it as an opportunity to further his research, expand his resume, and give Erin and the kids a chance to experience another country and culture. The kids could grow up bilingual. How could they not at least give it a try?"

"You sound jealous," Cole replied.

"I guess I'm kind of envious, in a way. But I'm not starting out."

"Too little, too late?" Cole asked with a melancholy sigh.

"You? Heaven's no, my darling. I just meant we are in the August of our lives, looking at the autumn of our years ahead. We have nothing to prove. We have each other, and we can do whatever we want."

"I do not want to go back to California. Period. I'm done. The kids are leaving. This move to Europe of theirs could be the beginning of half a dozen moves before we die. We can't follow them every time he gets a new opportunity."

"I agree. They will be an airplane ride away. No matter where we go. The big question is, what do you want to do?"

There it was, the thousand-pound buffalo sitting with them on the porch again. This is backward of the way Cole wanted this conversation to play out. Like having bet on the last hand of poker, he was having to show his hand first. He would be going into whatever happens next as the weaker of the two.

"It has been almost two months since you were offered the paper. What have you decided? You have to tell that man something. You can't just leave him hanging."

"I *have* decided. I don't want that paper. I just haven't worked up the guts to tell Abernathy. That would end the dream for good. But you know, sometimes the wishing is better than the getting. I had a good run at being a newspaperman. I think the dream of being an editor was that 'I could if I wanted' kind of dream. But when it really comes down to it, I don't want to be an editor. I want to be an author.

"I know you don't like it here, but I have fallen in love with this little town, our lives together here, and this house, I don't know, it just seems like home."

Cole didn't look at Kelly. He did it. He got it out. At least he let his feelings and desires be known. When he finally looked up at Kelly, he was surprised to see her staring at him.

"What do you mean I don't like it here?" Her tone showed she was not happy with his assertion.

"Well, do you?" Cole was direct and waited.

"Ever since my house in Sausalito burned, I have felt like a fish out of water. I'm a guest, a house sitter. I have no home. I have no possessions. Everything I knew in the material sense is gone. I have you, which is more than I ever expected in my life.

"Since we came here, you've found your place, your purpose. You are a writer, not just the reporter of news, but a novelist, and a fine one. You have walked taller, smiled brighter, and you have a contentment and an easiness I've never seen. You fit here."

"I think that -" Cole tried to interrupt.

"Let me finish. Seeing you happy to me is more important than a house or apartment anywhere in the world. I have come to love this little house. The memory of us working on it when we were first finding our way in our relationship fills my heart. It was then, Cole, that I knew I loved you. Now, three years later, we are back as husband and wife. So, it hurts a bit to think you feel I don't like it."

Are there things about the house I would change? Sure, Lottie's things are Lottie's things, not ours. I miss your big leather couches and that silly eighty-inch TV of yours. They *are* you. Besides, I already picked the paint." Kelly paused and smiled widely. "I never thought of that. I picked the paint for my new home with you and didn't even know it."

"So you want to stay?" Cole asked with delight.

"As it says in the Bible, *Where you go I will go, and where you stay I will stay. Your people will be my people.*"

Cole stood and grabbed Kelly's hand and pulled her to her feet. With an unexpected fluidity, he kissed her and spun her around, her hand held above her head.

"So this is where we'll grow old together?" Cole asked with excitement.

"I'm not sure about that. Who knows what the future brings? But it is definitely the turnstile to a new ride."

MICHEAL MAXWELL

THE END

SOUL OF COLE

Exclusive sample from Book 9

ONE

"What is the hold-up?"

"I'm putting on my shoes!" He wasn't, he was reading the news on his computer. Russ Walker wanted to be sure he was up on all the latest before his morning debate session.

"For fifteen minutes?" Sharon was now standing in the archway outside Russ' office. "Get off the computer!"

"Oh, for heaven's sake. They're not going anywhere."

"Nine o'clock means nine o'clock. Not nine-fifteen or nine-thirty." Sharon stood hands on hips, head cocked to the left and a scowl that would make babies cry. "Let's go already."

Russ stood, yanked at the back of his running shorts through his warm-up pants. He felt like an idiot. Running shorts? He hadn't run more than ten paces in the last twenty years, and that was when a rattler was in the back yard flower bed. The outfit Sharon bought him for his sixty-fifth birthday was an embarrassment and the butt of endless jokes from his buddies.

"Let's get this done," Russ grumbled as he closed the front door.

"You'll thank me someday for getting you up off your duff and out for some exercise. 'Sides, I think you're just teasing. Once we get going, and you and Warren get arguing about whatever it is you two argue about, you don't even know you're walking."

"We don't argue, we have meaningful, spirited, discussions." Russ went down the steps and off they went.

"OK, as long as you are enjoying yourself, that's all that matters."

"Be more fun over a cup of coffee and a cinnamon roll." Russ finally laughed. It was a daily ritual that eventually showed that all his bluster was just an act.

Sharon gave him a swat on the butt and picked up the pace.

Warren and Judy Poore lived two blocks from Sharon and Russ. The two couples met over forty years ago and they have been friends ever since. The Poore's came to Orvin as young marrieds. Warren was the assistant pastor at the Calvary Methodist Church where Russ and Sharon attended.

Sharon and Judy were pregnant together. Their kids grew up together. Brownies, Cub Scouts, ballet, swimming, dance, t-ball, little league, softball, soccer, Pop Warner football, piano, practices and recitals, Judy and Sharon were there. Rain or shine they carpooled through activities and ten years of school. The

Poore and Walker kids were often confused for each other, the wrong boys matched with the wrong sister. It was like one large cooperative family. That is until they reached Jr. High, then hormones, cooties, and peer pressure drove a wedge between the kids, and that was that.

The men bonded over their love of music. They traded recordings of their favorites, some of which, without a doubt, the members of Calvary Methodist would have raised their collective eyebrows at. They started with cassettes, moved to mini-discs (short-lived), then to CDs. With the purchase of their first computers, they entered the digital world. They learned to burn CDs, then DVDs. The ocean of music available to them on MP3s they found on the World Wide Web was a King Solomon's Mine to the Musicaholics. Now they pass flash drives in the foyer of the church, red for Warren and black for Russ. Like an info drop between spies, they were sly and silent, transferring their stash of new tracks with a quick handshake.

As Sharon and Russ made their way the last few yards to the Poore's, Russ couldn't help but admire the beauty of the morning. "Makes you glad to be alive!"

"Now there is a change of spirits!" Sharon grinned. All it took was to get Russ outside in the fresh air and he was a new man. She knew how much he hated exercise, but she was bound and determined to get him up and moving.

The Poore's house was like a photo from *House Beautiful;* the all-American white picket fence, manicured lawn, gigantic front porch with a swing on each end; Truly a dream home. Judy had a knack for decorating that Sharon could only dream of.

Sharon went up to the door first. After forty years, the formality of knocking was neither observed nor expected.

"Good Mornin'!" Sharon called out as she went through the front door. The house seemed unusually quiet. She moved to the bottom of the stairs and called up, "Let's get a move on, you two!"

"And you were rushing me!" Russ teased.

The faint sound of a radio announcer came from the kitchen/family room end of the house. Sharon turned and gave Russ what he would later recall as a concerned look. He moved toward the kitchen.

"Hey, are you guys here?" Sharon called, with a bit less enthusiasm than before.

As Russ entered the kitchen he noticed that the usual mess of breakfast dishes and coffee cups was nowhere to be seen. Walking past the snack bar, the first thing he saw was the family room wall and a three-foot splattering of blood, tissue and what appeared to be hair. Russ' eyes seemed locked on the circle. He was unable to process the nova of crimson that was spread across family photos and the *God Bless Our Home* stitchery.

"Russ? Whatcha doin' in there?" She peered across the kitchen, and out a back window to see if their friends had stepped outside.

Sharon's voice thawed Russ' frozen muscles. His eyes slowly moved down, fully aware of the carnage he would find.

Slumped on the sofa Warren Poore sat, head leaning in an odd, unnatural, position. A clotted, dangling, drip of blood hung from his bottom lip. The top of his head was an open mass of red and pink tissue. Warren's white Sooners t-shirt was a solid red from neck to waist.

"Russ!" Sharon was getting closer.

"Go home!" Russ shouted.

"What?"

"Leave, get out! Go home, call 911!"

Her voice was drawing ever closer.

"Damn you woman, do as you're told!" Russ screamed.

In all their years of marriage, Russ Walker never swore at his wife. He seldom, if ever, raised his voice. The combination of the two sent a wave of shock and nausea though Sharon. Not understanding or knowing the cause of the outburst she turned and ran all the way home. With each step, her tears grew. Her mind was grabbing at every memory, replaying every moment in the house, and every synapse searching for what just happened.

The reality of what he found began to sink in and Russ shifted his gaze from his friend's lifeless body and around the room. On the floor near the end of the sofa Judy was slouched, her head resting against a cushion. Her mouth was wide open. She stared with dead eyes at the ceiling. A large hole was surrounded by blood on the front of her white Cancun sweatshirt.

There was no blood behind Judy. Russ let his eyes slowly move from her head to her feet. She wasn't wearing shoes. Her bare feet were a strange hue of purplish blue. At her feet was a trail of blood. Russ followed the blood as its path led into the kitchen. There were several partial footprints from where he stepped in her blood. On the back side of the snack bar was a large pool of cordovan liquid, an ever-narrowing, ever thinning trail of her blood leading to where she leaned.

Russ felt his neck with two fingers. As the space in front of him began to twinkle and shift to black and white he realized he wasn't breathing. His heart was rapidly beating out the pounding in his head. He took a deep breath and held it. The vein on the side of his neck was thumping hard against his fingers. His heart was pounding.

Far away and in another world, the sound of sirens pulsed. As they grew ever louder Russ felt his hands tingle and his legs began to quiver and shake. He backed up from where he stood and collapsed in a thick leather recliner. Across the room, the circle of Warren's life matter was in Russ' direct line of vision. He closed his eyes.

With his eyes closed his memory took over and he saw an image of Warren and Judy sitting on the couch with brightly colored packages on their laps and surrounding them on the sofa. In his mind, he heard the laughter of a hundred gatherings. He heard Happy Birthday being sung accompanied with visions of Warren, Judy, Sharon, the children of both families at various ages, all surrounding the couch, all different seasons, all different years, all different ages.

Time was no longer a thing Russ was aware of so he couldn't determine how long he was in the chair when he heard a loud, deep voice come from the front of the house.

"Police!"

"In here!" Russ's voice broke with emotion.

Seconds later two police officers with guns drawn entered the room. From somewhere down the hall the booming voice of another officer yelled, "Clear."

"Mister Walker?"

Russ did not respond.

"Are you okay sir? Mister Walker?"

"Russ felt his head nod and his voice say, "Yeah, I'm okay."

"Let's get you out of here, alright?"

Russ felt the strong hand of the officer take his arm and help him to his feet. Out on the street a siren slowly wound down. He heard doors slamming shut with metallic thuds.

"We have some folks who are going to check you over. You've had a pretty bad shock this morning. Can you do that for me?"

Russ nodded the affirmative.

As the officer half led, half carried Russ to the front door and the waiting paramedics his eyes landed on something that looked strangely out of place. Not that he hadn't seen it before, and not that it wasn't something normal for the Poore home, but on the counter by the sink was Warren's open Bible.

"I wonder what he was reading," His voice was lost in the crackling chatter of police radios.

"What's that?"

Russ didn't respond.

About the Author

Micheal Maxwell has traveled the globe on the lookout for strange sights, sounds, and people. His adventures have taken him from the Jungles of Ecuador and the Philippines to the top of the Eiffel Tower and the Golden Gate Bridge, and from the cave dwellings of Native Americans to The Kehlsteinhaus, Hitler's Eagles Nest! He's always looking for a story to tell and interesting people to meet.

Micheal Maxwell was taught the beauty and majesty of the English language by Bob Dylan, Robertson Davies, Charles Dickens, and Leonard Cohen.

Mr. Maxwell has dined with politicians, rock stars and beggars. He has rubbed shoulders with priests and murderers, surgeons and drug dealers, each one giving him a part of themselves that will live again in the pages of his books.

Micheal Maxwell has found a niche in the mystery, suspense, genre with The Cole Sage Series that gives readers an everyman hero, short on vices, long on compassion, and a sense of fair play, and the willingness to risk everything to right wrongs. The Cole Sage Series departs from the usual, heavily sexual, profanity-laced norm and gives readers character-driven stories, with twists, turns, and page-turning plot lines.

Micheal Maxwell writes from a life of love, music, film, and literature. Along with his lovely wife and travel partner, Janet, divide their time between a small town in the Sierra Nevada Mountains of California, and their lake home in Washington State.

Made in the USA
Columbia, SC
08 July 2021